TH__ _____ N
OF
CULPEPER
COUNTY

JIM SMITH

Jim Smith (signature)

Words in
the Wynd
Publishing

The Cairn of Culpeper County
© Copyright 2003, 2012 James William Smith.
All rights reserved.

Published by Words In The Wynd Publishing, Everett, WA.

Visit www.wordsinthewynd.com for more information.

This novel is a work of fiction. Names, characters, places and incidents either are the product of the author's imagination or are used fictitiously. Any resemblance to actual events, locales, organizations, or persons, living or dead, is entirely coincidental and beyond the intent of either the author or publisher.

ISBN-13: 978-0-9851517-1-3
ISBN-10: 0985151714

Printed in the United States of America

For my friend and partner, my wife Angie, who never stops believing in me.

Acknowledgments

My thanks to the following people who helped this novel see the light of day: Heather Weir, my hard-working chief editor; Erin Brown for an inspired cover design; John and Sylvia Victor for planting the seed and inspiring the plot; my wife, Angie, my family and close friends for their moral support and enthusiasm for this creative project.

THE CAIRN
OF
CULPEPER
COUNTY

ONE

The curtain of darkness slowly receded, giving birth to a fresh Virginia morning. Lingering fog patches fought a losing battle with invading morning rays from the east. Already stirring sleepily to the promise of a new day, hills and valleys were suddenly jolted from their slumber by the thunder of horses at full gallop. A blood-pounding reminder of the shadow which hung over every Virginia morning in these dark days—the ceaseless nightmare of a bloody and tragic war.

As if fleeing the rising sun, the riders came, hunched forward over heavily muscled mounts. Some just lads of eighteen or nineteen. Others, grizzled veterans with weathered, leathery skin and eyes hardened by scenes of war and death. A tough band. Eighteen in all, clad in the unmistakable gray of the Confederate army.

They had broken camp before first light when scouts brought word of Union troops, commanded by Colonel Percy Wyndham, moving up along Johnson Creek. Within minutes of Lieutenant Stanton's order, the entire detachment was saddled and mounted, ready to move out. They tracked down to the creek, followed it west for about a quarter mile to hide their tracks, then turned sharply south and followed Pike Road. Like a crazed band of steeplechasers, they charged along the winding trail kicking up clouds of dust in their wake. Immediate destination—the Talawaga Bridge and beyond, the safety of the town of Culpeper.

Lieutenant John Stanton led the column. Hand selected by Colonel John Mosby himself, Stanton was proud to lead this detachment of Mosby's Rangers. Their partisan band had wreaked havoc on Union encampments and supply trains for over a year. They were the thorn in the Yankees' flesh. Hard to track. Unpredictable. Nearly impossible to defend against. So disruptive were they to the Federal army's cause that General Ulysses S. Grant himself had advised General Philip Sheridan that if any of Mosby's men were captured, they should be hanged without a trial.

Armed with their chief weapon—surprise—Mosby's Rangers struck like lightning: derailing trains; kidnapping officers for information; robbing and burning supply wagons; stealing horses, weapons, ammunition, payroll funds, anything and everything of value to the Confederate cause.

Stanton relished the thrill of guerrilla attacks. He and his cohorts were making a name for themselves, carving a niche in this bloody war, making a mark for the Confederacy. War suited John Stanton's disposition just fine. Aggressive to a fault, he would stand up to any man over any issue. An imposing physique intimidated most who crossed Stanton. The broad shoulders, heavily muscled, tapered to a thin waist and cut a fine figure in the gray officer's uniform decorated with the bars of his rank. A square jaw, shock of blond hair and ice-blue eyes had turned many a woman's eye and left an indelible impression on anyone who saw him.

Stanton's big break had come on the notorious raid led by then Captain Mosby, in which they penetrated Federal Headquarters at Fairfax Court House, dragging Brigadier General Edwin H. Stoughton out of bed, and taking him and thirty-two others captive. Captain Mosby was so impressed with Stanton on that raid that he made the young man one of his most trusted officers. Thus Stanton had followed Mosby up the ranks, finding himself promoted to the rank of lieutenant when Mosby became a colonel.

Stanton smiled as he pictured his good friend now. Though slight of build, the wiry John Singleton Mosby was a dashing guerrilla leader. He shunned the traditional saber and instead always wore two pistols. His coat was lined with scarlet, and he wore a hat with gold cord, a gold star and an ostrich plume. He was a brilliant strategist and as tough as they came. He could spit nails, if pushed. No one doubted who was in charge when John Mosby was present.

That formed part of the answer as to why eighteen brave and daring Confederate guerrillas were running from a Federal column. Stanton had never run from a fight in his life. His choice now would be to spill some Yankee blood. Take some prisoners and spoils of war–not turn and run. But he had his orders, from Colonel Mosby himself, not to engage Colonel Wyndham's troops. So they ran.

Squinting into the morning mist, John Stanton could see the road ahead funneling through a narrow pass between two low hills. He knew this road well. It fed out on the other side close to the riverbank and only a few hundred paces from the Talawaga Bridge. Accompanied by the thunderous clamor of horseshoes pounding the dirt, Stanton and his men shot through the narrow opening into the winding approach to the bridge. Dense brush and undergrowth lined the road here. Enough cover to disguise a sea of blue-shirted sharpshooters. None of the rebel riders suspected ambush until the forty-odd Burnside carbines began to spit lead. They had walked right into a Yankee trap. The tables were turned. Surprise was on the bluebellies' side this time. And it proved fatal.

The whole attack lasted only a few minutes. Gray uniforms, tattered and bloodied, dropped from saddles like dead flies. Horses staggered and rolled, cut out from beneath stunned boys in gray. John Stanton flinched at the searing pain in his right leg as he caught a bumblebee. The lead ball ripped the flesh and exploded into bone, leaving the leg a crimson, soggy mess. Another round smashed into the head of Stanton's horse. The mortally wounded beast lurched forward, twisted sideways and, falling, threw Stanton down the embankment bordering the river. The officer hit the water face down and stayed there motionless as the current gathered him up and swept him downstream around the bend and out of sight of the bushwhackers.

None of the Rangers had made the Talawaga Bridge. Seventeen bloodied bodies lay in the dirt, frozen in the grotesque contortions of death. In the muddy waters of the Rappahannock River, another struggled to survive. By sheer willpower, John Stanton raised his head, gasping for air, and clutched at branches overhanging the swirling waters. Slowly and painfully, he dragged himself into the weeds and out of sight. The leg was numb now, but the damage clearly evident. Stanton began to fade as a wave of unconsciousness rushed to overtake him. Instinctively, he reached to his waist, unbuckled the leather belt and fashioned a crude tourniquet. A desperate measure to curtail the bleeding and spare his life. His last conscious act was tugging at the belt.

When Stanton's detachment failed to show as expected, Colonel Mosby dispatched a search party led by Sergeant O'Sullivan. The burly Irishman had ridden under Stanton's command on numerous raids and, like so many others, had taken a liking to the cocky young officer. Finding the lieutenant's horse slain and the seventeen fellow rangers in his command dead on the road, O'Sullivan and his party feared the worst. After sending for a burial party, they scoured the area in search of Stanton's body but to no avail. A bespectacled young private named Benson suggested they bring in dogs to assist with the search. He said that back home in Mississippi they used hounds in the bayous once to search for ol' man Carter who had gotten hisself lost.

"Them dogs took one or two sniffs of one of ol' man Carter's tattered old shirts," Benson said, "and dashed off into the bayou. After yelpin' and sniffin' fer about an hour, they led the search party right to the ol' codger."

And so, with the help of Rawley Swenson's bloodhound and the scent from an old bandana in Stanton's saddlebags, O'Sullivan's party finally located Lieutenant Stanton's bloodied body in the weeds, unconscious. He was barely alive.

It was mid-afternoon when they brought him into the Willis house just three miles from the scene of the ambush. Aristides Monteiro, a surgeon in Mosby's regiment, had been summoned. Dr. Monteiro confirmed that the belt had saved

Stanton's life, but the leg was a mess. The entire knee was shattered. Damage was extensive. The limb would be useless. Monteiro knew amputation was the only course of action. He surveyed the room.

Sometimes he wondered why he had accepted the offer of his University of Virginia classmate, John Mosby, to transfer to Mosby's regiment. Seeing Stanton lying on the couch, his smashed right leg dressed in a pile of blood-soaked rags, he remembered why. As a surgeon in the regular Confederate army, this scene was played out day after sickening day. Young men in the prime of life carried in on stretchers moaning and bleeding. They left maimed, crippled, less a limb or an eye. Many died on the operating tables. The makeshift clinics were slaughterhouses disguised as field hospitals. Blood flowed freely. It stained the surgeons' tables, gowns and instruments. It ran off and tinged the soil—silent testimony of the deadly cost of this hellish war. Though casualties were proportionately high in the risky guerrilla warfare business, many raids were carried out successfully with little or no bloodshed. In fact, today's massacre at the Rappahannock was the worst of the war so far. At least with Mosby's Rangers, the bodies he patched up and fought to save bore familiar names and faces. Not like the endless stream of unknown wounded in the regular army.

"Put him on the table," Monteiro ordered as he gestured toward the solid oak dining table in the middle of the room. "I need hot water and blankets, and a good lamp," he said, while rummaging in the black bag that accompanied him on every official trip.

Mrs. Willis, a plump but pleasant enough woman in her early fifties, leaped into action at the doctor's orders, Silently vanishing to another room, she soon reappeared, arms laden with blankets and clean white sheets.

Rangers Munson and Crawford grunted at the strain of lifting Stanton's sizeable limp body onto the table. The rough transfer to the table elicited a painful moan from the lone survivor of the ambush. Everyone in the room knew the seriousness of the situation. Stanton's life hung in the balance. The doc was all business. As he laid out the shiny, steel instruments – scalpel and saw – the wounded officer began to emerge from his unconscious stupor.

"Three rocks. Markers. Culpeper County," he mumbled. At least that's what it sounded like. The voice was barely audible – weak and muffled. "Three rocks. Culpeper County." Yes, they heard it more clearly this time. Strange words, but not surprising. The poor soul was delirious from pain and loss of blood. Stanton fought to be heard again. "Three ro . . . s . . . Mar . . . Cul . . ." He collapsed.

Wasting no time, Dr. Monteiro tightened a tourniquet high on the thigh of the shattered leg and ordered Munson, Mr. Willis, who had just arrived, and Crawford to hold Stanton down. He inserted a wedge of rawhide between Stanton's teeth. Then, wielding the razor-sharp scalpel, the experienced hands of the veteran surgeon carved a clean cut just above the knee and quickly separated the layers of skin and tissue until the white of bone lay exposed. Stanton was writhing in pain now – teeth clamped on the rawhide, stifling the screams of agony. Monteiro pressed ahead with crude saw in hand, deftly drawing its jagged teeth back and forth across the opening until the limb fell free. Stanton was out again, retreating to the painlessness of oblivion.

TWO

The **computer** had kicked into screen saver mode hours before. The monitor continued the light show, flashing through asteroid fields, constellations and floating planets, and casting an eerie, flickering glow across the room. The customized workstation built into the wall was flanked by massive floor-to-ceiling birch bookshelves well-stocked with primarily historical volumes. Several books lay open next to the keyboard, some hidden by sheets of lined paper crammed full of scribbled notes.

A massive walnut desk stood in front of the workstation. Coffee stains marred the small sections of the green blotter barely visible beneath scattered papers and books. An empty Pepsi can and crumpled Snickers wrapper shared desktop space with a green banker's lamp and pens and pencils standing upright in a faded Redskins mug.

The antics of The Three Stooges filled the screen of a 20-inch TV on a stand in the corner. Judging by the heavy snoring emanating from an ancient plaid sofa, Ambrose Lapain had done it again. For the second time this week, he had failed to make it to bed. One of the privileges of bachelorhood, though it was murder on the clothes. From the argyle-clad, size twelve feet on one armrest to the partially balding head on the other, the long, skinny frame of the 47-year-old history professor provided maximum couch coverage. Heavy, dark-rimmed glasses, perched halfway down Ambrose's long, pointy noise, were still aimed at a half-read copy of *Mosby and His Rangers*. The book had collapsed on Lapain's chest and rose and fell gently with every deep breath.

Since beginning research for his book on guerrilla warfare in the Civil War, Ambrose Lapain often looked as worn and weary as the wrinkled suit he still wore after a full day of lectures, a TV dinner, six hours of research and six more of sleep. The only deadlines sparking such a heavy workload were self-imposed. His passion had always been Civil War history and the move to Georgetown University six years ago had planted him right in the center of the land where the bloodiest historical battles had occurred. This was Mecca. Gettysburg. Manassas. Bull Run.

Though he taught American history day in and day out, the lectures became more intense, more animated, whenever the topic happened to be The Civil War. Professor Lapain required no notes for his lectures on the Blue-Gray conflict. He was an expert who knew the ins and outs, participants, strategies and outcomes of each and every major battle. His latest fascination, and the subject of his new book, was guerrilla tactics of Colonel John Mosby of the Confederate Army.

Lapain bolted to a sitting position as the telephone broke the early morning silence. Book and glasses went flying. In a groggy stupor, the professor grasped for the handset.

"Yeah," he mumbled in a coarse, half-awake whisper.

"Dr. Lapain, it's me, Holly."

The voice was far too cheery for 6 a.m. This better be good, Lapain thought.

"I couldn't wait any longer to call you, Professor. I didn't call last night because I knew you'd be working on your manuscript. I hope I'm not calling too early."

"Nnnn."

"Oh, did I wake you? I'm sorry, sir."

"It's all right."

"Well, anyway, since you're awake, I've just got to tell you! I've been in contact with a Marie Palmer of Front Royal. She answered our ad in the *Post*. Seems she has some artifacts that might be of interest—one in particular. It's a letter written by a Confederate soldier, the brother of this Marie Palmer's great-grandmother. May have been one of Mosby's men."

Lapain was awake now, hanging on every word, a bloodhound on the trail of a scent. Holly was good. The 23-year-old Ph.D. student was the best research assistant ever to work for him. Energetic and self-motivated, she thrived on the quest for information. With thoroughness unequaled among her peers, she would pore over documents exhaustively, extracting the minutest facts pertinent to the project at hand. An all-nighter in the campus library was not a vigil but an adventure for Holly. And she was gifted with people. Her bubbly, outgoing nature oozed a rare warmth and charm. She could sell sunblock to Eskimos.

"Dr. Lapain, I took the liberty of scheduling a 3:45 appointment for this afternoon at Mrs. Palmer's home in Front Royal. I've got the address. And I lined up Richard to sub for you in your two o'clock lecture. Everything's set. I'll see you in the office later, OK?"

"Yeah. Thanks, Holly. See you later."

"'Bye."

A flick of the 14-kt gold butane lighter and a yellow flame engulfed the bulbous tip of a giant Havana cigar. Special occasions call for their small indulgences. And this was a very special occasion. Not only had Holly uncovered a new and potentially groundbreaking source, but she would be accompanying him to Front Royal for the interview. Professor Lapain paced nervously back and forth beside his navy 1986 Volvo, not sure which event he most anticipated. The interview and findings—especially the possible link to Mosby's Rangers—could be a breakthrough discovery for his book. And the thought of the three-hour roundtrip by car, alone with Holly, was almost too much to bear.

Just as his mind was shaping an image of the striking goddess disguised as research assistant and coed, out from behind the brick and ivy General Arts building emerged the real thing. Her golden blond, shoulder-length hair bounced and swayed as she practically danced into the staff parking lot. She wore white Keds, short navy shorts that exposed maybe the best pair of legs on campus, and a patterned kelly-green silk blouse. As she approached the Volvo, her perfect porcelain complexion and aqua blue eyes burst into the radiant smile that immediately melted all she greeted. God, she was beautiful!

Lapain was tempted to drive below the speed limit just to lengthen the trip, but mere survival on Washington expressways dictated at least minimum-posted speed.

Across the Potomac on the Francis Scott Key Bridge and west on Interstate 66 they headed, chatting as the Volvo clicked off the miles. Mostly small talk. Research, teaching assignments, likes and dislikes in movies, clothes and food. It was fun just to be with Holly. The professor basked in the sunshine of her personality until they arrived—all too soon for him—at the neat little cottage a few blocks off Pickett Road.

A frail but friendly old lady greeted them at the door and ushered them into a stuffy sitting room. Holly's charm quickly set Mrs. Palmer at ease. Over coffee the wrinkled, gray-haired woman told how she had been widowed for nearly a year now. It was after her dear Gerald's death, as she sorted through old cartons of junk, that she ran across the items of interest to Holly and Dr. Lapain. With bony hands, Marie Palmer lifted the lid from a sturdy Xerox carton. Scooping up a yellowed, brittle sheet of paper, she began to read.

> Dear Ma,
>
> I been real sick. Got shot up real bad and lost a leg. This ain't my writin' cuz I'm too sick to write. Nurse Hancock is puttin' down my words for me. I may not make it on account of complications, they say. Lost a lot of blood and got some gangrene. Anyway, I

guess I been out of my mind pretty much with fever but today's not bad.

I want you and Patty to know I love you more than anything in the world. I hope that some day Patty finds her a good husband who will take care of both of you.

My last raid was a disaster. Ended in an ambush by Yank sharpshooters. Only I survived, but we accomplished our mission. Buried the booty near our camp the night before the ambush. Marked by three rocks in Culpeper County near Johnson Creek. Don't tell no one. Not sure yet how this war's gonna turn out.

I miss you both. Wish I could see you again. Know that I did my best for Colonel Mosby, the Confederacy and General Lee. Maybe God will yet spare my life.

Your son,

John Stanton

Ambrose felt his pulse race at the news of buried booty. Could this secret have been hidden for over a hundred years? If so, it meant there was a Civil War treasure out there somewhere, still interred beneath a crude but unobtrusive marker of three stones. Wouldn't Mosby have searched out and recovered the booty? And what about the Union army? Couldn't they, wouldn't they, have tracked down their own goods? Then again, maybe this John Stanton had carried the location to his grave. Maybe Mosby never heard that the raid was successful. And maybe the Union army gave up looking and was too embarrassed about the loss to record it anywhere.

Lapain was preoccupied the rest of the visit with Mrs. Palmer. Though present in body, his mind was far away, wandering fields of fantasy and possibility—obsessed with Stanton's letter and the mysterious reference to buried spoils of war.

As soon as the doors of the Volvo slammed shut, the car was racing for the campus.

"What's the big hurry, Professor?"

"We're on to something here, Holly. You heard that letter from the Confederate soldier, John Stanton?"

"Yeah. That was really something. Really touching."

"It was more than touching."

"What do you mean? I didn't pick up on anything useful in the letter for the book."

"Forget the book. We may be on to something a lot bigger than a research breakthrough. I remember reading something just recently that may tie in with the letter. I'll need your help when we get back to campus."

Supper would be greasy burgers and fries from a drive-thru on the fast food strip adjoining the campus. Professor Lapain tossed the bag on his desk and began to leaf through yellow legal pads.

"It's here somewhere. Check that stack of notes over there."

Obediently, Holly began to rummage through a mountain of scribbled pages, pausing only long enough for a quick mouthful of burger and a few fries.

The campus office of Dr. Lapain bore a striking resemblance to the disorder of his den at home. The man was brilliant in most ways, but his filing skills were definitely flawed. Holly had given up trying to get him organized. He seemed to work best amid the chaos of disorganization.

Sure enough, only ten minutes into the search, they hit paydirt. Dr. Lapain began to scan a page halfway into one of the legal pads.

"Monteiro . . . Doctor . . . Surgeon . . . transferred into Mosby's command . . . published memoirs of war years . . . Noted several curious anecdotes . . ." Lapain hurriedly flipped the page and continued.

"One story of a surgery performed on an officer in Mosby's command . . . Uh . . . no name mentioned here . . . cf. page 168 . . . Holly, check that reference will you? Monteiro's memoirs are in that stack of books beside you."

Holly fingered through the pile and snatched a thin, gray-covered book. Flipping it open, she leafed to page 168, searched, and began to read.

"The sobering realities of this bloody war were underscored for us all in the tragedy of Lieutenant John Stanton's command. Victims of a cowardly Yankee ambush, Stanton's entire command was wiped out. The Lieutenant himself, one of Mosby's favorites, succumbed to complications stemming from the amputation of his right leg. I performed the surgery on a table in a farmhouse a few miles from the Rappahannock River. Odd thing about it, Stanton, delirious from pain and half-conscious, kept repeating a garbled message. Something about three rocks and Culpeper County. The poor lad was obviously beside himself, but the words have stuck in my mind. Such a strange utterance they were. After the amputation we shipped him off immediately to a hospital in Richmond where I'm told he died quite suddenly a week later. Probably a massive blood clot . . ."

"You don't suppose . . ." Holly queried.

"I sure enough do," Ambrose answered. "It looks to me like there's a damn good chance this Stanton guy buried a treasure out there somewhere in Culpeper County, and it's never been recovered."

"Wow. Awesome!" Holly gasped, now feeling the rush of their discovery.

"There could be anything buried out there. Guns. Ammo. Supplies. Money. Gold . . ." His voice trailed off as his mind raced down the corridors of possibility. "Why, there could be enough to make someone very, very wealthy."

"But professor, you don't even know if there really is anything out there. It's been such a long time. Never mind trying to find the exact location. It would be like trying to find a needle in a haystack."

"Oh, it's out there. I know it. I can feel it. I can feel it in my bones." His eyes narrowed as a faraway look came over his face.

Holly did not like that look. There was something disturbing, something sinister, about it.

"I gotta go, Professor. I have a whole stack of papers to grade for tomorrow."

Lapain snapped out of his trance. "Oh. Okay, Holly. See you tomorrow."

He watched as she spun around and headed for the door. "Oh, by the way, Holly, let's keep this discovery as our own little secret, OK? We wouldn't want to cause a big stir over nothing, now would we?"

☙

Ambrose Lapain's hand quivered as it traced the Rappahannock River on the map spread across the oak study table in the main hall of the Georgetown campus library. Only the serious students were here now as the clock approached 11 p.m., and they were too occupied with algebra, chemistry, and American lit. to notice the professor's agitated demeanor or his finger tracing the northward meandering of the Rappahannock, following it to a bridge labeled in tiny block letters—TALAWAGA. The finger stopped there, glued to the spot, as the index digit of the other hand scanned the surrounding area for more obscure bodies of water. Lapain searched his memory banks. The surgeon's memoirs had clearly stated that Stanton's surgery was performed not far from the Rappahannock, and the Confederate Lieutenant's letter had identified Johnson Creek, so it must be nearby—certainly no more than a day's ride. The finger roamed the map. It picked up Pike Road and slowly traced its graceful curves. And there it was—Johnson Creek. Lapain felt his pulse quicken.

The creek wound its way through the countryside for about 12 miles. There were three main crossovers but only one near enough to the Talawaga Bridge. Assuming that Mosby's men were running to the safety of the south, Pike Road would be the logical route since it crossed over the Rappahannock and turned directly south heading straight to Culpeper.

Hardly a head turned as a whistling Lapain sauntered to the door.

❧

Nothing like a Sunday drive in the country. Professor Lapain drank in the beauty of the sunny Virginia day. He wished he had invited Holly along for the ride. After refueling in Culpeper — gas for the car and a cheeseburger for himself — he turned his attention to Pike Road and the Talawaga Bridge. Swirling and churning in muddy torrents, the waters of the Rappahannock River rushed by below as the Volvo traversed the wooden bridge. Another mile or so on Pike Road and Lapain slowed as he approached a newer concrete bridge. A green sign with bright white letters announced Johnson Creek. This was the place. He pulled off the road onto a sandy turnout just before the bridge.

With all the excitement of a gold prospector, he jumped from the parked car. For three hours, Lapain walked. He explored the south side of the bridge on both sides of Pike Road, then crossed to the north side and did the same. He stood on the bridge and surveyed the land in every direction, trying to guess where Confederate troops might have camped 150 years ago. Finally, when clouds moved in from the southwest and rain began to fall, he conceded failure. It was a dreary ride home.

After hitting such an abrupt dead end, Lapain could hear Holly's words echoing in his mind: "It would be like trying to find a needle in a haystack." But this could be the discovery of a lifetime — a life-changing historical find. He refused to throw in the towel, so he handed the problem over to the best researcher he knew — Holly Fenton. After a brief but intensive investigation, she dispatched him to the Culpeper archives located in the bowels of the stately Culpeper Public Library. She had discovered that a wealth of vintage maps lay hidden there—virtually unknown to the general public.

Lapain descended the stairs to the lower level where a faint mustiness permeated the air. The archives desk was manned by a shriveled, elderly lady named Blanche Stevens, according to the nameplate on the desk. Blanche looked like she had been dried and pressed between the pages of one of the thick tomes in the archives surrounding her. And, as Lapain quickly discovered, she quite obviously did not believe in smiling.

"So, it's maps you want," she said suspiciously, glaring over thin reading glasses perched on her nose.

Lapain immediately sensed a possessiveness toward her valued treasures.

"Yes, Ma'am. In particular, I'm looking for maps of the region near Johnson Creek and Pike Road from the Civil War Era. My assistant recently discovered that the road has undergone some rerouting in recent decades, and I'm keenly interested in confirming the old route."

"Hmm. Let me see. Johnson Creek. Pike Road. Seems I recall a bit of controversy over rerouting that road. It was back about 1949 as I recollect. Folks around them parts were against any such change, but local politicians wanted a new bridge. The old one was beyond repair, they said, so it seemed like a good idea to straighten out the road and construct a new bridge at the new location."

"Do you have any maps that would indicate the location of the original road?" Lapain asked.

"Just give me a few minutes, sonny. I'll pull what I can find."

She led the way to stacks of map drawers lining the wall. This corner of the basement smelled mustier as they approached it. Consulting a card catalogue for a moment, Blanche then wheeled and pulled open a wide drawer. Several brittle, yellowed charts lay flat in the drawer. The aging keeper of the archives gently pulled the third map from the top and laid it across a table as carefully as if it were a beloved infant about to have its diaper changed.

"Here is Johnson Creek," she said, pointing a finger to an upper quadrant of the circa 1876 map. The meandering line identifying Johnson Creek clearly bisected Pike Road at a point where road and creek had run parallel to one another in an eastward direction for several hundred yards.

"Can't tell from this map where the new road fits in, young fella," she said. "You're going to need a more modern map to compare with this one."

Lapain was too impatient to think of having to make a return visit to confirm details.

"Well, would it be okay if I just borrowed this map for a couple of days?" he asked.

Blanche Stevens looked like she'd been shot. Lapain realized it was going to take some heavy-duty convincing, and perhaps some groveling, to wrestle the map from her protective custody.

"I could sign it out, couldn't I?" Lapain began, but her head was already shaking.

"I promise I'll have it back here in two days," he persisted. The head shook just as vigorously, and Blanche pulled the map closer as if to protect it from any abduction attempt.

"But, Ms. Stevens, I am a respected professor of American history at Georgetown University.

"Georgetown University?" She repeated the words thoughtfully.

"Yes, Ma'am—Georgetown. So can I please borrow the map?"

"No, you may not," Blanche replied. "But you can use the one in the library at your university."

"What do you mean?" Lapain asked. "I didn't know we had any vintage maps like this."

"Talk to the librarian, Ethel Waters. She's a good friend of mine. In fact, tell her I sent you. She has what you need."

Blanche was grinning broadly—no doubt relieved, thought Lapain, that she would not have to surrender her precious map to this stranger.

"Ethel Waters." Lapain repeated the name as he recorded it on a slip of paper. "Thanks, Blanche." He hugged her and headed for the stairs.

"Say hi to Ethel for me," Blanche yelled after him. Lapain waved.

It was Holly's brilliant idea to visit the nursing home to interview elderly residents in hopes of gleaning information that might help locate the buried treasure. But now, as he made his way to the entrance of the Peaceful Valley Care Facility, Lapain was wishing he had sent Holly instead. She had done the legwork, but he—wanting to keep full control—had insisted on doing the interviews himself.

Peaceful Valley was, well, peaceful. The grounds were a virtual garden of Eden—a splashy flourish of perennials and annuals, in a kaleidoscope of color, texture and fragrance. Lapain entered through sliding glass doors and found a receptionist at the Administrative Offices.

"I'm here to see a Mr. Sweat," he said.

"Welcome," said the cheery receptionist. "Mr. Sweat is in Room 186. Just follow this hallway and turn left at the water fountain. His room is on the right side, about halfway down. You can't miss it."

Lapain dodged wheelchairs and patients in various states of mental acuity as he made his way to Room 186. The overpowering stench of urine emanating from several rooms kept him moving in search of fresh air. He hoped the 104-year-old Mr. Sweat had good bladder control. Upon entering the room, Lapain discovered that Henry Sweat was in firm control of not only his bladder but also his mental capacities. The centenarian was sharp as a tack. His weathered, black face—deeply creased—bore testament to over a century of worry and hard work, but the bloodshot eyes glowed like the fanned embers of an old fire as he spoke of days past.

"Ma grandpappy were a slave on de plantation at White Hall," he drawled. "Home o' Massa Henry Clay. Ah 'memba ma pappy tellin' how he seen da riders comin' up da lane durin' da big war. Dem Bluecoats done marched right up ta da front door o' de big house. Grandpappy so scare' he say he shakin' from head ta toe. Pappy say afta' da war, dey come ova' ta Vuhginia when Massa Clay give 'em dey's freedom."

"So you were born here in Virginia?" Lapain asked.

"Yessuh. Bo'n and rais' right here in Culpepa County. Done lived here all ma life so fars and ah don't thinks ah be plannin' no moves no place now."

"I understand that when you were just a boy you lived in this area?"

"Why, we was livin' just north o' Culpepa 'bout wheres Johnson Crick and Pike Road meets up. Had us a piece o' land in dem parts."

"Was there a bridge near your house?"

"Yessuh. But it ain't there no mo'. They done move dat road west apiece. Don' be askin' me why cuz ah ain't got no idea. Left dat ol' bridge ta rot and done buil' dem a fancy new one."

"Do you remember where the road used to go as you traveled north on Pike Road from Culpeper, Mr. Sweat?"

"Henry. Jus' call me Henry, suh. Shore ah 'member. Use' ta fish off da ol' bridge back when dey was lotsa watta in da crick. Dat road use' ta go east jus' afore da crick," he said, waving a leathery hand in no particular direction. "Foller'd da crick fer a ways, den turnsed north ag'in ova da crick on da ol' bridge. Hell, anybody roun' dem parts could tell y'all dat much, mistuh." The bushy, white eyebrows merged beneath a furrowed brow. "Why y'all so interested in dat ol' bridge anyways?"

Lapain decided it was safe to confide in Henry Sweat. "I'm searching for buried treasure from the Civil War days. I have reason to believe it may be located near that bridge."

"Well, ain't dat sumpin'." Mr. Sweat's eyes were glowing again. "Ah know'd dey was lotsa soldiers campin' 'round dem parts durin' da big war. Seen da remnants o' mo'n a few of dem with ma own eyes. Folks says dem soldiers made demselves circles. Built demselves a campfire in da middle and they done slep' all 'round it."

Lapain pressed for specifics. "Henry, any idea how far from the road the camps were?"

"Well, lemme see." The brow furrowed again. "Da ones I seen was 'bout 500 paces, mebbe mo', mebbe less. From da bridge dat is."

Lapain suddenly jumped to his feet.

"Mr. Sweat, I mean Henry, I have to run. I want to thank you for the information. You've been a great help to me. Thanks for your time." He shook the old man's hand firmly.

"Well, time's 'bout all ah gots anymo'," Sweat said. "Time, lotsa time and nuthin' ta do wid it. Ya'll come back sometime, pufessa, so's we can jaw some mo' 'bout dem good ol' days."

The dark blue Volvo slid quietly off the road onto the sandy turnout just before the familiar concrete bridge spanning Johnson Creek. Pike Road and Johnson Creek—the desired crossover—but it was modern Pike Road. Lapain had no further interest in this new section of the road. He glanced across the front seat to reference his cherished photocopy of Ethel Waters' vintage map. Pike road originally veered off to the east just south of the creek. This must be the spot. The land leveled off along the south side of Johnson Creek forming a natural roadbed that followed the sweeping curves of the creek. Lapain tried to imagine what this area must have looked like over a hundred years ago when Union and Confederate troops marched these roads.

The professor followed the creek for several hundred yards, glancing warily about, not wanting to be spotted on this reconnaissance mission. The water level in the creek was low. Grasses, weeds and small trees hung over the banks as if bending to drink. Lapain kept walking until he spotted old rotting planks hung up in the far bank. Could be timbers from the remains of an old bridge. This may have been the crossover point for the old Pike Road. If so, Stanton's party must have camped somewhere in the vicinity.

Several hundred yards from the creek, the ground rose sharply to the crest of a hill. The entire hill was heavily treed except for a large clearing where an impressive modern home stood. A well-worn path circled the base of the hill and the trees thinned out on this lower table. After exploring the creek bank for about a mile, Lapain turned back. Nearing the site of the washed out bridge, this time combing the underbrush farther from the creek, he nearly tripped over a piece of cast iron lodged in the soil. Next to the hunk of iron were three rocks stacked one on top of another. Lapain's heart leaped to his throat.

This was no freak of nature arrangement. Someone had purposely placed the stones in this manner. Lapain snatched up the piece of iron. Definitely a crude casting. Pre-twentieth century for sure. It was a T-shaped channel, open on the bottom, with holes near the ends for connecting bolts. Might have been used on a wagon or caisson to attach the tongue to the crossbeam. It could easily be a relic from the Civil War Era. The rocks were up to 18 inches across, six to eight inches high. Judging by the accumulation of dirt and dead leaves around them, they had not been disturbed for some time.

The crouching professor was too absorbed in his discovery to notice the pair of yellow eyes zeroing in on him. The only warning was a ferocious deep growl and a broken twig as a massive beast lunged at him. The snarling brute knocked him on his back, then sunk its canines into Lapain's left arm, tearing flesh. Lapain was too shocked to scream. He grabbed a broken limb next to him, and began clubbing the animal over the head. It was life or death. Lapain struck with ferocity as his own survival instinct kicked in. The foaming grip on his arm only tightened. Huge paws ripped at his chest. Smack! He clubbed it again and again. Finally, one crashing blow hit the mark, leaving the beast lying motionless in a pool of blood.

His immediate instinct was to turn and run, but Lapain's keen mind quickly overrode that impulse. He looked at his fallen attacker. A Rottweiler—and a big one. Must be at least 130 pounds. A massive chest, with beautiful tan and black coat. If he left it here, someone would surely come looking for it and would undoubtedly discover the marker and its buried secret.

Though his knees still shook and his arm throbbed, Lapain grabbed the animal's hind legs and dragged it a hundred yards or more alongside the creek. Then he returned to the site of the battle and meticulously brushed away every sign of struggle, every footprint and every trace of blood.

He knew his own crudely wrapped wound needed medical attention, so he headed back toward the car. Halfway there, the quiet of the forest was disturbed by the light patter of footsteps. Turning, Lapain spied three more magnificent Rottweilers closing the gap on him! He would never make the car. They would run him down easily. The only other option was the creek. He dove in feet first up to his waist and desperately waded to the far shore. He clambered up the bank just as the dogs reached the other side, snarling and growling. Strange thing, though. They did not pursue him across the creek, as if an invisible fence held them there.

Shaken and sore, the professor scrambled back to the main road and followed it back to his car. He headed for home and a hospital.

THREE

A sleek, black Lincoln Mark VIII with personalized plate bearing the letters V-I-C-T-O-R, purred as it left the sleepy southern town of Culpeper behind. The familiar voice of pop singer John Denver gushed from all eight speakers, "Country road take me home . . ." as the elegant coupe veered off County Road 46 onto Pike Road. Across the Talawaga Bridge it sped, leaning into the curves and devouring the straightaways. Catlike, the black machine slowed as it approached a stylish rural mailbox, a miniature mansion on a post, with the name Johns emblazoned on its foundation. With a sudden leap, the Lincoln veered onto a narrow tree-lined driveway. Victor Johns was home.

The land still stirred something deep within him after all these years. This was his pride and joy. Tenacity and hard work rewarded. A dream come true. Twenty-two years ago he had purchased this wooded 30-acre parcel of land. It would be his retirement haven. For nearly a quarter of a century it had been his sanctuary, a place of rest and relaxation, a retreat from the hectic executive lifestyle in the

Capital. He had hunted and camped here, built a small cabin, dug a well, and cleared a site on the highest point of land for his dream home.

As the Mark VIII emerged from the towering oaks into a large clearing, the dream house came into view. It was a striking wooden structure with dramatic, sloping roof lines and expansive banks of windows offering panoramic views of the surrounding trees and grounds. An impressive deck stretched out over the lower level patio and entry.

The Lincoln crawled past a phalanx of Rottweilers into the two-car garage and grew silent. From the driver's side door, a compact athletic man in his mid-fifties emerged. Victor Johns took pride in his trim body. He had continued a rigorous daily workout regimen since his stint in the Marines back in the '60s. He shouted a greeting to the dogs, then disappeared into the house.

"Any mail?" he asked, entering the country-style kitchen and depositing a brown grocery sack on the counter.

"Yes, Vic, there's another letter from that real estate agent. It's on the breakfast bar. Says they're willing to up the offer by $10,000."

Victor snatched the envelope off the counter and skimmed the letter. He had to see for himself. There it was in black and white, a $10,000 hike over the previous offer. The signature was Homer Townsend's, that pompous wheeler-dealer, real estate whiz — a scavenger feeding off the carcasses of hard-working, honest people doing business with one another. Even Townsend's letterhead reeked of ostentation. Homer N. Townsend, B.A., M.A., King of Realty. The man was a fool but somehow managed to charm his clients into lucrative deals that paid him handsome fees. He cared little for their needs or happiness. The bottom line was his profit margin.

"What's with this guy, Sal?" Victor asked as his wife, Sally, appeared in the doorway. "I've told him three times already that I don't intend to sell for any price. Can't he get that through his fat, little head?"

"Knowing Homer Townsend, he probably boasted to some client that he could arrange a deal for this place, and now he's trying awfully hard to keep his word."

"You're probably right. I've had about enough of Homer Townsend."

The telephone abruptly interrupted the conversation. Sally grabbed the receiver from the wall.

"Hello?" She listened. "Yes, he's here. Just a minute." Covering the handset, Sally whispered, "It's the King of Realty, asking for you," and handed it to Victor. He scowled.

"Hello? . . . Yes, I got the updated offer but the answer is the same, Homer. I don't want to sell. I am not going to sell — for any price. Got it? By the way, what's the big interest in my property, anyway? There are a dozen properties in the area as nice as this one. Why not go after one of them?"

The conversation ended quickly after that. When Victor hung up, Sally asked, "What did he say to that?"

"Oh, something about an anonymous out-of-town client who specifically wants this property."

"Well, I can understand that. It's quite a love nest," she said as she slipped into Victor's arms for a hug. "Trouble is, they don't understand how much sweat and blood you've put into this place over the years."

"Yeah, I've poured heart and soul into this chunk of land, haven't I? We've got a truckload of memories here, don't we?"

"You bet," Sally said, as they embraced in a long, passionate kiss.

Ambrose Lapain's roots were not in the north. He had been raised in a staunch Southern Baptist family in Black Mountain, South Carolina, a conservative town tucked into the shadow of the Blue Ridge Mountains and bordered by the towering expanse of the Pisgah National Forest. It was a wondrous place to grow up, but Lapain soon felt the urge to expand his horizons. As a teenager, he longed to explore life beyond the shadow of the Blue Ridge Mountains and what he saw as the oppressive Baptist life. So, upon completion of high school, he threw off the shackles of the genteel southern life for the more unabashed secular leanings of the north. Michigan State University became his home for the next eight years as he completed his undergraduate degree in history, then a Ph.D. with special emphasis on The Civil War.

He had never returned to the south, at least not to live, but the memories never faded. He remembered attending the Mount Zion Baptist Church with the entire family, the whole clan packing a couple of pews every Sunday—morning and evening. In Sunday school, he heard all the old stories about Jesus walking on the water and feeding the five thousand with five loaves and two fish.

His grandmother was the matriarch—a spit-and-polish churchwoman who wouldn't dream of missing services for any reason short of deathly illness. She regularly preached against the immorality of the changing times — frequently quoting Scripture to back up her views. No one dared question Granny's authority on matters religious or moral.

Ambrose recalled that church services afforded sensational theatrical entertainment, especially twice a year when the traveling evangelists would come to town for a week of revival. With their white suits, white shoes, slicked-back hair, and a giant-sized Bible tucked under their arm, these saintly men of the cloth would launch into animated hellfire-and-brimstone sermons on the evils of drinking, dancing and womanizing. Brother so-and-so was, by all indications, on intimate terms with the Lord, getting his sermons straight from the mouth of Jesus — and people listened. Lapain remembered a particularly colorful sixty-minute treatise on the evils of playing cards. Though he had never found the actual scriptural reference declaring playing cards evil, he never picked up a deck of cards again without some pangs of conscience.

Now, in the weeks since hearing of the Culpeper County secret treasure, one recurring Biblical image was haunting Lapain. It was the parable of the merchant who found the one pearl of great value and went and sold all that he had in order to buy that magnificent gem. Daily, Lapain's own luminous pearl — buried treasure — entranced him. It dangled in his conscience, like the hare chased by racing greyhounds, always just ahead, barely out of arm's reach — attainable, if only he could grasp it. It was all he thought about these days.

The strategy he had embraced with respect to his 'pearl' came from a companion parable that he recalled about a man who found a treasure in a field and hid it, then went and bought the property. Like the man in the parable, Lapain had sold out to the singular, all-consuming pursuit of procuring the parcel of land containing the treasure.

That quest had him peering through a blue haze of cigar smoke enveloping the Volvo's interior, searching the business establishments along old Route 42. The yellow pages had it listed at 4069 Route 42. There was King's Lumber Yard, 3800. Must be getting closer now. Dilapidated buildings, junk-strewn grounds and pot-holed driveways were standard fare on this stretch of old 42, but Lapain did not mind one bit. He smiled at the thought of laying out his proposal to some poverty-ridden redneck and watching his eyes light up and his mouth drool at the mention of the financial returns at stake.

Lapain had not wanted to resort to Plan B especially when Plan A had held such high promise. He was still stewing over the botched efforts of that boasting little fat man, Homer Townsend. The hollow, unfulfilled promises to secure Victor John's property rankled him. No more sitting back, waiting for the Homer Townsends to deliver. He wanted results.

Oh, he had repressed the real anger and impatience quite nicely. "Thanks for your efforts, Mr. Townsend. I have some other options I plan to pursue on the Maryland side, but please notify me immediately if Mr. Johns ever changes his mind and decides to sell. I am extremely fond of that piece of land." But once outside the door, out of earshot, he had cursed that pompous ass, Townsend, and immediately set his mind to Plan B.

❧

There was the sign now.   Weather-beaten and faded, its letters barely legible, Lapain could decipher the words, Crazy Jake's Salvage Company.   He guided the Volvo through a maze of chuckholes into a compound surrounded by ten-foot-high chain link fence.   If the drive looked like the scene of mortar shell practice, the compound resembled the rest of the battlefield.   Mere shells of once-stylish automobiles lay strewn all over the yard, rusting, in row after row of shattered windshields, dented fenders, crushed roofs. Some stripped down.   Doorless.   Sagging on flattened rubber. Others piled two or three high. Squashed. A graveyard of steel, glass, rubber and plastic.

Lapain butted out the stub of the cigar, tossing it on the ground and stomping it under his size 12 wingtips.   As he strode to the door marked entrance, a monstrous black beast emerged from behind the building and charged.   Not again! Lapain froze at the sight of foaming mouth and bared teeth lunging and snarling at him.   Instinctively, he cowered, drawing his recently wounded left arm close to his body for protection.   Then he heard the snap of a heavy steel chain as the massive, ugly dog was intercepted in mid-air and yanked to the ground, still barking madly. Lapain ran for the door and burst into a dingy outer office, slamming the door behind him.

"What the hell kind of monster is that out there?" he asked no one in particular.

"Oh, that's just Rex," replied a husky female voice. "He's our watch dog. Hey, relax. He hasn't eaten anybody yet."

The plump redhead exploded into a belly laugh that ended in a hacking coughing spell. She wheezed, took a long drag on a cigarette stuck between her chubby fingers and blew a cloud of smoke in Lapain's general direction. "What can I do for ya, mister?"

Having regained his composure and ignoring the cloud billowing around his head, the professor got right to the point.

"I'm Dr. Ambrose Lapain. I'm here to see Jake Crapper."

"Ooh, a real, live doctor right here in our little old office," cooed the receptionist sarcastically. "Have a seat, Doc. I'll get Mr. Crapper for you." She giggled as she disappeared through a door bearing the sign 'Employees Only.'

In a flash she was back. "He'll be with you in a couple of minutes, Doc. You can wait in his office," she said politely, gesturing toward an open doorway in the corner.

The professor stepped through the doorway into a shabby little office with a décor matching the basic drab of the outer receptionist area. An ancient steel desk hogged most of the floor space. It was flanked by tall, green file cabinets with vertical doors. A vinyl armchair on casters sat behind the desk. The walls were plastered with pin-up girls and stock-car and motorcycle posters. Everything was coated with a layer of dust and grease.

Lapain pulled up a chair with torn upholstery, ignoring the stuffing dangling from the seat cushion. It was important to look cool and controlled. He would dictate the terms. This was his project. He would call the shots. As Lapain mentally rehearsed his presentation, a bear of a man filled the doorway. Coarse black hair, drawn back in a ponytail, and a thick beard wreathed his round face. Matching eyebrows shadowed piercing brown eyes. An ample belly hung over his over-sized belt buckle and massive, tattooed forearms extended like pipes from the sleeves of a black and silver Harley T-shirt. A ragged scar ran from his right temple down across the cheekbone.

"Sorry to keep ya waitin', mister," growled the bear. "Not often we get fancy folks like yourself out our way. Name's Crapper. Jake, my friends call me." He extended a greasy paw. "What can I do for ya?"

Ambrose shook the hand firmly and sat down again. "I'm Dr. Ambrose Lapain, history professor at Georgetown University. I'm working on a secret project and need some special help."

"What kind of help?"

"Well, we'll get to that in a minute, but let me bring you up to speed first. I won't bore you with all the fine details. Here's the condensed version. In researching my latest book, I have stumbled upon some information about a buried treasure and I want to recover it . . ."

"Wait a minute," Crapper interrupted. "You're tellin' me you found a buried treasure? Like in pirates and such? You feelin' okay, mister?"

"Listen, Mr. Crapper . . . Jake. This is no joke. I've located the site of buried booty from the Civil War. The spot is undisturbed as far as I can tell. It's in a wooded section of a private estate."

"And you want us to go and dig it up for ya, right?"

"Well, not exactly. You see, there's a catch. I'm not sure what is buried there. It could be money—gold from a payroll. Or it could be guns or ammunition or supplies. But whatever it is, it has to be worth a fortune after all these years. We're talking seven figures, Jake. If you help me out, you'll get a handsome return for your labors."

The mere mention of big bucks reeled in Jake Crapper — hook, line and sinker. Desire — no greed — was etched all over his hairy face.

"Just tell us where it is, and we'll go get it."

"That's the catch, Jake. Highly trained killer dogs guard the property. I nearly had my arm ripped off just confirming the location. But the dogs are not the only problem. Since this is such a profound historical discovery, I am going to have to document it all very carefully. That means identifying the burial site and detailing the recovery of the goods. I cannot do that if someone else owns the property. I would be charged with trespassing. The legal owner would probably get custody of the goods, and my reputation would be dirt."

Jake was reaching for a cigarette now, hanging on every word. He lit up as Ambrose continued.

"I've tried anonymously, through an agent, to purchase the property. So far, every offer has been rejected and the word I get is that the owner stubbornly refuses to sell — at any price. Jake, I've got to have that property. That's where you come in. I need a little muscle to convince this guy to sell. I assure you, you will be well-compensated for your trouble."

Jake's mind was racing. Lapain could see it and, like a mind reader, he knew exactly what Jake Crapper was thinking: "This could be my big break, my ticket outta this God-forsaken dump."

"Whaddya want me to do?" asked an obviously interested Jake.

"We can work that out later," replied Lapain. "Right now, I just need to know whether to count you in."

"Professor," the bear grinned approvingly, extending a greasy paw. "You've got yourself a partner."

They shook hands vigorously to seal the pact. Both men were beaming from ear to ear.

FOUR

Aren't you proud of Kim, Vic? It's hard to believe, isn't it? Our baby all grown up and head trauma nurse at the Alexandria Hospital. She is such a responsible young lady, isn't she?" Sally broke the long silence.

"Yes. I just hope she isn't working too hard. There's so much stress on the ER trauma team. I know she's made of strong stuff, but the shifts are a real killer, too, on top of the stress."

"I know I couldn't handle it, but then I'm not twenty-eight years old anymore," confessed Sally.

"And you don't need any more stress in your life. You have enough trauma putting up with the likes of me everyday," joked Vic.

"You've got that right, mister. I have the gray hair to prove it, too."

The journey home marked the end of a pleasant day spent with daughter Kim. A leisurely lunch at Red Lobster had followed a tour of Kim's plush new condo in Alexandria. Still single, though quite attractive, Kim had invested herself in career, moving up the ranks at an astonishing pace. There had been a few relationships along the way—all casual, however.

The high-stress, fast-pace Emergency Room nursing was her first love. The solitude of her condo, with its muted greens and soft pastels, was Kim's oasis away from work. The apartment exuded a peaceful tranquillity.

The Johns were turning into the narrow lane now. Sally's seat was in reclining position. Her eyes were closed so Vic was the first to see the dogs. Tiger was staggering across the yard like a drunk emerging from a roadhouse bar in the wee hours of the morning. Duke looked agitated, parading back and forth, nose to the ground. Sarge lay motionless on the ground alongside the lane.

Not again, thought Vic! He had mourned Prince's death after finding the poor beast lying in a pool of blood at the far side of the property, his head smashed in. These dogs were part of the Johns family. He nudged Sally gently and jumped from the car to kneel beside Sarge's still body. The big guy was still breathing. Thank God for that. In a stupor, Tiger dragged himself to his master.

"What's wrong with them, Vic?" an awake Sally asked.

"I'm not sure, Sal. Seems like they've been drugged or something."

"Vic!" screamed Sally, pointing in horror toward the house.

Lying not more than a couple of feet from the east wall of the house, was a massive oak. The towering tree had been deliberately felled with a chainsaw. The brunt of its bulk had dropped across the rear deck, reducing it to kindling.

Vic ran to check the damage. He stooped to pick up a handful of sawdust and fired the particles into the air. Who would have done such a low-down, mindless thing? Fortunately, the tree had missed the actual house. A few of the longer branches had scratched the brick and wood siding, but there was no structural damage other than the deck.

Vic's anger quickly channeled into questions. Who did this? And why? Sally, however, was nearly hysterical. Tears ran down her cheeks at the sight of the damage and the thought of the near calamity. She felt violated and vulnerable. This was their private property. What kind of sick personality would do something like this? She shivered even in the warmth of the late afternoon sun.

"Come on inside, Sal," said Vic, as he took her by the hands and led her inside. "Don't worry about it. I'll clean it up tomorrow. We can rebuild the deck. Everything will be okay. You'll see. Here, make some coffee. I'll bring the car up and tend to the dogs."

Once outside again, Vic scoured the area around the fallen tree looking for answers, clues, anything. Sawdust was scattered like snow on the groundcover of dead leaves. The aroma of freshly cut wood hung in the air around the stump. There were no clues to be found. No clothing items left behind during a hasty retreat. No visible footprints. No way to tell how many perpetrators there were. Nothing . . . except . . . what was this? A single footprint in a bare patch of soft ground where the leaves had been shoved aside. It looked like the soleprint from a workboot. The right foot. Must be a Red Wing boot, thought Vic. He could barely make out the imprint of the wing logo about halfway along the sole. It was an average size — maybe a ten. The only other distinguishing mark was a definite groove in the heel along the right side.

Vic retrieved the Polaroid camera from the bedroom and snapped several pictures of the fallen tree and surrounding area, including the demolished deck and the solitary footprint. Now he needed a good, strong cup of coffee.

It was a long night. Sally, beneficiary of a tranquilizer, dozed like a baby. Vic spent most of the night staring at the stars through the skylight above the bed, listening for the sound of intruders, straining to hear the tiniest whimper from the canine patrol. All was quiet except for the gentle whisper of the wind in the trees, a hooting owl and the incessant serenade of the crickets.

The first light of dawn was a welcome sight. A quick breakfast and Vic jumped right into the clean-up. He lopped off the smaller branches with a hatchet and stacked them to be burned.   Not wanting to alarm Sally by using the chainsaw, he swung the ax instead. It was tedious and tiring but therapeutic, too. Each blow drained off another ounce of the deep anger boiling inside.

By the time Sally emerged from the house, the sun was peeking over the treetops and Vic had a small mountain of tree parts stacked in the clearing.

"Want some help, Vic?"

"No, I'm doing okay. I'll get the chainsaw out now that you're up. That will speed things up quite a bit. How are you feeling, anyway?"

"Not bad. I slept pretty well. I'm still a little nervous, though."

"That's understandable."

"Vic, what is going on? Who would have done this? And why? We have never hurt anybody or done anything to make anybody mad at us. It just doesn't make any sense."

"I don't have any answers either, Sal. Listen, let's just go on with our lives as normally as we can and hope this is the end of it."

"All right. We need a few things at the grocery. I think I'll take a run into town now. Need anything?"

"No, I don't think so. On second thought, maybe you should pick up a tube of BENGAY."

"How about some horse liniment?" suggested Sally with a laugh. It was good to see her smiling again.

Sally backed the red Honda Pilot out of the garage and eased the sport utility along the winding drive. She waved at Vic who was busy planting some shrubs across a freshly-dug front garden bed. She loved her excursions into Culpeper to explore the quaint shops. On her list today was the Book Emporium where she hoped to find John Grisham's latest legal thriller, and the Gourmet Coffee Shop which carried an extensive line of imported specialty coffees, a treat both she and Vic enjoyed during quiet evenings lounging on the deck or snuggled up in front of a crackling fire in the den. The scene that loomed before her as the vehicle reached the end of the lane obliterated that romantic thought. Sally slammed on the brakes, and the SUV skidded to a dusty halt on the gravel. Across the road was their rural mailbox, a perfect replica of their dream home, engulfed in a ball of flames. In horror,

Sally leaped from her vehicle, screaming at the top of her lungs.

Vic arrived in seconds on a dead run and took Sally into his arms to console her. As the hysteria calmed, Vic noticed something nailed to the post, beneath the flaming house. Stooping to get a closer look, he found a charred note bearing the scribbled words: NEXT TIME THE REAL THING! A cold shudder swept through Vic's body. So, the felled tree was no isolated incident. This was no coincidence. Someone was orchestrating a deliberately planned series of scare tactics. But why? Who was behind this?

Sally was still sobbing and shaking uncontrollably as Vic led her back up the lane, across the yard and into the house. He tried not to let his own apprehension show. He had to be strong for her now, but all the time his nerves were frayed with fear. His hands were shaking and his heart racing.

"Come and lie down, Sal. I'll get you a glass of water and a tranquilizer. We have to stay calm. I'm sure there's some explanation for all this. Probably just some teenagers getting their kicks."

"But why us, Vic?" Sally's voice quivered. "Why don't they pick on somebody else? We don't deserve this. We've never hurt anybody," she whimpered.

"I don't know, Sal, but I intend to find out."

Sheriff Sam Bodie heard dispatcher Chester Muldoon's voice as the radio in his cruiser chattered away. He smiled as he heard Deputy Nate Peters acknowledge Chester's call for an officer on duty to respond to a domestic disturbance at the

Peterson place out on Fowler Road. Old man Peterson must have been hitting the bottle again.

The sheriff had weightier issues to deal with this morning as he chewed on a toothpick and cruised along Pike Road with his left elbow sticking out the window. Sam Bodie wore a certain arrogance much like a second uniform that warned others — this was not a man to be crossed.

He pulled the cruiser over to the side of the road, flattening the weeds that bordered the shoulder. He swung the door wide and sprung to his feet, adjusting his gun belt and hat as he swaggered over to the charred remains of a rather fancy mailbox. Stooping with considerable effort on account of his paunch, he read the note nailed to the post. No doubt somebody's idea of a practical joke. He almost snickered at the thought of Vic Johns going into apoplexy at the sight of his fancy mailbox going up in flames. Sam Bodie did not hide his disdain for the rich city folk who had invaded his turf over the past few years. They came out here to the outskirts of town from D.C. with their big-city ways and influence and built large houses on prime real estate. They were different. Not like the simple southern folk who had grown up hereabouts. They were foreigners as far as he was concerned, and he couldn't stomach any of them.

As the cruiser crept up the lane to the house, Sheriff Bodie recalled the policing controversy 18 months ago. The town council was considering hiring out the town's policing to the State Police as a cost-cutting measure. A number of the newcomers, including Vic Johns, had campaigned loudly for the new arrangement. In fact, Vic Johns and that former D.C. judge, Fred Hamilton, had nearly swayed the vote in their favor. Had he not held such a tight grip on the business community, Bodie might have been out of a job. From that day forward, he had marked Vic Johns and Fred Hamilton as threats to his little empire. How ironic to now be responding to a citizen's complaint from Vic Johns, the very man who tried to oust him from his job.

Bodie parked the cruiser in front of the double garage doors and stepped from the car. He swaggered to the door and knocked loudly. Glancing about, he caught a glimpse of his reflection in the side window next to the door. Not too shabby, he thought. He looked good in the brown uniform and striped pants with the bold holster hanging at his hip. His piercing brown eyes, thick black eyebrows and mustache made him look downright serious. Just needed to lose a few pounds around the middle — too much beer consumed as an armchair quarterback.

He heard the deadbolt slide and the door began to swing open. He took his hat in hand as Sally Johns appeared in the doorway.

"Mornin', Ma'am," he said. "I'm Sheriff Bodie. Is your husband home?"

"Why, yes, he is, Sheriff. Come in. I'll get him for you."

Sam Bodie glanced around at the impressive entry as he crossed the threshold. Ceramic tile floors blended with fine oak trim. A circular stairway drew his gaze to the heavily beamed cathedral ceiling. An abundance of green plants and dried flower arrangements added a touch of warmth and elegance. There were expansive banks of windows and skylights. Sam felt a little out of his element here, and it only fed his irritation at being called to the Johns' residence.

"Ah, Sheriff, how are you? Come in. Thanks for coming out," gushed Vic Johns, showing no sign of any animosity toward the sheriff.

"All in the line of duty, Mr. Johns. So what can I do for you?"

"Well," Vic responded, "did you see the mailbox on your way in?"

"Yes, as a matter of fact, I did."

"Then come on over here and see what's left of our deck on the back of the house," Vic said, as he turned to lead the way to the bank of windows in the great room that looked out on the rear of the house.

Sheriff Bodie took in the shattered remains of what had been a huge deck area. Now it lay in splintered pieces strewn across the ground.

"So you say you arrived home to find the tree cut down and lying across the deck? And you have no idea who might have done this or why?"

"That's right, Sheriff. Obviously the two incidents must be related. Somebody is trying to put a scare into us. Why, I don't know, but the note on the mailbox post is definitely a threat."

"Now, listen here, Mr. Johns. You all don't wanna go jumpin' to conclusions about this. Looks to me like some good ol' boys is just havin' a little fun with you city folks. I don't think there's anything to get alarmed about. I'm sure they've had their fun now, and that'll be the end of it. They'll move on to some other prank somewhere else. I've seen this sort of thing before. I'll keep my ear to the ground and see if I can't come up with a lead on who might've done this. In the meantime, just relax. It ain't nothin' to get all riled up about."

"Well, I'm glad you can be so calm about it all, Sheriff, but I've got a wife in there who's on the verge of hysteria every time she hears a strange sound outside." Vic began to lose his composure. "We've had our privacy invaded, our personal property destroyed, our dogs drugged, and all you can say is, relax? Come on, Sheriff, surely you can do better than that."

"Believe me, Mr. Johns, I am truly sorry for the property damage that's been done, but there's not much I can do 'til I have a suspect. Now, me and my deputies will ask around and sniff out a few clues if we can, but until then, all you can do is carry on as normal as possible. I'm sure this'll all blow over."

Bodie, sensing Vic's rising anger, made his way to the door. "If we come up with anything we'll let you know right away. Have a good day, now." And with that, he closed the door behind him, stepped to the car, tossed his hat on the seat and climbed in.

Sally immediately read the anger in Vic's face as she entered the room.

"What did the sheriff say?" she asked.

"Not much. He said we should relax; that it's probably just some pranksters getting their kicks and we've probably seen the last of it already." Vic paced the floor. "He said he'll try to track down the locals who did this."

"Well, that's a little comforting to know that he thinks it's just some pranksters," offered Sally. "Maybe he's right. Maybe that will be the end of it. And maybe they'll even catch the people who did this."

"I hope you're right, Sally. I hope you're right," Vic replied almost absent-mindedly. His mind was racing. An unsettled feeling had lodged in his gut, and he couldn't shake it. It kept him awake late into the night. Wide-eyed, he stared at the ceiling as he lay next to Sally, listening to her rhythmic breathing. None of this made any sense. What possible motive could anyone have for intruding on their private lives? What did they hope to gain from such mindless vandalism?

Not since trudging through the rice paddies of Vietnam in the face of sniper fire, had Vic felt so vulnerable. He had always prided himself on providing a safe, secure environment for his family. Now that had been stripped away. It tore a piece of his manhood with it. He took it as a personal failure. He had failed in the line of duty. The red numbers on the alarm clock flipped to 2:00 AM. Vic continued staring at the ceiling.

FIVE

The meeting took place in Jake Crapper's dingy little office. His stove-pipe arms dominated the desktop, and a toothy grin revealed bad teeth. Ambrose Lapain reclined in the client chair with the dangling stuffing.

"So, how did it go?" he inquired of the big man.

"Went off like a well-planned huntin' trip," replied Jake with that big toothy grin. "Not a hitch. We got the phone line tapped and the house bugged and they won't even suspect nothin' on account of that tree crushin' that big ol' deck of theirs. It was a perfect diversion, Doc. Good thinkin'."

"Now, remember, Jake, the bugs are just for surveillance, so we can keep track of their coming and going and maybe pull off a few more shocking surprises to get more leverage. You and your men have to be careful not to give them any reason to suspect the bugs."

"Don't you worry none 'bout us, Doc. Me 'n' the boys are havin' a real good time with this project of yours. In fact, we're ready for a little more of that creative destruction.

Kinda get a kick out of picturin' that rich guy goin' out of his head tryin' to figure out what's happenin' to him."

"Well, that's a good start, anyway. So what have you picked up on the surveillance so far?"

"We got Whitey out there in a beat up old van that looks like it's abandoned in the weeds. He says the old lady's been pretty upset with everything, but the guy's mostly pretty calm. Sometimes he gets madder than a hornet, especially when they called in the local sheriff and he did squat for them. Just said it was some good ol' boys havin' a little fun. Boy, was he right! Anyway, this Johns guy seems like a pretty tough bird. He doesn't rattle too easy from the sound of it. Ex-marine type, says Whitey."

"He'll crack," Lapain shot back. "He has to. I need that land. We're going to make him beg us to take it off his hands. He'll be ready to give it to us before we're done."

"And then we get the big payoff, right Doc?"

"You've got it, Jake. The BIG payoff."

"So, what's next, Doc?"

"Well, I think maybe we should tighten the screws a little bit on our tough guy Vic Johns. We have to exploit his biggest weakness right now."

"What's that, Doc?"

"The little lady."

Crazy Jake grinned again. "The boys are gonna like this."

Two weeks had passed since the mailbox incident. Maybe the sheriff was right. Maybe they had seen the end of the pranks. Sally felt free and relaxed again, though she worried about Vic. He seemed to brood a lot. He was having trouble letting it go and getting on with his life. Of course, he had the rebuilding of the deck as a constant reminder of the incidents. She had left him hammering and sawing this morning as she headed into town. Better pick up a six-pack for him — he'll be hot and tired by late afternoon. Maybe a couple of T-bones, too, to throw on the grill.

Sally wheeled the shopping cart past the fresh produce and headed for the meat counter. She didn't notice the burly man in the Harley T-shirt hiding behind a jumbo box of corn flakes. His eyes slyly followed her as she passed by. When Sally stopped to chat with Mrs. Hamilton, the judge's wife, the big man coolly walked right on past the two ladies and pretended to examine the ingredients listed on a package of Oreo cookies.

"We really must have you and Fred over for a barbecue soon, Esther."

"Why that would be nice, Sally, and maybe we could play some cards, too. You know how the boys like their euchre."

"I think they'd prefer poker, if we let them choose."

"But we wouldn't want to take all their money, now, would we?" They both laughed and parted, promising to call one another to get a date on the calendar.

Sally swept down the meat counter, grabbed two steaks, and headed for the checkout. She squinted as she stepped through the automatic door into the bright sunlight and crossed the parking lot. She unlocked the driver's door and hopped in, reaching to set the bag of groceries on the floor of the passenger's side. As she returned to an upright position, a hand clamped tightly over her mouth from behind. Sally panicked and struggled to break loose, but the hands that held her were too powerful.

"Just relax, sweetheart, and no harm will come to you," a voice whispered in her ear. The pungent smell of stale beer hung in the enclosed space of the vehicle. Sally stole a glance at the rear view mirror to see her assailant, but the mirror had been flipped up toward the roof.

"I've got a message for that husband of yours, dearie. You tell him it's time to pack up and move away from here while he still has all his valuables. You got that?" Trembling, Sally nodded, panic in her eyes. The hand over her mouth was chapped and smelled of grease. The rough skin grated her face.

"Now, you're gonna sit right here like a good little girl when I get out and you're gonna look straight ahead and count to 100 before you look around. See that car next to us with the black windows?" He roughly jerked her head to the side to make sure she got a good look at the car. "There's a fella in there with a gun pointed at your head and he's got an itchy trigger finger. He'd love to blow your brains all over this seat, but he won't shoot unless you do somethin' stupid like turn around or honk or scream or get out of this truck. So you start countin' to 100, then slowly drive out of this parking lot and go straight home to give your husband that special message, OK?"

And with that the man was gone. Sally sat shaking and sobbing. For a long time, she couldn't move at all. Finally, a teenaged boy and his girlfriend approached the car with the black windows. They hopped in, and as they drove off, Sally read the license plate. S-H-A-D-O-W.

Hands still trembling uncontrollably, Sally fumbled with her keys, got the engine started, and slowly exited the parking lot. She drove home in a daze.

When the garage door closed behind her, the dam broke. Sally's chest heaved with great sobs, and tears poured down her cheeks in little rivers. She was numb. Her limbs were leaden. She stared, unseeing, at the windshield for a long time. When Vic flung the door open, she bolted in fear.

"Sally, what's wrong? What happened?" Vic searched her face for answers. Her eyes were wide with fear. Folding her into his arms, he carried her into the house, laid her on the sofa, and pleaded for an explanation. Her words came out jumbled between sobs as she clung to Vic's neck.

"He . . . he . . . grabbed me!"

"Who grabbed you? Sally, who grabbed you?"

Sniffling and more tears. "I don't know. He was . . . hiding . . . in the truck. When I got in he . . . he . . ." More sobbing.

"He did what, Sal?"

"He told me to tell you . . . sniff . . . that it was time to pack up and move away from here . . . while you still had all your valuables."

"What did he look like?"

"I don't know. He told me not to turn around or a man with a gun in the next car would . . . would . . . blow my brains out." More sobbing. "I was so scared, Vic. I . . . I . . . I just did what he said. Oh, Vic, I thought he was going to kill me." She was bawling now.

Vic held her close, trying to comfort her. Now there will be hell to pay, he thought, as he cradled the woman he loved so dearly. It ripped his insides to see her suffering like this.

❧

The Culpeper County Police Department was located in the courthouse, an older, three-story red brick building with a flag pole in front bearing the stars 'n' stripes and the flag of Virginia. The sidewalk in front was flanked by a row of reserved parking spots for the sheriff and his deputies. There were two spots for visitors, and it was into one of these that Vic Johns' Lincoln shot, coming to an abrupt halt. The door swung open; Vic jumped out, raced up the steps, and blew through the door. Not even hesitating, he strode down a short hallway to the left, pushed his way through the swinging gate, and marched straight for Sheriff Bodie's office. The desk sergeant was too surprised to react in time. "Hold on there," he barked too late.

Vic was already pushing his way through the door into the sheriff's office. A surprised Sam Bodie looked up from behind the desk.

"Sheriff, we have to talk . . . NOW . . ."

The sergeant reached out to impede Vic. "Mister, you can't come barging in here like this. This is a private office." But Vic shoved the hand away. Sheriff Bodie motioned to the sergeant to stay calm, then nodded to send the officer back to his post in the outer office.

"So, Mr. Johns, since you're not big on knocking, what's the reason for the intrusion?"

"It's my wife, Sally. Some hoodlum accosted her in the grocery store parking lot an hour ago and ordered her to give me a message."

"What message?"

"He said that it's time to pack up and move . . . while I still have all my valuables."

"Your valuables? What's that supposed to mean?"

"Beats me, but I want something done and now."

"It's probably just an idle threat. Is your wife hurt?"

"Well, not really. Not physically, anyway, but she's an emotional wreck again. I've got her over at Doc Nelson's office right now to try to get her calmed down."

"Did she see the assailant? Can she give us a description?"

"No, he hid in the back seat and grabbed her from behind. She never saw his face. Said his hands were rough, and he smelled of booze."

"Hmm. Not much to go on. What about a vehicle?"

"Well, he told her there was a man in the car next to her with a gun pointed at her head. Sounds like he used it as a ruse to keep her from turning around to ID him, while he was getting away. He said if she didn't sit still and stare straight ahead while he got out, the man would blow her brains out. Sally said that a young couple came out of the store a few minutes later and got into that car and drove off. She saw the license plate. It was a personalized plate with the word SHADOW on it."

"OK, we'll check it out. Anything else you can tell us?" He jotted the details on a pad of paper.

"Not really. But I want to know what you're going to do about this. Obviously, this is no prankster. We're talking serious threats now, Sheriff. I want to know what's going on, and I want it stopped."

"Now hold on, Johns. Don't get carried away here--"

"I won't hold on. I want to know what kind of protection you're going to give my wife and me. You can't just slough this one off, Bodie, and make some feeble explanation, then run and hide behind your desk."

"Listen here, Johns. I resent you bargin' in here like you're the only person in this town with a policing need." He rose to his feet as his temper flared. "Who do you think you are to come waltzin' in here makin' demands, and implying that I don't do my job? There are lots of folks in these parts that hold the same sentiment as your wife's assailant. They'd just as soon see all you rich city folk pack up and leave us alone."

"I suppose you're one of them, Sheriff," Vic said coldly.

"All I know is this is MY town. I run this town the way I see fit, and nobody, I mean NOBODY, questions me. There are lots of people who appreciate the first-class police protection they get in this town, and they pay quite well to enjoy that security. So I don't need your kind comin' in here and rocking the boat. In fact, I won't stand for it. Do you understand that, Mr. Bigshot?"

"Oh, great. I'm standing here trying to get help from a bigoted, redneck sheriff who'd just as soon run me out of town himself. That's just great." Vic started for the door, then stopped. "Well, Sheriff, sorry to barge into your office like this and take up your precious time. Next time I'll take a number. Only, there won't be a next time." With that, he stomped out the door. No sense wasting any more time with this pitiful excuse for a law enforcement officer.

❧

Vic took the stairs two at a time, hitting the top floor in seconds. He stalked down the hall, making a beeline for the Mayor's suite of offices behind the frosted glass and gold lettering. His face was red, not so much from the exertion of the stairs as from the anger of the frustrating encounter with Sheriff Bodie. As Vic approached the door, the Mayor emerged, turning toward the elevator. Mayor Quint Adams was thin and of average height, with a severely receding hairline. Vic had always thought Adams looked like a chipmunk with glasses. His cheeks were well-rounded, and his mouth was undersized with a tiny mustache perched beneath a very small nose. Rumor had it, Sheriff Bodie had the mayor in his back pocket, but Vic had to rattle somebody's cage. Might as well be the mayor's.

"Mr. Mayor. Excuse me, but I was just on my way in to see you about an urgent matter."

Quint Adams was already shaking his head. "You'll have to schedule an appointment with my secretary."

"But it will only take a moment of your time, sir. Please. Just give me two minutes."

"I'm on my way to an important meeting--"

"Sir, it involves Sheriff Bodie and the welfare of good citizens of your town."

"Oh, all right. Here, ride the elevator with me, and we'll walk to my car."

By the time they reached the parking lot, the mayor's interest was piqued. He had heard enough to know this had to be quashed, and right away. It would be political suicide to allow such willful destruction to go unchecked in

Culpeper. What was Bodie thinking? Getting a man like Victor Johns riled up would be like tossing a grenade into an ammunition factory.

"Mr. Johns, I am truly sorry to hear what is happening to you and your wife and I assure you this sort of thing, as a rule, simply does not go on in Culpeper. I am going to give Sheriff Bodie a call right now and tell him to make this case a priority."

"Thank you for listening, Mr. Mayor."

Mayor Adams extended a hand to Vic.

"I thank you for bringing this to my attention, Mr. Johns. I am sure the sheriff will wrap this matter up in a hurry." He slid into the driver's seat of his BMW convertible. "Now, you go and take care of that good wife of yours. And don't worry. We're on the case."

With that, the mayor whisked out of the parking lot. He reached for his cell phone as he turned onto Main Street.

"Yes, Chester, it's Mayor Adams. Put me through to Sam, will you? Tell him it's important." He strummed his fingers on the steering wheel as he waited. "Sam, what the hell are you doing over there? I've just had Victor Johns all over me like a sweat because he claims you won't do anything about the vandalism and threats happening at his place."

He loosened his tie as he listened to sheriff Bodie. "I don't care what you think. I'm worried. We have to appease this guy. He could be a threat to our program."

"No, do not tell me to calm down. We don't need Vic Johns pointing fingers at us, especially with an election coming up." Beads of perspiration broke out across his forehead.

"Okay, well maybe it is just 'some boys havin' some fun.' But can't you do something? At least make it look like you care?"

"Well, I don't know. You're the sheriff. Come up with some little personal protection plan to keep him happy until this blows over. But get on it right away, will you? Listen, I have to go. Talk to you later." He snapped the phone closed and tossed it on the seat.

He had been so jumpy lately. His nerves were frayed. Even his staff had noticed. His thoughts floated back to the morning conversation with his secretary, Rose Taylor. He could hear her gentle voice alerting him to the staff scuttlebutt. "Sir," she had begun, "I've overheard the staff. They feel you've not quite been yourself lately. I'm only telling you this because I know you have always been sensitive to the office staff. Lately, you have been edgy and short with all of us. Everyone feels they're walking on eggshells because they're worried you may blow up at any minute."

"Have I really been that bad, Rose?"

"Well, sir, in all honesty, yes."

"I guess it's the election coming up. You know I always get a little uptight when election time rolls around."

"Are you sure that's all it is, sir?"

What was he supposed to say? Tell her the truth? That he was worried that he and Sheriff Sam Bodie might be exposed for their strong-arm tactics that kept the town in their tight-fisted control? That he was taking kickbacks from Bodie, a share of the revenues extorted from the good townsfolk in return for a safe and secure business community? He'd wanted to scream, "I have every right to be touchy! I'm scared! The guilt hounds me day and night, and I hate myself for knuckling under to Bodie all the time." But, of course, he said none of it, only mumbled an apology, thanked her for pointing it out, and promised to try to be more sensitive in the future. Rose had left the brief meeting with an approving smile on her face.

Mayor Quint Adams. He loved the sound of it. When he first aspired to the job twelve years ago, it was with high ideals of serving the community in return for the status and title of mayor. Now he longed for a way out, a chance to start over. The decision to team up with Sheriff Bodie had secured his re-election for two more terms, but now he wished he'd done it on his own. He longed to govern with honor and integrity, to make decisions in light of the facts and for the good of the community, not out of ulterior motives dictated by Bodie. He felt cheap. He was only a pawn in Bodie's game plan.

SIX

When the bear is away, the cubs will play. The atmosphere was seldom too serious at Crazy Jake's Salvage Company, but today, with Jake out of town on business, the boys were being boys. The '66 Mustang being surgically disassembled in Bay One lay untouched since the morning coffee break at ten o'clock. Zeke, Willie and Charlie, Jake's underlings, had gotten into the beer early. They sat, eyes glazed by the liquor, around the table in the mechanic's kitchen. Newspapers and empties littered the table. Zeke Patterson, tall and muscular with wiry blond hair and a two-day stubble on his square chin, was describing a hot night with his latest girlfriend, Flo, who worked the diner out on the highway. Zeke was leaving out none of the lurid details, and Willie and Charlie were drinking in every word. They idolized Zeke and actually believed his graphic stories of romantic encounters with the local women.

Willie Wilson, the youngest of the three at just eighteen, was a rebel at heart. His shoulder-length black hair was always greasy and usually tied back in a ponytail. His often sullen face was cratered with acne scars. He wore muscle shirts to show off the bold tattoos on his upper arms. Willie was street smart. He knew how to survive. He had run away from home when he was thirteen because he couldn't take the beatings any more. He'd been on his own ever since. A cauldron of anger brewed just beneath the surface of this young man and often erupted at the slightest provocation.

He laughed as Zeke told of getting caught skinny dipping with Flo at Hook Lake on the weekend. A group of girl scouts had wandered onto the beach just as Zeke had emerged from the water clad only in nature's finest. Zeke said the girl scout leader was shocked and embarrassed and nearly fainted, but her little cohorts stared wide-eyed and giggled. The leader was comical, he said, as she tried to shield eight sets of little eyes from viewing forbidden parts.

"Hey, Zeke," Willie asked, "how long do you think we're gonna be on this special assignment?"

"Don't know," came the reply. "I think Jake is gettin' tired of waitin' around for this Professor guy to come through with the goods."

"I think it's fun," Charlie said. He always had a vacant look in those large brown eyes, set beneath a wide forehead. His cheeks were chubby and freckled, and he had very short, bristly red hair. "I liked choppin' down that big tree!"

"It beats slavin' away in this dump everyday," Zeke said as he took another swig of beer.

Willie nodded. "Whitey sure likes that surveillance stuff. He's been spendin' somethin' like twelve hours a day in that ol' van. Gets a blast out of nosin' in on other people's private business. Come to think of it, maybe we should set up one of those gadgets in your apartment, Zeke, to catch some of the live action."

"Yeah, you wish, Willie. You might actually learn somethin'. Hey, Boyd, how'd you like torchin' that fancy mailbox?"

Charlie Boyd's face broke into a broad grin. He liked fires; in fact, he seemed to take great pleasure in most forms of property destruction. There was nothing sadistic about him, he was just a simple young man who enjoyed the adventure. "That was fun, too, but I got scared when that lady was screaming."

"Well, maybe you'll get a chance pretty soon to make a bigger fire, Charlie."

"You think so, Zeke? I'd like that."

Willie played a drum solo on the tabletop. The beer was gone. "I guess we'd better get to work, boys." Zeke was the natural leader of the group when Jake was not around. "Don't want Jake thinkin' we slacked off while he was gone."

The other two followed Zeke back to the bays. Jake had assembled a motley crew, but they could do wonders with a set of wrenches and a few power tools. Soon, the drone and twang of country music gave way to the rat-a-tat-tat of the air compressor.

Doctor Nelson's office was actually a turn-of-the-century Victorian home on tree-lined Turner Street. While maintaining the exterior architectural style, the doctor had completely renovated the interior. Much of the original oak woodwork had been preserved and complemented the modern upgrades in tiled flooring and wall-coverings. The office where Doctor Nelson received and interviewed patients was a spacious round room on the front of the building. A wide bank of windows facing the street made it bright and cheery. Vic waited in one of the red leather wing-chairs facing a huge walnut desk. Mounted on the wall behind the desk were several diplomas and certificates. Doc Nelson was a 1969 graduate of the Georgetown Medical School.

The door opened, and a striking gray-haired man of average build entered. He wore a white lab coat over an open collar blue denim shirt, and khaki slacks.

"Sorry to keep you waiting," he said as he stepped briskly to the desk. He dropped an open file onto the desk and sunk into his chair.

"Oh, no problem," said Vic. "So, how's Sally?"

"Well, I've completed my assessment, and I believe she is suffering from post-traumatic stress disorder. She's been through a harrowing experience, as you well know, Mr. Johns. I've given her a strong sedative to calm her, but I'd like to admit her to hospital overnight for observation."

"Is she going to get over this, Doc?"

"In time, yes, but she will feel extremely vulnerable for a while. You must realize, she feels violated even though no physical harm was done to her. Psychologically, she feels quite defenseless right now--"

"Well, I'll look after her."

"I know you will, but that may not be enough for her right now. Until she gets her confidence and sense of security back, she will be skittish."

"What can I do, Doc?"

"Let us check her out thoroughly overnight. Then, if I send her home tomorrow, she should be under constant supervision for a week or so. Just don't leave her alone, especially at night. And give her time. I'm sure she'll come around."

"Thanks, Doctor."

"Glad to help," he said as he rose and extended a hand to Vic. "Call or bring her in right away if you have any concerns. You can take her to admitting now; I've made all the arrangements. They're expecting you. I'll look in on her in the morning when I do my rounds."

"Thanks again, Doc."

Once the paperwork was done and Sally's hospital-issue plastic I.D. bracelet was attached, an attractive nurse wheeled her to Room 310 on the psychiatric ward. Sally was a little groggy from the sedative but managed to stay awake. Nurse Hollins tucked her into the bed by the window.

"Since you're probably only in overnight, we're putting you in here so you can have the room all to yourself, Sally."

"That's nice." Sally's tongue was thick and her speech slurred. Her eyelids kept wanting to close, but she fought the sleep.

Nurse Hollins picked up a cord at the head of the bed. "If you need anything, just press the button on this cord to summon us. The nurses' station is right in the middle of the ward, so we're not far away," she said with warm reassurance.

As soon as Nurse Hollins left, Sally flatly declared, "Vic, I want to move."

"What do you mean, Sal?"

"I mean I want to move away from here—back to Washington."

"But, Sal, everything we've worked for and dreamed of is right here."

"I don't care. I want to move."

"Sal, listen, I know you're a little upset right now. Give it some time. This thing will blow over, and you'll feel better again. Everything will be the way it used to be. You'll see."

"Vic—"

"No, we'll talk about it later. You just rest now." He took her hand in his. "The doctor said it's important that you rest and relax." He brushed back the hair from her forehead and planted a kiss. Sally was asleep.

The familiar road heading home, out of Culpeper, gave Vic time to think. He couldn't believe what had happened in a few short weeks. Their dream life was unraveling—the years of planning and hard work tossed aside like rubbish. Their security and happiness threatened by senseless acts of violence. They were not random acts. Each incident was carefully orchestrated, part of a bigger plan. But the real mystery was the motive. Why would anyone want their property after all these years? And, so badly that they would stoop to vandalism and threats to get it? Unanswered questions. Loose threads. If only he could tie them together. Even the sheriff was not above suspicion. He'd already registered his hatred for outsiders like us. You could see it in his reluctance to get involved. And there was obviously some sort of corruption going on behind the scenes. He was a dirty cop for sure. Practically came right out and admitted it in his office.

Vic's thoughts drifted back to the hospital room where Sally lay in a drug-induced sleep. Her words had pierced him. Moving was out of the question. Nobody was going to drive him off that land. Too much of his own sweat and blood mingled in the soil. The land was a part of him. Sally would be okay. It was the stress and the drugs talking. She'd come around. Just give her time. Let her get over the trauma of this latest incident, and she'd see things his way.

In the rear-view mirror, Vic glimpsed flashing red and blue lights approaching in a hurry. He glanced down at the speedometer. He wasn't speeding. The cruiser pulled up behind him, so Vic slowed, and pulled off onto the shoulder of the road. The lights followed. In the side mirror, Vic could see the sheriff hauling his bulk out of the car and hiking up his belt. What was this all about? He jumped out of the car to meet the sheriff between the vehicles.

"What's this all about, Sheriff? I wasn't speeding. Or is this just some kind of harassment?"

"Now, just stay calm, Johns. I'm not happy doin' this, but I guess you have some pull with the mayor. He wanted me to give you some protection until this thing blows over. I'll admit, maybe I lost my temper a bit back there in my office, but here's what I'll do. I'll post an officer in an unmarked car on stakeout just up the road from your place. If anything unusual happens, you can call us and we'll send him in. We'll also give him orders to investigate if he sees anything out of the ordinary. You'd best stay close to home for awhile, and don't let your missus go runnin' around town alone. That's about the best I can do for now."

"So you came all the way out here, chasing me down on the highway, to tell me that? What's the matter, Sheriff, didn't want people in town seeing you talk to the scum from Washington?"

"Now listen, Johns, I'm tryin' to be nice here--"

"Save it, Sheriff. Nice isn't in your repertoire. For what it's worth, I'll accept the help. Thank the mayor for me. Now, how soon will one of your boys be stationed there?"

"In about two hours. I'm sending Nate Peters out for the first shift. He'll be in an unmarked white sedan."

"OK. You'd best tell your men to be careful if they come onto the property—I've got the guard dogs on duty most of the time, and they can be vicious. But, I guess I could keep them penned up for awhile."

"Nah, I wouldn't worry 'bout it. I'm not expectin' any more trouble out your way, anyhow."

"Professor Lapain. Professor." Holly tried to get the professor's attention. Lately, he seemed eternally preoccupied, frequently lapsing into a trance-like state, his mind a million miles away in another world. The lectures Holly had attended were flat and lifeless compared to the former exuberance of his teaching style. Maybe he was working too hard on the manuscript and not getting enough sleep.

"Professor."

"Oh. Uh, yes, Holly. I'm sorry, my mind was wandering. Where were we?"

"I was talking about the generally poor grades the Civil War class received on the mid-term. I've graded all the papers, and only about 10 students scored better than 75%."

"That's pretty low. Was the exam too hard?"

"I don't think so, sir. I think the class wasn't properly prepared."

"What do you mean?"

"Well, sir, I've noticed a big change lately in your lectures. You don't seem to be yourself. It's as if you are preoccupied or something. I don't think the students have been getting your best over the last few weeks in any of your classes."

The professor stared at the floor and shifted his feet nervously.

"Forgive me for being so blunt, sir, but for the sake of the students I need to say this. Your teaching should take precedence over your new book, shouldn't it? I mean, the writing is a sideline, a hobby, whereas teaching is what you are paid to do—"

"OK, enough said, Holly. I've got a lot on my mind these days. Maybe I have been a little negligent. I'll try to do better. Just don't harp at me about it."

"I wasn't harping, sir."

"Well, whatever you call it, I don't need any more of it, understand? I'll work through this. You just do your job, and I'll do mine."

Holly's face went white. He had never talked to her like this before. He had always treated her with respect and kindness. What was happening?

A loud knock at the door halted all discussion. The door swung open and a huge bearded man filled the door frame. Professor Lapain was visibly shaken at the sight of the man.

"Uh, Holly, let's take this up later, shall we?" he stammered. "I need to talk to this gentleman right now."

"Sure," Holly said as she departed, feeling the big man's eyes probing her body. She was glad to get out of there. But who was that guy? He looked like some rough biker.

Ambrose Lapain shoved the door closed behind Holly. "What the hell are you doing here, Jake?" He turned on the big man.

"Just headin' down to Culpeper, so I thought I'd stop in and say hi, Professor. You mean you're not glad to see me?"

"Jake, I told you never to contact me here. That means don't call and certainly don't ever come here in person."

"Oh, come on, Doc. What's the harm in a little visit?"

"We shouldn't be seen together. Understand?"

"You're a might skittish today, aren't you, boss? What's the matter? The little lady there refusin' your advances?"

"Shut up, Jake. Now what are you going to Culpeper for?"

"I've got a little business to take care of."

"What do you mean? You don't take any action without consulting me, you hear? I'm calling the shots. This is my project."

"Well, Doc, let's just say me 'n' the boys are gettin' a little impatient waitin' around for somethin' to happen. We want to see some of this money you're talkin' about us gettin'."

"Okay, listen, I'll give you another advance. Let's say a grand apiece. That's all I can afford right now."

"All right. That might keep the boys happy awhile longer, but make it two for me."

"OK, just go on back home and wait. I'll get the money and the next plan of attack to you ."

"Sure, Doc, that sounds just fine. Hey, you wanna do lunch?"

"Get out of here, Jake. And don't let anybody see you leaving my office."

Jake lumbered back to his pickup. He left the parking lot and headed south toward the Francis Scott Key Bridge and Virginia. He imagined himself as the proud owner of a big house in the classy subdivision of Parkview Estates, where the upper class lived. He could see himself driving around in a shiny Cadillac, like a big shot, and everybody kissing up to him. He could get used to that.

When visiting hours end at eight o'clock each evening, the hospital reverts to a skeleton staff. The hallways grow quiet and deserted. It becomes a lonely, eerie place as lights are extinguished and patients drift off to sleep.

No one noticed as a large hand pressed open the heavy wooden door of Room 310. A hulking figure of a man stepped quietly to the bed and pressed a strip of duct tape across Sally's mouth as she slept. She startled awake and looked up into the sarcastic grinning face of a bearded man. Sally bolted as if to climb out the other side of the bed, but a big hand reached out and shoved her back onto the pillow.

The faint light caught a glint of steel as the bear-of-a-man brandished a knife before Sally's eyes. Her eyes widened in terror. One big hand groped her body, pausing to touch her private parts through the thin hospital gown. He made direct eye contact as he touched her suggestively and waved the knife in her face. He leaned forward and whispered in her ear.

"Get out of town, or I'll carve you like a Thanksgiving turkey. And if you tell anyone about this little visit, I'll blow that husband of yours away. Understand?"

Sally's terrified eyes told him she knew exactly what he had said. He reached back and slugged her, knocking her out cold. He ripped the tape from her mouth and dumped her body onto the floor. He slipped out of the room as quietly as he had entered and ducked into the stairway.

"Kim, it's Dad. Listen, I just finished talking to the doctor and apparently Mom's not doing well at all. The nurses found her on the floor last night. She's hallucinating about somebody trying to get her. They think she fell out of bed during an episode in the night."

Not surprisingly, Kim — the nurse — wanted details. Vic paced the floor as he listened to her questions, then answered, "Yes, they have her restrained now, and they upped her meds to try to calm her down . . . No, I haven't been in to see her yet, but I wondered if you could come down and spend some time with her. I have some important business to take care of." He listened again.

"How many days off do you have? OK, Kim, that would be great. See you later today, then."

SEVEN

A **look of relief swept across Sally's face** when Vic walked into the room. Her arms and legs were strapped to the bed, though she appeared to be perfectly calm at the moment. A nasty bruise colored the left side of her head in the temple area, no doubt a result of her fall from the bed during the night. She seemed quite lucid as Vic engaged her in conversation.

"Sal, I talked to Kim this morning. She's going to come down to see you later today, after her shift. She has three days off, so she'll be able to spend some time with you."

Sally flashed a bright smile. She and Kim were very close—friends—not just mother and daughter. As the only child, Kim had received special attention from Day One. She and her mom had spent countless hours at the park on the swings and slides, then later on the tennis courts as Kim had matured. They shopped together, walked and played together, and even now chatted on the phone almost daily. Their lives were intertwined as only kindred spirits can be bound together.

When Vic broached the subject of the hallucinations, a brooding cloud shadowed Sally's face.

"I don't want to talk about it," she flatly stated. "Nobody believes me anyway."

"Believes what, Sal?"

"That someone came into the room last night and threatened me." She shuddered at the memory, and tears welled in her eyes.

"Tell me about it, Sal. You know I'll believe you."

"Well, I woke up and saw a big man with a black beard staring at me in the dark. I tried to scream, but he had taped my mouth shut. He . . . he had a knife, and he . . . he touched me." The tears were flowing freely now.

"Touched you where, Sal?"

"You know, all over."

"Did he hurt you?"

"No, but he said he would cut me up if we didn't get away from here. That's all I remember. I must have passed out after that because everything just went black. Next thing I knew, I woke up on the floor, and the nurses were helping me up."

"You're sure about the details?"

"Of course, I'm sure. It was real, Vic. There was really somebody in here and I'm afraid. Next time, maybe he'll kill me. Vic, I want to move. I want to get away from here—far away, so they'll never be able to find us."

"We can't just pick up and move away."

"Why not? Who says we have to stay here?"

"No one does, but this is our dream, Sal. We've lived for this. We've planned and worked all these years to make this dream come true. We're not walking away from it now."

"That's easy for you to say. You're not the one they keep threatening. I don't see them sneaking into your bedroom to tell you to move or they'll slit your throat."

"Now, Sal, stay calm — "

"I won't stay calm. I've had enough. I'm not staying in this town any longer. If you want to stay, fine, stay by yourself. I'm moving."

"Sal, listen, don't be too hasty. You've been through a lot, and it's the emotion talking. It's understandable, but you'll feel better in time. Just give it a chance, give it some time, will you?"

"My mind's made up, Vic. It's only land and a house. Our lives are more important."

"But it's OUR land and OUR house, Sally. Our lives, our memories are all wrapped up in that land and that house. How can you separate us from them?"

"No, Vic, it's too late. I'm not going to change my mind."

Further argument would be futile. Sally was getting too upset so Vic left the subject alone. He assured Sally that Kim would be in to see her later, then made an excuse about going to see the doctor, and left.

It was time for action. This whole thing was getting out of hand. It made no sense to start with. Now even his wife had turned against him. There must be a loose thread somewhere that would tie it all together. Time to investigate. A determined Vic Johns hustled across town to Poplar Avenue to pay a visit to the King of Realty.

Homer Townsend was a rotund little man with rosy cheeks and a cheery disposition. He extended a chubby hand to Vic and invited him into his posh office.

"So, have you changed your mind about the latest offer on your property?"

"Not at all," Vic answered a little testily. "Actually, Homer, I'm here to find out who this anonymous person is who wants my property so badly that he's willing to suddenly up the offer by $10,000."

"I'm afraid I can't divulge that information, Victor. It would be against my client's wishes."

"I don't care about your client's wishes, Townsend. I want a name, and I want it now."

"Sorry, that's privileged information, Mr. Johns." Homer's smug smile brought Vic's blood to a boil. He leaped to his feet and grabbed Homer by the throat, shoving him against the wall and twisting his tie until the fat man began to turn blue.

"Who is it, Homer? Tell me!" He twisted the tie a little tighter. Homer tried to shake loose, but Vic's grip was too strong. Vic shook his victim and slammed him against the wall again. "The name, Homer, the name," he practically screamed. His face was beet red, and the vein on his forehead was about to explode.

Homer's secretary stepped through the doorway and gasped as she saw her boss pinned to the wall by a raging madman. When he heard her, Vic loosened his grip. Homer shoved the hands away from his throat.

Coarsely, he said, "You can't walk in here and threaten me like this, Johns. Now get out of here before I call the sheriff." He straightened his tie and smoothed his shirt as he moved a safe distance from his attacker.

"Look, Homer, I'm sorry. I lost my temper. I've got a wife in the hospital whose being threatened by someone. I've had my mailbox burned and a tree chopped down that narrowly missed flattening my house. Somebody wants us off our land, and I think there might be a connection to the offers you've been bringing me."

"I can understand what you're going through, Mr. Johns, but I simply can't give you what you want. All I can say is that this fellow is from D.C. and he is also pursuing property in Maryland, so I doubt that yours has any special significance to him. In fact, he may have already bought over there instead."

"Isn't it a strange coincidence, Homer, that shortly after I get ballooning offers on my place, my wife and I receive death threats and orders to move away or else?"

"It does sound strange, but maybe that's all it is, a coincidence. I'm sorry, but I can't help you."

"Can't or won't?" Vic sneered. He turned, stomped past the secretary and slammed the door behind him on the way out.

"I tell you, this guy is dangerous, Sam. You'd better keep an eye on him. He's a tiger on the prowl."

"He does have a short fuse, doesn't he?" Sheriff Bodie adjusted the ever-present toothpick. He was enjoying this. Let Victor Johns dig himself a hole. Give him enough rope and maybe he'll hang himself.

"Short fuse! Why, he went ballistic on me! Grabbed me by the throat; nearly choked me to death."

"You wanna press charges, Homer? I can have the boys pick him up right now."

"No, I reckon I'll overlook it this time, on account of all the guy's going through."

Oh, a touch of sympathy for Johns. We don't want too much of that, thought Bodie.

"Well, if you change your mind, let me know." Bodie relished the thought of slapping cuffs on Vic Johns and escorting him to the county jail. That would be a source of supreme pleasure.

"I just wanted to let you know what's going on, Sheriff, but if he gives me any more trouble, I'll throw the book at him."

Gotta like the sound of that, Bodie mused. "If you ask me," he said, "we'd all be better off if Johns and his kind just packed up, ran back to Washington, and left us alone. Then you could re-sell their property and make yourself another bundle of money, Homer."

Both men enjoyed the laugh as Homer stood and headed for the door. "Thanks for your time, Sam."

"Anytime, Homer. Don't forget, now, if you decide to press charges, let me know."

"I will."

Ambrose Lapain carefully skirted Rex's territory in the compound and nervously hurried into the first bay where Willie and Charlie worked underneath a wrecked Subaru.

"Where's Jake?" Lapain demanded.

Zeke emerged from the mechanic's kitchen, wiping greasy hands. "He ain't here," he answered.

"Where is he? I told him yesterday to stay here."

"Said he had some business over in Virginia. Left yesterday mornin'. Ain't seen him since." Zeke turned his attention to a carburetor on the workbench. He didn't care much for this professor guy.

Lapain stuck his head through the doorway to the office. "Hey, Lil', when do you expect Jake back?"

"Actually, that's him just pulling in, Doc."

As soon as they had retired behind closed doors, in the privacy of Jake's office, Lapain lashed out.

"Where the hell have you been?"

"I told you, I had a little business in Culpeper."

"What kind of business?"

"Had to make a friendly hospital visit to a mutual friend. Now what was her name? Oh, yeah, Sally Johns. You know her, don't you, Doc? Nice lady. Very nice."

"What did you do?"

"Just paid her a little visit and reminded her that she needs to get out of town." He grinned.

"I told you I was calling the shots, Jake. I told you to come back here and wait until I brought the money and gave you instructions."

"Too bad, Doc. I guess I'm not too good at waitin' around."

Lapain reached into the breast pocket of his sports jacket and drew out a bulky white envelope. He slid it across the desk to Jake.

"Maybe this will make waiting a little more attractive to you. It's the money you wanted. There's two grand for you, one for each of the boys."

Jake fingered the cash. "OK, so what's next, Doc?"

"I want you to lay low for a few days. Let this thing play itself out a little to see what effect it will have on Mr. Johns."

"Well, OK, but me 'n' the boys are gettin' a little impatient, Doc. We're beginnin' to wonder if you've got a plan. We wanna get this thing done and get the big payoff."

"That'll come, Jake. It's just going to take a little time. Be patient, all right?"

"All right, Doc," Jake replied, at the same time thinking, the clock's ticking, Doc, and your time's almost up.

The radio bleated, "Sheriff, we've got a match on that SHADOW plate. Registered to a William Rosemont of 1327 Sycamore Street."

"Great, Chester. I'll head over there now. Have Nate meet me there in five."

By the time Sheriff Bodie arrived, Deputy Nate Peters was already waiting in his cruiser parked at the curb in front of 1327 Sycamore. The two officers walked briskly to the door together. Nate Peters was slimmer than the sheriff but just as muscular. With a football player's neck and piercing dark eyes, he stood 6 foot 3 inches tall and weighed 225 pounds. Nate had a Mediterranean look—dark olive skin and jet-black straight hair. He was a handsome, but fierce, figure. This was an intimidating duo for anyone to face at their front door. The apprehension was clearly etched on the face of seventeen-year-old Billy Rosemont as he cracked the door and peered out at the big men in uniform.

"What's your name, son?" the sheriff demanded.

"Billy. Billy Rosemont."

"You the owner of a black sports car with the license plate SHADOW?"

"Yes, sir."

"Would you step out here on the porch, young man? We'd like to ask you a few questions."

"What's this all about, Sheriff? I haven't done anything wrong."

"We'll decide that," came the abrupt reply.

Billy, trembling slightly, stepped out onto the porch. He was just a skinny teen with acne. The policemen towered over him.

"Two days ago, your car was parked in the Foodtown shopping plaza parking lot. Is that right, son?" The Sheriff handled the interrogation.

"Yes, sir, I was there to get a few groceries."

"Was anyone with you at the time?"

"Yes, my girlfriend, Tanya. She went in the store with me."

"Was there anyone else in your car at the time?"

"No."

At the Sheriff's nod, Nate Peters stepped forward and grabbed young Billy by the arm, twisting it behind his back.

"Are you sure, boy?" Sheriff Bodie glared at the frightened teen, and Nate Peters tightened his grip until Billy winced with pain.

"I'm sure," Billy cried. "It was just me and Tanya. You're hurting my arm."

"Boy, I don't like bein' lied to, you understand? Now tell me who the hoodlum was in the back seat of your car."

Nate Peters shoved Billy hard against the wall of the house and gripped him by the throat. "Answer the Sheriff, boy," he commanded.

"I'm telling the truth," Billy blurted as tears welled in his eyes. "There was only Tanya and me, nobody else. I swear it. We parked and were shopping for maybe an hour. Then we came out, got in the car, and drove back here."

"OK, kid, I believe you. But if I ever find out that you were lyin' to me, Deputy Peters and I will be back here in a flash, and there'll be hell to pay, you understand?"

Billy nodded and was relieved when Nate Peters released the iron grip on his throat. Sheriff Bodie nodded to the deputy and they headed for the cars.

"Kid's tellin' the truth, Sam."

"Yeah, I know. So either Mrs. Johns fabricated her story or the assailant used young Billy's car as a ruse to scare Mrs. Johns into lettin' him get away without her seein' his face."

"He probably saw the car sittin' there with the privacy glass and decided on the spur of the moment to use it for his getaway."

"Yeah, that's what I figure, Nate."

"Now what, Sam? There ain't much else to go on."

"Yeah, I know. Maybe we'll come up with a lead from the stakeout."

They parted company and drove off in their cruisers.

EIGHT

Holly Fenton was a responsible young woman. She took her studies and her work seriously. She felt some responsibility for the undergraduates' education and also a certain concern for her mentor, Professor Lapain. That's why she could not sit back and watch the deterioration of the professor's teaching without doing something about it.

She had raised the issue on a couple of occasions lately but saw little change despite his promises to the contrary. The professor was preoccupied, maybe even obsessed, about something, and it wasn't his new book. The manuscript had been left untouched for weeks. He had given her no new research assignments, no chapters or pages to proofread. His attention had been diverted elsewhere, and Holly intended to find out where. She suspected it had to do with his theory about the buried Civil War booty. Professor Lapain had acted so strangely the day of the interview with Mrs. Palmer in Front Royal, when they had discovered the connection to possible buried treasure.

The time had come to confront the professor again. But now, as she stood poised to knock on his office door, an ominous foreboding swept over her. He had not reacted well the last couple of times she had raised the issue. There was little hope that this time would be any different. She knocked, despite her reservations.

"Come in," came the muffled reply.

Holly entered the familiar setting to see professor Lapain staring out the window from behind his desk.

"Professor, I want to talk."

"Come in and have a seat, Holly. What is it?"

"Well, it's the same old issue. I'm concerned about our classes and about you. You've hardly written a word on your new book in the last month, and your lectures, as I said before, have been sub-par over that period."

"As I told you before, Holly, I've got a lot on my mind lately, but I'm trying to do my best."

"Sir, you've said that repeatedly but, frankly, I see little change. What's bothering you, sir? Can I help? Is it this buried booty theory that you're so preoccupied with?"

"What do you know about that?" Lapain asked sharply. He glared defensively at Holly.

"Nothing, really. You said it would be our little secret, so I haven't told anyone about it, but you haven't told me anything more about it either. What's going on?"

"Nothing you need to know about." He looked away from her, hiding something. "I've done some preliminary research, and at the right time, I'll bring you in on it, Holly."

"So that's it! You're really on to something. Have you located the site?" She was getting excited about it.

"Holly, I'd really rather not say just yet. I want to verify certain things first. And please, whatever you do, keep this quiet, will you? I don't want this thing blown out of proportion."

"Oh, don't worry about me, I'll keep it a secret, but I want to know about this. It could be a huge discovery! Don't keep me in the dark, Professor, please tell me what you know."

"All in good time, Holly. There is no better research assistant on the planet, so rest assured I will definitely use your talents when things are in place."

Holly's appetite for adventure and discovery was whetted. No wonder Lapain had been so preoccupied lately. She would be, too. This kind of discovery came along maybe once or twice in a lifetime. She wanted in—now. The suspense would kill her. What did he know? Had he actually located the site? Why not let her in on it at this point? She was his ace assistant. He confided in her on matters of research and discovery. Why was he keeping her at arm's length on this one?

"So, how long do you think it'll be before you can tell me about this in detail, Professor?"

"Maybe just a few days or a week or so, Holly. Just hang on, OK? I've got a few details to wrap up, then you're in."

Well, at least we made some progress this time, Holly thought, as she left the office. But she had to know more. She couldn't wait. She wanted in now. As she stepped out into the sunshine, a plan began to brew in her mind.

Whitey Thompson was nearing the end of another long day monitoring the surveillance equipment which intruded on the home of Victor Johns. The tight quarters in the old van didn't bother Whitey, for he loved tinkering with the electronic equipment. A headset pressed into the white locks for which he was named and covered his oversized ears. His pale complexion was heavily freckled across the cheeks and nose. He stretched the kinks out of his five-foot-ten-inch frame as best he could in the limited space of the van and began to think about closing down for the night. It was nine o'clock already and little seemed to happen in the evenings at the Johns house.

Just as he was about to shut down the monitor, Whitey heard a new voice. He had come to recognize Victor Johns' and his wife Sally's voices, but this one was different— younger, he thought. Instantly, Whitey was sharply tuned to every word. He raised the volume and listened intently.

"I'm glad you're here, Kim. How was Mom tonight?" That was Vic's voice.

"Pretty good, Dad. She seemed a little anxious when I got ready to leave, but the nurse came in to give her a sedative." That must be the daughter, thought Whitey. She was supposed to arrive today sometime. He continued to eavesdrop.

"I hope she's going to be OK," Vic said. "The doctor seemed to think she might come home tomorrow since you'll be here to help me with her."

"Mom's hoping. I don't think she likes that hospital too much, especially after that episode the other night."

"What do you think about that, Kim? Have you ever heard of such a thing? Do you think she was hallucinating?"

"I don't know. After the parking lot thing, she may just be paranoid. That's what the staff believes."

"But the details were so vivid."

"Yeah, that's what got me, too. Her description was so clear."

"Did she say anything about wanting to move?" Vic changed the subject.

"Yes, she did. And I think you should listen to her, Dad."

"Kim, you know we can't move from here. Our lives are too rooted in this land."

"Rooted or not, you need to listen to Mom. She's been through hell these last few days. Her health has to come before any consideration of land and buildings."

"She's just under stress. She'll pull out of it in time. We don't want to do anything rash."

"You just don't see it, do you, Dad? This has emotionally scarred Mom. She may never get over it. You need to think about her."

"No. We're not giving up the land."

"How can you say that so matter-of-factly without considering Mom's feelings and her needs? She's your wife, your partner."

"And we are tied to this land. Our memories are here; our future is here. This place is the essence of who we are. It's our dream, and we're not giving it up just because some crazy tells us to get out of town."

"Dad, what's the matter with you? You're obsessed with this land. Aren't we more important than property?"

"It's one in the same, Kim. You, Mom, the land, our dream house. It's one big package. I'm not giving it up."

"Sometimes you can be so stubborn. I'm tired. I'm going to bed."

Whitey was grinning from ear to ear as he dialed the cell. Wait 'til Jake hears there's trouble in paradise.

The wives retreated indoors as twilight's grip on the day loosened and the temperatures dropped as quickly as darkness approached.

Retired Judge Fred Hamilton filled his lungs with the aroma of freshly cut wood and admired the workmanship beneath him.

"You did a fine job rebuilding this deck, Vic."

"Thanks, Fred. I'm just sorry I had to do it."

Vic glanced at his long-time friend reclining in a wooden Adirondack chair, tapping his fingers on the wide armrest. Fred was a decorated Vietnam war hero. A strapping black man with distinguished gray hair and small glasses, he had a deep, booming voice that echoed with authority. One of the first black judges in D.C., his integrity and fairness was known far and wide. He had a reputation for toughness, but it was tempered by a great sense of humor. When The Judge, as his friends liked to call him, laughed, his whole body shook.

"How's the restoration project coming?" Vic asked, thinking of the judge's passionate hobby of restoring vintage automobiles. "Are you still working on that '56 Chevy?"

"Sure am. I dropped the tranny the other day. Figured I'd best do the job right the first time around. You should come over and check it out. I might even let you pull on a wrench or two." His big smile revealed a solid fence of white teeth.

Vic suddenly grew serious. "I'm trying to get to the bottom of this harassment thing, but I can't seem to get any help from the sheriff."

"That doesn't surprise me, Vic," the judge said, as he shifted his ample weight in the chair. "Bodie has poisoned the attitudes of the people of this town toward us 'outsiders'. He's convinced them that we're here to ruin their town."

"That's ridiculous."

"Sure it is, but not in their minds. He has a lot of control over them, especially the business sector. I just wish we'd been able to oust him at the last election. He's a dangerous character, and he's running a corrupt little empire."

Vic straightened in his chair. "What do you mean?"

"This is strictly confidential, Vic, but I've been approached by a local businessman who claims that Sheriff Bodie is using threats and brutality to extort protection money from the business owners in town. Apparently, Bodie demands a monthly payment in return for the guaranteed protection of their business establishments from crime. They have to pay up or face the consequences. My source tells me, those who refuse have been brutally beaten and their businesses ransacked. No one will speak out against him. They're afraid of what Bodie will do to them and their families."

"Some racket. So, Bodie collects each month and the town remains crime free."

"Something like that."

"I can see why he wants to keep us 'outsiders' on the fringe — so we don't go rockin' the boat and spoil his take."

The judge nodded. "Exactly. My source can't prove it, but he believes the mayor is in on the game, too."

Vic let out a slow whistle.

"I'm doing a little surreptitious investigating of my own, Vic, to see if I can get some dirt on these guys that will stick in a court of law."

"Watch your backside, Fred." Vic said with genuine concern for his friend.

"I will," the judge replied with a grim smile. "If I were you, Vic, I wouldn't expect much help from the sheriff, and I certainly wouldn't trust the man."

"I'll keep that in mind," Vic said, as he stood and motioned to the door. "The girls are waiting to take our money, Fred. Let's go in and take our lumps."

The judge's barrel laugh echoed across the darkened yard as the two friends stepped into the warmer confines of the great room with its crackling wood fire.

Holly's heart was pounding as she followed the blue Volvo from a safe distance. A mix of excitement and apprehension gripped her. The sheer adventure captured her imagination, but the risk of being caught filled her with fear. Of course, the risks were minimized the minute she donned the brown wig and glasses and hopped into her friend Jennifer's VW Beetle. Her own bright yellow sports car would have been a dead giveaway.

The sun was setting quickly. Holly was thankful for the additional cover of the gathering darkness but worried about losing sight of Professor Lapain's car up ahead as the daylight faded. The Volvo made a sudden right turn onto old Route 42. Where was he going? This was a pretty seedy part of town, but she followed on, hanging back to avoid detection.

Soon, the professor turned into a business establishment along Route 42. From what she could make out on the faded sign, it looked like Crazy Jake's Salvage Company. Holly slid her car onto the shoulder of the road, just beyond the driveway, to a vantage point where she could see past the main building, which was in darkness, to the service bays where bright lights bravely cast their glow onto the compound. The professor's car was parked in front of one of the bays.

Holly waited, wondering what she hoped to accomplish and even questioning this silly plan to follow the professor. This was a desolate stretch of the old highway at this time of night. Chills ran up her spine. She wished she had brought Jennifer along for moral support. The uneasiness grew. Forty-five minutes had passed, and Holly was ready to retreat to safer confines. She reached for the ignition to start the engine and cast one last look toward Crazy Jake's establishment. She froze. Professor Lapain stepped out of the bay into the glow of yellow light, followed by a huge bearded man. There could be no doubt—she would have recognized him anywhere—it was the same man who had visited the professor on campus. Holly shuddered as she remembered his probing stare. Her flesh crawled at the memory.

How she wished she could eavesdrop on their conversation. What was the professor doing out here on this god-forsaken stretch of road with a slimy character like this bearded guy? The two were worlds apart. What could they possibly have in common? Now Holly was really curious.

She watched as Professor Lapain bid the big man farewell and hopped into his car. As his headlights illuminated the driveway, she ducked out of sight in the front seat and stayed down until she heard him pull out of the compound and drive off toward home on Route 42.

Now what? Should she confront the professor again and demand to know what was going on? If he found out that she had followed him, her cover would be blown, and he would watch his backside from then on. Chances of uncovering information on the sly would be greatly reduced. No, she would have to continue in secrecy for now. Not tip her hand. But what was the next step? She had to find out about that big man. Who was he? And what was the connection between him and Professor Lapain?

City streets, bathed in the soft glow of streetlights, passed unnoticed as a preoccupied Holly headed for home, deep in thought.

The thwack of ax splitting wood reverberated through the woods. That Vic Johns would retreat to the forest was no surprise. It had been his haven for over two decades. The canopy of arching branches above and the bed of dried leaves beneath his feet usually engulfed Vic in tranquil peace. On countless weekends during his thirty years in the employ of the Department of Agriculture, he had retreated to these woods, exhausted, stressed, worn to a frazzle, and had found here the balm of solitude and rest to rejuvenate his flagging spirit. The pressures and deadlines of work evaporated in this natural cathedral. The land had been his spiritual anchor through all the hard times. Rocks, trees and soil siphoned off the poisons of city life and restored his soul. Clarity came here. And peace.

So now, with the household charged with growing tension over Sally's demand to move, it was no surprise to find Vic Johns retreating to his cathedral. He didn't need the firewood — four or five cords stood neatly stacked next to the shed — but he needed to chop. Thwack. The deft stroke split another log, sending wood chunks flying on either side of the chopping block. Today, the therapy was not working. Polarized emotions tore at his insides. Anger at the mere thought of moving boiled over and ran down the shaft of the ax with every blow, only to reload and discharge again. At the same time, a quiet but persistent voice kept asking, What about Sally? What's best for her? Vic's body tightened as his refusal to move clashed with love for his wife. The battle raged on. No soothing balm could be found to tame this tempest. Vic knew he was hiding out here, like a coward, refusing to face Sally and Kim, not wanting to make a decision. The plan was to avoid them long enough to stall the decision-making until Sally recovered enough to see things his way.

This was a departure from standard Vic Johns problem solving. Normally, problems were met head-on. Decisions made promptly. None of this stewing over options. No inner turmoil. Just make up your mind and go for it. No looking back. For some reason, Vic could not pull the trigger on this decision. The repercussions ran too deep. He knew what he wanted to do but lacked the resolute courage to take action. At every turn, Sally's tearful face haunted him. He could not block her from his consciousness. She had been his high school sweetheart, the one and only true love of his life. He had committed his love to her for life, in sickness and in health. He believed in commitment and duty. But his affections were split. A mistress vied for his heart and laid claim to his loyalty. Seductively, she whispered to him in the gentle rustling of the leaves. She had been his friend, his refuge, his strength. She had given him roots, a place to call his own. Separation was out of the question. He needed her. He could never turn his back on her now. Sally and the land. That was the only way he could live.

Finally, the fatigue of shoulders and arms matched the weariness of mind, so Vic laid aside the ax and trudged slowly back to the house. As soon as he opened the door, the tension engulfed him. It hung in the air like a stale aroma. Vic grabbed a cooler from the refrigerator and sat in one of the big easy chairs in the great room. Before he sank into the cushions, Sally coldly declared, "Vic, we need to talk." He braced himself for the storm.

"What's to talk about?" he said, with more defiance than he intended.

"Us. The land. Moving away from here, so we can have a life again."

"Sal, we've covered this ground already."

"No, you've covered it. You haven't listened to me at all. You don't care what I think or feel, it's just this house and the land, that's all that matters to you."

"That's not true, Sally — "

"Just look at yourself. You've been hiding out there in the woods for two days now because you can't face me. You can't tell me to my face that the land comes before me."

"Sally, don't say that. It's not true."

"Then why aren't we packing our stuff and getting out of here?"

"Because I don't think we have to move to solve this. I think we can stay and this thing will blow over. You'll feel better again soon, and you'll see things my way."

"Your way. Your way. That pretty well sums it up right there." Sally rose to her feet and walked to the fireplace. She spun around, anger and hurt flashing in her eyes. "It's always been about you, Vic, hasn't it? Whatever you wanted. You made all the plans and decisions, and I was always supposed to follow along like some obedient little puppy dog."

"We made the decisions together. You were always excited about this dream like I was."

"That was before it turned into a nightmare. Now I can see the truth."

"What truth? Sally, I love you. I always have. I always will."

"Then take me away from here."

"I—I can't do that—not yet." Vic started to pace. His heart was pounding.

"See? Where do I actually rank on your list of priorities, Vic? Do I even make the top ten?"

Then Sally's tone suddenly changed. "Vic, I'm leaving today. I'm going to stay at Kim's until I can sort things out in my own head." Tears welled in her eyes.

Vic rubbed his forehead. "Sally, don't do this. Give it some time, I beg you. You'll see, everything will work out just fine. We'll be happy again." But he could see that her mind was made up.

"I'm leaving as soon as I get packed."

NINE

Her departure was cold and mechanical. Two proud and stubborn individuals set on their own course of action, a wall erected between them. Vic did offer to drive her to Kim's, in fact, would have insisted on it, but Sally flatly refused. A clean, quick break was what she wanted so Vic could not talk her out of going. Besides, she reasoned, she wanted her own vehicle with her, anyway.

Vic, looking totally lost, stood at the door and watched her drive away. Sally managed to suppress the tears until the end of the driveway, but as home disappeared behind her, the dam broke. She wiped the flood of tears with the back of her hand and peered at the road through blurred eyes. The urge to go back gripped her, and she almost turned the car around, but pride and fear pushed her on.

By the time she reached County Road 46 and turned north to head for the highway, she was regaining her composure. A sense of relief poured over her. The Culpeper nightmare was behind her now, banished forever. She could start afresh and build a new life, liberated from fear and anxiety. But what would it be like without Vic? He had always been there—secure, dependable, tender and loving, a strong shoulder to lean on. Her identity was tied up in their relationship. Who was she apart from Vic? Talking to Kim would help. She seemed to understand Sally's feelings even before they were verbalized and was always supportive and caring. Yes, Kim would be her refuge until she and Vic got things sorted out.

Sally's train of thought was broken by a wildly blaring horn behind her. Glancing into the rearview mirror, Sally could see a carload of young men waving and honking at her. They were riding in a big blue sedan, a fifties car with the big fins. It loomed large in the mirror as it tailgated her vehicle. She sped up a little to move away from them, but the big car quickly closed the gap. They were waving her over to the side, wanting her to pull off or let them pass or something. A wave of panic swept over Sally. What if they were the ones who threatened her before in the parking lot? What would they do to her if she stopped? She stepped on the accelerator and the sport utility surged forward, but the blue beast kept pace, hanging just behind her bumper. Sally pressed the accelerator to the floor—she had to get away from them. The speedometer shot up to 70 miles per hour, but still she could not gain on them. It inched up to 80, and Sally frantically turned her head to glimpse her pursuers. They were still waving and shouting and honking as she opened a gap of about four car lengths. Thinking she would outrun them for sure, Sally turned back to the front and froze. She was hurtling toward a sharp bend in the road. Her vehicle was going too fast to make the turn. She slammed on the brakes, and the SUV skidded and spun sideways as she tried to steer into the turn. The wheels caught the gravel shoulder, and she lost control. Over the embankment the vehicle shot, going airborne for a brief moment, then crashing to earth and rolling three times before slamming broadside into an oak tree. Shards of glass and twisted metal spewed everywhere. A wheel flew off. The roof caved in. The vehicle was a tangled mess wrapped around the trunk of the old tree.

The big blue sedan, having slowed enough to make the turn safely, backed up to the brow of the embankment. It paused for a few seconds then raced away, tires squealing.

Within minutes, the wail of sirens broke the eerie silence. Deputy Nate Peters was first on the scene, followed closely by an ambulance and two fire trucks. Emergency vehicles soon clogged the roadway, flashing their ominous lights.

Nate Peters took charge. One glance at the wrecked vehicle told him this was a bad one. Bounding down the embankment, he doubted that they would find any survivors. The ambulance crew, stretcher in tow, followed him and silently shared his assessment. In the tangled wreck was one victim—female, bloodied from severe head trauma and deep lacerations. The ambulance attendants found a faint pulse, but the Jaws of Life would be needed to extricate the woman's badly battered body.

Firemen were already spraying the remains of the vehicle with foam as a precaution in the event of a fuel leak. Officer Tom Porter had arrived and was taking charge of traffic and crowd control. Curious bystanders, passing motorists and local residents were beginning to gather at the top of the embankment. Tom Porter gently corralled them a safe distance from the rescue team.

The extrication process was underway now. Under the trained hands of the firemen, the mighty Jaws of Life pried twisted metal apart. What had been door and pillar were separated. A power saw was maneuvered into position to sever the steering column, which had the victim pinned to her seat. Quickly and methodically, the rescue squad peeled the vehicle open like a tin of beans. The paramedics gently eased the woman's broken body onto the stretcher. She was unconscious but alive—just barely.

Sheriff Bodie arrived on the scene just as the woman was being extricated from her vehicle. One glance at the victim's face, and he turned to Nate Peters.

"That's Victor Johns' wife."

Nate exhaled slowly through pursed lips. "They don't know if she's gonna make it, boss. Just hangin' on by a thread."

With Sally Johns blanketed and strapped to the stretcher, the paramedics gingerly loaded her into the ambulance, still working feverishly to stabilize her condition. The rear doors slammed shut, and soon the wail of the siren faded away in the direction of Culpeper.

The emergency room was a flurry of activity as a distressed Vic Johns approached the reception area. A gurney sped by, pushed by paramedics, a doctor and two nurses. Vic heard a paramedic reeling off the vitals. "Eighteen-year-old female, ingested sleeping pills, quantity unknown; unconscious, pulse faint, breathing shallow, blood pressure . . ."

A kind nurse greeted Vic and immediately prepared him for the sight of his seriously injured wife.

"It was a terrible accident, Mr. Johns. We are still trying to stabilize your wife. She is in critical condition, but we are doing everything possible to save her life."

"Can I see her?" Vic's voice was trembling.

"Of course, but I must warn you, she is in rough shape." The nurse led the way down the hall. "Your wife has multiple fractures," she continued, "some serious lacerations, and we are most concerned about head trauma, but the doctor will explain things to you once they get her stabilized."

Vic could not speak. The words were choked off in his throat. He followed the nurse blindly, awash in a sea of emotions. "You can wait here," the nurse pointed to a tiny lounge that served as the ER waiting room. "It should only be a few more minutes. By the way, my name is Cindy, Cindy Calloway. If I can be of any help, please ask for me, Mr. Johns. Is there anyone I can call to be with you?"

"No, but thanks." Vic managed to force the words out.

Waves of guilt and anger crashed over him. Why didn't he insist on driving her to Kim's? He should have seen to her safety. He wanted to punch something, anything, to vent the frustration and anger. He desperately wanted to change the situation but knew he could do nothing about it. Why did she have to be so unreasonable as to leave, anyway? None of this would have happened if . . . He fought the tears. None of that mattered now. Sally was clinging to life by a thread. She had to live; he needed her. What would life be without her? He didn't even want to think about it. Everything was happening in slow motion like some bad dream unfolding.

Every muscle felt weak, as if a huge syringe had sucked all energy from his body.

With rubbery legs, Vic followed Nurse Calloway to Examination Room Three. Two more nurses hovered around the bed, adjusting equipment and assessing the operation of the various machines and monitors hooked up to the patient that Vic hardly recognized as his wife. Sally's head was heavily wrapped in white gauze bandages. Her face was swollen and red, with scratches and cuts all over. Her eyes were closed. She was unconscious. The respirator tube spilling from her mouth made her look like an alien life form. Tubes and cords were everywhere. A monitor gave a green-line readout of her heartbeat and recorded pulse and other vital stats. The rhythmic pumping of the respirator and the accompanying rise and fall of Sally's chest was surrealistic. Several bags of fluids hung on a nearby intravenous pole.

Denial swept over Vic. Someone had made a mistake. This couldn't be Sally. This wasn't happening. He couldn't accept it. Yet, deep inside, he knew that this was Sally's barely alive, broken body before him. He wanted to reach out, pick her up, and take her home. How he wished he could make this all go away, make her well again and smiling. But he knew he could not.

As the nurses stepped back to give him some privacy, Vic reached out to touch Sally's limp hand, and gave it a gentle squeeze, but there was no response. Grief tore at his chest, shaking him like a rag doll. He couldn't stand to see her like this.

"Sally, if you can hear me," he whispered, "hang in there. Fight this, Sal, for me, for us. You're going to be okay, you'll see. I love you, Sal. I love you. Don't leave me, don't give up on me now."

After a few moments, the nursing team stepped forward to continue their vigil around Sally's bed. They directed Vic to the hallway where a young, dark-haired surgeon, Dr. Moffat, was scratching notations on Sally's chart. Nurse Calloway made the introductions, and Dr. Moffat, clad in a white lab coat with the obligatory stethoscope wrapped around his neck, launched into an explanation of Sally's condition.

"As you have already observed, Mr. Johns, your wife has been badly injured. She is in stable but critical condition right now. She has sustained serious head injuries including a fractured skull. There is swelling of the brain, which is our most serious concern at the moment."

Vic nodded with understanding.

Dr. Moffat continued, "As you know, she is unconscious, but we don't know for how long. It is not unusual, in cases like this, for the victim to remain unconscious for days or even weeks. We will not know the full extent of any effect on her brain until later. I have called in Dr. Evans, a top neurosurgeon, for further assessment."

"You mean she may have brain damage?"

"I honestly can't answer that at this point, Mr. Johns. Only time will give us that answer. Meanwhile, we are tending to several fractures and lacerations, which will heal. There was some internal bleeding, but it appears to be under control now. We will keep you updated on her condition, but for now it's a waiting game. I'm sorry, I wish I had better news."

"So do I," Vic stared at the floor. "Thanks, Doctor."

The surgeon nodded. "We're doing everything we can for your wife, Mr. Johns." And with that he was gone, leaving Vic standing alone.

It was risky to show her face at Crazy Jake's Salvage Company, but Holly's curiosity far outweighed her sense of caution. She had to know what was happening. Her wristwatch showed 11:55. She waited and watched the entrance to Crazy Jake's. At noon, a rusty pickup with a large bearded man driving, tore out of the driveway and sped off down the highway. It was the moment Holly had been waiting for. She slipped her car into drive and eased into the compound, pulling up in front of the main building. A black hole in the dash, where the glove compartment door should have been, glared at Holly. She smiled, hoping this plan would work.

The outer office was vacant when she entered. The work bays were silent. Everyone must be on lunch break. Holly poked her head through the doorway marked 'Employees Only' and shouted, "Anybody here?" Instantly, a tall, blond young man, holding a sandwich in one hand, emerged from another doorway. The greasy mechanic's overalls he wore draped a muscular body. The young man's lustful stare immediately told Holly that her wardrobe selection for today — the low-cut top and very short skirt — was perfect.

"Yes, ma'am, what can I do for you?" he said, his eyes never leaving her.

"I have a little problem and thought maybe you all could help me with it." Holly tried to sound as helpless and pitiful as possible.

Gallantly, the man stepped toward her. "Name's Zeke, ma'am. I'll do what I can. What's the problem?" He was still staring at her.

"Well, Zeke," she smiled as she pronounced his name, "my name is Holly. Someone broke into my car last night and stole a part from it."

"That's too bad, Holly. What kind of car is it, and what's missing?" he asked.

By now, two other young men in matching overalls were peering from the same doorway behind Zeke and whispering to each other.

"Why, I'm not sure, but I've got it here if you care to take a look."

She led the way back to her car, aware that behind her Zeke was giving the other two some macho sign. He followed her, and she could feel his eyes on her body. Holly purposely opened the passenger door, leaned in slightly, flashing considerable cleavage before Zeke's young eyes, and pointed to the glove compartment missing its door. Zeke tried to focus on the dashboard.

"Oh, I see," he said, obviously enjoying the view. "I'm afraid we don't have a glove compartment door for a model this new. You'll probably have to order one from the dealer."

"That's too bad," Holly replied seductively, "I was hoping you could help me." She closed the passenger door and walked around to the driver's door, knowing Zeke would follow. His eyes were on her exposed thighs as she got in. She reached out her right hand to Zeke, thanking him for his help. He was eyeing her cleavage again.

"You seem like a nice young man, Zeke," she said. "I'm having a little party at my place tomorrow night. Would you like to come? I'd love to have you."

"Sure," he blurted out.

"Great. Say eight o'clock? Here's the address." She wrote it on a slip of paper and handed it to him with one of her classic smiles. She knew he could hardly contain himself, that he figured this was his lucky day. Holly felt a tinge of guilt as she drove away.

When darkness descends, the deserted streets of Culpeper trade their friendly daytime garb for an ominous, eerie shroud. The judge felt it as he coasted his car to a stop on Main Street and got out to walk the two blocks to the rendezvous site. Hands jammed into the pockets of his overcoat, his footsteps echoed off the sidewalk and ricocheted off the brick buildings. A dog barked somewhere in the distance. The shadows threatened to swallow the dim glow of the streetlights. The judge stepped more quickly, uneasy about being the lone pedestrian on the street. He strode one more block then, furtively glancing about, ducked into a litter-strewn alley. Past trash cans obviously full, judging by the smell, around stacked crates, skids, and abandoned boxes, he continued at the same brisk pace, into the darkness and around the corner to the back of the building. Beneath a dim light fixture, the judge knocked on a battered, old door with more confidence than he felt.

A short Oriental man with a round face opened the door and bowed deeply, inviting the judge to enter, then securely locked the door behind them. He motioned to the judge to follow and led him through a shipping-receiving area, past a dark storage room and into a poorly lit office. Around a small table sat three others, their faces strained as if they anticipated some impending doom. They managed faint smiles when the judge introduced himself and shook their hands.

The Oriental man was Kai Chiu Wong, owner of the Chinese Restaurant in which this meeting was taking place. His wife, Cecilia, sat at the table along with Findlay Ralston, owner of the hardware store on Main Street, and Patricia Long, a widow, who ran the fabric shop. The judge grabbed a chair, swung his leg over to straddle it and rested his arms across the back. He wanted to set these people at ease right away.

"Just relax, folks," he said. "Everything you say tonight will be kept completely confidential. I'm just here to get some information to see whether there is anything I can do to help you."

They seemed to relax a little as the judge's powerful voice instilled renewed confidence.

"As I tell you before, Mr. Hamilton," Kai Chiu Wong spoke first, "Sheriff Bodie — he threaten us. Tell us pay money or he hurt us. He say if we pay, he keep business safe. No choice, have to pay, but this wrong, no?"

"Yes, very wrong," the judge assured them.

Findlay Ralston summoned up the courage to speak next. "I was late with my payment one month, and they came at night and turned my store upside down. It took me a week to get it back in order."

"They beat up my late husband one night when he refused to pay." Patricia fought back the tears. "My Johnny came home with a broken nose, two broken ribs and a black eye. He said they threatened to hurt our kids next time, if we didn't toe the line."

"Who can we turn to?" asked Findlay. "They're the law. We can't prove it, but we believe that even the mayor is part of it. We have to knuckle under or suffer the consequences."

"How much money does he demand from each of you?" asked the judge.

"Two hundred dollars a month," Patricia volunteered. The others all nodded. "Sometimes more."

The judge shook his head in disbelief. "So, how many businesses do you think he controls like this?"

"Most them, maybe all," Mr. Wong guessed.

The judge felt his blood begin to boil at the injustices meted out on these innocent people. This town needed a good cleaning up. He would do whatever he could to rectify this situation.

"Folks, you have to remember that what the sheriff is doing is wrong, illegal. It's extortion, pure and simple. But he has a lot of power backing him up, including the entire police department, I suppose, and, like you said, maybe even the mayor. I want you to realize, though, that his biggest ally is your fear. As long as all of you refuse to stand up to him together, in large numbers, he has you whipped."

"We realize that, Mr. Hamilton, but how do we break that cycle of fear?" Patricia asked. "Every time someone resists, they get badly beaten or their store gets vandalized."

"Yes, because it's only one person at a time." The judge spread his massive arms wide, "If you could somehow band together and consolidate your stance against Bodie, you might stand a better chance of getting somewhere."

"What do you suggest?" Findlay asked, nervously tapping the table.

"How about approaching some of the others very cautiously, and only those you know you can trust. Let them know that a whole group of you is planning to stand up to Bodie. See if you can get their commitment to join in. I'll try to arrange some help for you from the outside."

The judge could see the change in their expressions right away. Hope, for now at least, had replaced the doom in their faces. They needed a leader, someone to take up their plight, to implant the seeds of optimism, to inspire them to action on their own behalf. The judge already knew that he would be that leader. A fight against gross injustice was always his fight. He left the meeting as he had come, via the back door and the smelly alley. As he drove off in the euphoria of having made a difference in a few lives on this night, the judge failed to notice the police cruiser with its lights off, silently creeping along Main Street three blocks behind him.

TEN

J ennifer and a few friends pitched in to flesh out the party. Raucous rock tunes blared from the stereo, and a generous assortment of liquor sprawled across the kitchen counter. When Zeke rang the doorbell, the party was in full gear. People danced, kissed and embraced.

Holly greeted Zeke with her patented winning smile, took his arm and led him into the center of the action. Beer was his beverage choice, and Holly kept them coming. She lavished attention on Zeke all evening, treating him like a prince who had found his sleeping beauty. She showed great interest in his life, especially his job at Jake's. Zeke had one thing on his mind—making out—but Holly held him at bay, teasing him with an occasional suggestive kiss to maintain interest. Between kisses, she continued the stream of probing questions under the guise of genuine interest in him.

Soon the alcohol began to work. Zeke's speech became slurred, and his inhibitions evaporated. He spoke more boldly and openly, bragging about personal exploits.

"So what do you do for excitement?" Holly probed.

"You mean aside from women?" Glassy eyes stared back at Holly.

"Yeah, besides women."

"Well, right now we've got us a special project goin' on."

Holly didn't have to feign interest now. "A special project! That sounds exciting." She planted another hard kiss on his lips. "Tell me about it, you sexy thing. I bet you're the top gun on the project."

Now ego, fueled by alcohol, took over. "Me, Jake 'n' the boys are all in it together. But don't tell nobody, Holly, 'cause this is secret stuff."

"Oh, I wouldn't dream of telling anyone, Zeke. It'll be our little secret."

"We're after hidden treasure," Zeke continued, looking suddenly very tired. "We're gonna be filthy rich real soon."

"I love mysteries," Holly said. She had to keep him awake awhile longer. "How are you going to get rich?"

"There's this buried treasure from the Civil War, you see, and this professor who's supposed to be runnin' the project found out where the treasure's buried—" Zeke's eyelids were closing.

Holly shook him excitedly. "Go on, Zeke, this is so exciting, don't keep me in suspense. Where's the treasure?"

"On some rich guy's property over in Virginia. Culpeper, Virginia. Johns is his name. Vic Johns." Zeke was nearly unconscious now. "Me, Jake 'n' the boys are the muscle tryin' to make this guy get off the land—" He was out cold on the couch. Holly tried to revive him without success.

At her signal, the party ended abruptly. She checked his wallet, pulling his driver's license to get the address. They hauled Zeke's drunken butt to his car, and Holly drove him home, followed by Jennifer and her boyfriend Dan. They dragged him inside and laid him on the bed, then Holly left an ego-stroking note declaring what a stud he'd been.

"Thanks for letting me use your apartment, Dan," Holly said from the backseat as they returned to Dan's to clean up.

"Anytime, Holly. Glad to help out."

"So you got the goods?" Jennifer asked.

"I got it all," a beaming Holly replied. "Names and places. The poor guy probably won't even remember telling me. He'll wake up with a hangover."

"And a swelled head when he reads your note," Jennifer added. They laughed the rest of the way home.

Ambrose Lapain was furious. He'd caught news coverage of the accident on the local NBC affiliate out of Richmond, Virginia. They made a big deal out of testimony from eyewitnesses that a second vehicle was harassing the victim from behind just prior to the crash. Police were continuing their investigation to determine whether this second vehicle had forced Sally Johns' vehicle off the road.

That idiot, Jake Crapper, was going to ruin everything. That's all they needed now — statewide attention focused on Vic Johns. The whole bloody eastern seaboard would soon be on the lookout for the car and, eventually, for Jake and his misfits, and that would lead right to him, Ambrose Lapain, respected professor of American history at Georgetown University.

Lapain stomped into Crazy Jake's Salvage Company like an angry gunfighter itching for any excuse to pull the trigger. He slammed the door and scowled at the curious glances of the losers in Jake's employ. A smiling Crazy Jake emerged from the mechanic's kitchen. Lapain started on him with six guns blazing.

"Jake, what the hell do you clowns think you're doing?"

"What're ya talkin' about, Professor?" Lapain's anger surprised Jake, and the venom kept coming.

"I'm talking about that stupid accident and you idiots nearly killing Sally Johns."

"Now hold on there, Professor—" But there was no stopping Lapain. He was a machine gun out of control.

"Now the whole state of Virginia knows who Vic Johns is and sympathizes with him because his wife is lying half dead in a hospital in Culpeper!" Lapain grabbed a wrench from the cluttered workbench and fired it against the back wall of the garage. It clattered around on the floor. He wasn't finished yet.

"You bozos are supposed to be taking orders from me! I hired you and this is my project, got it? I told you no one was to be hurt and no one was to act without my authorization. So why the hell do you keep playing lone ranger, Jake? I've just about had enough of it, you hear? I don't even know if we can salvage this thing now after this asinine performance."

"Cool down, Professor." Jake's smile was gone now. "We had nothin' to do with that accident."

"You're lying."

That accusation clearly didn't sit well with Jake. Now his temper was flaring. "Why you—" His bulging arms grabbed Lapain by the front of the shirt and practically lifted him right off the ground, pinning him to the wall. The professor's anger drained quickly. His face suddenly registered fear. Jake was a formidable adversary.

"Now you listen to me, Professor," Jake began. "We had nothin' to do with that accident, you hear that? We didn't do it. But as far as I'm concerned, somebody did us a big, fat favor." Lapain felt Jake's fiery eyes boring into him. "We've waited around long enough for this Johns guy to tuck his tail between his legs and run back to Washington. It's time to really tighten the screws, and I don't think you've got the guts to do it, Professor."

Lapain knew he teetered on the brink of a leadership crisis. The misfits were watching the action closely. He had to exert himself now or all was lost. "Let me go, Jake," he barked with as much authority as he could muster, while pushing Jake away. The big man loosened his grip. Now for some damage control.

"Jake, you and I both know that I'm the brains behind this operation. You wouldn't even be involved if it wasn't for me. What do you think happens when we dig up the treasure? I'm the one who's going to authenticate the discovery and turn it into a big payday for all of us. You can't do that on your own. You need me for that."

"Maybe so, but I'm tired of waitin' around for the payoff. Me 'n' the boys are gettin' restless, Professor, and I say it's time for action, not more waitin' around, eh, boys?" He turned to get their response. Every head was nodding. "So you have a choice, Professor. You can get out now and forget about your precious historical discovery, or you can follow my orders from now on."

Lapain glanced around the garage. Jake's boys glared at him, waiting for his answer. Jake's stare was cold and unyielding.

"All right, I understand your frustration. Let's say we share the leadership, Jake. You call the shots right now, and I'll take the lead again when we get the property. But I still get some input along the way—kind of like co-captains. What do you say?"

Lapain knew he was on shaky ground but hoped Jake would at least accept this compromise. If so, he could save some face before Jake's boys. That might help down the road. They all waited for Jake's response. Finally, a big smile broke across Jake's bearded face.

"Okay, Professor, you got it. Now, let's convince our man Johns to take a permanent vacation in Washington, D.C."

The forest was his shrine of escape, so as soon as the rains stopped, Vic headed out under ominous gray skies. The stiff autumn breeze in his face had a soothing effect, transporting his spirit to another realm where stress and worry were forgotten, at least for awhile. He walked the circular path that roughly followed the perimeter of the property. Tiger, Duke and Sarge, the loyal Rottweilers, followed. Vic filled his lungs with the fresh scent of rain-soaked foliage. He remembered happier days strolling this same path with a young Kim giggling as she rode on his shoulders and a laughing Sally at his side, tossing fallen leaves at them. The memory brought a tear to his eye. Where had the time gone? It seemed only yesterday that they had been so happy and carefree. Now, Sally lay fighting for her life in a hospital bed, and guilt hung over him like a dark cloud. He felt like he was falling helplessly into a bottomless black pit, reaching, groping for something, anything, to stay the fall, but to no avail. The darkness sucked him downward, as the light above receded.

Vic finished the loop around the property and settled down to splitting wood. The only sounds were the rustling of the wind in the treetops and the echo of the ax blows. After only five minutes, Vic peeled off the rain gear and rolled up the sleeves of his flannel shirt. He was breathing heavily now, and beads of perspiration formed on his forehead.

Kim knew exactly where to find her father. He'd been hiding out there for the past three days, as if ignoring the situation would make it go away. She strolled along the path and, shivering in the chill air, pulled her fleece jacket closed, holding it in place with arms crossed. She passed the old cabin that her dad had built here over twenty years ago. They used to come out here on weekends to get away from the big city. The cabin was their retreat for years. Even in the snowy winter months, they had sat around the old woodstove, playing games and singing silly songs. They'd even spent a few Christmases here. She remembered wondering how Santa Claus always knew where to find them.

Vic was chopping feverishly as Kim approached the clearing behind the cabin. "Dad," she shouted, startling him. He turned to see her.

"The sheriff called," she said. "Just an update. There's nothing new yet on the second vehicle. He said the eyewitnesses corroborate one another. There definitely was a second vehicle, but whether it actually caused the accident is not yet clear. He said they have to find the car before they'll know any more."

"If they find the car, they'll find the perpetrators of this whole fiasco. I'd like five minutes with them to show them how it feels to be bullied. But don't hold your breath, Kim, Sheriff Bodie couldn't find his own nose if it wasn't attached to his head."

"Dad, I know you're angry but it sounds like the sheriff is trying his best."

"Then his best just isn't good enough. Look where your mother is today, thanks to Sheriff Bodie." Vic split another log right down the middle.

"What's gotten into you, Dad? You spend the days pining out here in the woods, avoiding me, chopping wood you don't even need. You're so full of anger, you can't even be civil."

"Well, how would you feel if your life was falling apart?"

"What are you talking about? You're not the only one suffering here. That's my mother in that hospital bed fighting to stay alive. Don't you think I feel the pain like you do? I'm just as afraid as you are. I don't want to lose her either."

"It's different."

"What do you mean, different?"

"I mean, you weren't here. There wasn't anything you could have done to prevent it."

"Dad, it's not your fault."

"Yes, it is. I should have been able to protect her from those killers. I should have driven her to your place. I shouldn't have let her leave here alone."

"There's no way you could have known, Dad. She's driven to my place alone hundreds of times. You can't punish yourself like this. It won't change anything. And this hiding out in the woods won't help, either. What's gotten into you? You don't even go to the hospital to see Mom."

"I can't. I can't handle it. I can't stand to see her like that."

"But she needs you, Dad. She needs to know you're there for her. She needs to hear your voice, to know you care."

"She might not even make it." Vic stared at the cutting block.

"That's right, she might not." Kim fought back the tears. "But we have to do our best to give her every reason to keep on fighting."

"No, I can't do it." Vic kept shaking his head.

"You have to do it — for Mom and me."

"Kim, I said no, I can't do it. I'm not going to that hospital." Kim had heard that declaration of finality before. It always meant end of discussion, my mind is made up, I don't want to hear any more on that subject. Laboring the point now would be useless, but she was angry and had to get in the last word.

"Dad, it hurts me to say this, but you've become such a stubborn, selfish, old fool, I hardly even recognize you anymore. I'm telling you, if Mom dies while you hide out here in the woods, you'll regret it for the rest of your life, and I'll never speak to you again." With that, she turned and stomped back to the house.

❧

In Vic's mind an earthquake had so violently shaken his life that a huge gash had opened in the ground. The deep chasm ran between him and his loved ones. Kim and Sally were on the other side, out of reach; Vic was cut off from them, isolated, alone in his pain. At least that's how he felt. The real rupture was inside. The pain bubbled up from a broken heart. Vic fought back tears and wrestled with anger at the same time. He buried the ax head deep into the chopping block. He needed a long walk.

His head hung low as he made the turn at the end of the lane, left the dogs behind, and followed Pike Road. He shuffled along, aimlessly kicking stones, watching them skitter out of control across the road. He had a lot in common with those rocks. Life was kicking him pretty hard. He was bouncing along crazily, propelled by forces beyond his control.

This was Nam all over again. The lurking danger. The fear that gnawed away at your guts every waking hour and even in your dreams. The not knowing what might happen next, where Charlie was hiding, where he would strike. Fear. Inner turmoil. You couldn't shake it. It was tattooed to every moment of every day. The pain, the anxiety, grew unbearable. At times, you wanted to eat a bullet just to get it over with, to be rid of the relentless anguish. Or have someone pinch you to wake you from this horrible nightmare.

At least in Nam you knew who the enemy was and occasionally had a chance to wreak some serious punishment, to get in a few punches, to fight back. Here, the winds of fortune held sway. They blew, and Vic toppled, helplessly, passively, like the heads of wheat in the next field, bending before nature's blast.

How he longed to know the enemy, to see the whites of his eyes, to lash out and bind the bearer of adversity, to stem the bleeding and begin to turn things around. He wanted to spring into action and fight the foe, not drift passively down this river of slow destruction. He clenched his fists as the combat desire fired his blood. Instinctively, all senses were on alert as years of training and combat experience kicked in.

Vic was only a few hundred yards from his own driveway, hugging the weed-lined side of Pike Road, when he saw the footprint. The impression was clearly stamped in the soft mud on the shoulder of the road—a carbon copy of the footprint next to the fallen tree in Vic's backyard. The Red Wing insignia distinctly stood out, as did a pronounced groove in the heel along the right side. Vic would recognize that footprint anywhere. It was indelibly etched in his mind.

The print, he discovered as he surveyed the surroundings, was located at the end of a short, apparently unused, farm entry off Pike Road. It led into the back acreage of Ted Jensen's farm. There was nothing there except a thin line of trees along the fence row, a gate blocking vehicle access to the property, a pile of old brush waiting to be burned, and an old, abandoned white van.

Vic seldom drove this section of Pike Road. Access to town was from the other direction, so he rarely passed this stretch of the old road. Funny place for Ted to leave an old van like that, thought Vic. Curiosity sent him over the fence to investigate. As he approached the vehicle, the side door suddenly swung open with a loud creak. Vic dove for the tree line, out of sight. He sprawled flat on his belly, heart beating rapidly, and waited, listening, hoping he had not been detected.

A white-haired young man of average height and build, wearing a green and black checked hunter's shirt and dirty blue jeans, circled around the back of the van and relieved himself behind a tree. With not even a glance in Vic's direction, he returned to the van, slamming the door behind him. Vic crawled silently on his stomach along the tree line, toward the rear of the van. A quick search turned up a visible footprint. There was the Red Wing insignia and the unmistakable groove in the heel. This guy was the terrorist who had downed the tree. A surge of anger boiled in Vic, but the calm thinking of his combat experience overrode the heated desire for revenge. He took a deep breath and inched his way to the rear of the van. Like a cobra uncoiling, he stealthily raised his head and peered into the rear window. Vic gasped. The rusted-out wreck was decked out for surveillance. The white-haired kid wore headphones and sat at a console.

Vic ducked down quickly and inched his way back to the tree line. He hopped the fence and hurried back down the road to his own driveway. They have the house bugged, Vic thought. They've been eavesdropping on everything that has gone on in the house. He had to warn Kim, but they had to act as if they didn't know. Everything had to seem normal to avoid suspicion.

He burst into the house and shouted, "Hey, Kim, come outside for a minute, I want to show you something." When she emerged, he took her arm and practically dragged her from the house.

"Dad, what are you doing?"

"Kim, they've got the house bugged. They've been listening to our conversations at home. That's how they know where we are all the time."

"How do you know?"

"I just stumbled across an old white van across Pike Road at the back of Ted Jensen's property. They've got it rigged out for surveillance. They've probably been monitoring our conversations for awhile now."

"I don't believe it." Fear crept across Kim's face as the news sunk in.

"Kim, we have to go back in there and act like we don't know anything about this. I don't want to create any suspicion on their part. Do you understand? We have to act totally normal and go about our activities as if we didn't know they were listening in."

"OK, I'll try," Kim replied hesitantly. She felt exposed, vulnerable all of a sudden. But she noticed that her father had a new fire in his eyes. He looked more alive than he had for weeks. "What are you going to do?" she asked.

"I'm not sure yet, but I'm working on a plan."

"Be careful, Dad."

"I will, but for now, let's just keep them thinking that they have us totally fooled."

ELEVEN

The peppy, little Neon rental car would do nicely, thought Vic, as he ran one last errand before launching his plan. He turned into the Dominos Pizza lot and claimed his medium with extra cheese and pepperoni, then returned to the dilapidated Shamrock Motel. Earlier in the evening, he had followed the white van here and watched as the mysterious surveillance operator had parked and entered Room Seven.

Now, Vic stood knocking at the door of Room Seven with a steaming hot pepperoni pizza in hand. He pulled his cap low to shadow his eyes. The door opened, and there stood Vic's target.

"Pizza," Vic said, disguising his voice.

"I didn't order no pizza," came the reply.

"You're kiddin' me," Vic said with genuine frustration and disbelief. He jabbed a finger at the bill. "It says right here, Shamrock Motel, Room Seven. This is the Shamrock, isn't it?" The young man nodded.

"And this is Room Seven, isn't it?" Another nod.

"Are you sure you didn't order it?"

"Yup."

"Great. I'm in big trouble. Somebody's playing some kind of joke on me, and it's not funny, 'cause now I gotta pay for this pizza. Sure you can't take it off my hands, buddy? Tell you what, I'll give it to ya for five bucks instead of the regular price of eight. You'd really be helpin' me out here. Whaddya say?"

By now the aroma of fresh, hot pizza filled the room. It did smell good.

"Oh, OK, I'll give you five bucks for it. Just set it there on the table. I'll get my wallet." He turned his back on Vic.

In one fluid motion, Vic slid the pizza onto the table and lunged for the younger man. He grabbed him in a headlock and twisted his arm painfully into his back. One hard shove, and he pinned the young man to the floor.

"Be quiet and you won't get hurt, pal."

Working quickly, Vic held him down with one knee, pulled a piece of rope from his jacket pocket, and tied the assailant's hands and feet behind his back. Finally, he handcuffed him to the headboard of the bed.

"Now, I want some answers and I want them fast. Cooperate and I'll go easy on you, understand?" The young man was nodding, tear written in his eyes.

"What's your name, boy?" Vic demanded.

"Whitey. Whitey Thompson, sir."

"Live around here, Whitey?"

"No, sir."

"Where do you live?"

"D.C."

"What are you doing way out here, Whitey? Why the van and all the surveillance equipment?"

It was clear Whitey didn't want to answer that question. Maybe he couldn't decide who he was really more afraid of — his captor or the boss he was going to be asked to betray.

"Whitey, I don't want to hurt you, but I will if you don't answer me." Vic glared at the lad. The kid was already sweating profusely. Vic could smell his fear. This would be easy. He slammed his fist on the table and turned on Whitey in anger.

"Why are you spying on me and my family, Whitey?" He made a move as if to attack the kid and that was all it took.

"Jake. He told me to do it." The kid was spilling the beans already.

"Who's Jake?" Vic demanded angrily.

"My boss. Jake Crapper. Listen, Mister, don't go messin' with Jake — he can be mean as a junkyard dog."

"You haven't seen mean until you see me angry, Whitey." For effect, Vic snatched a glass from the table and fired it across the bed into the wall behind Whitey, sending a shower of glass shards in all directions. The bound young man cowered on the bed.

"Now, where can I find this boss of yours, Whitey?"

"Old Route 42 on the outskirts of D.C. Crazy Jake's Salvage Company."

"Salvage Company, huh? What are you guys doing harassing my family, Whitey?"

"Listen, mister, I don't know nothin'. I just do what I'm told. Jake — he knows everything. Go ask him. He's the one with the plan and all. I just take orders, mister. C—Can I go now?" The kid was practically begging.

"What's your hurry, Whitey? Anxious to make a little call to Jake?"

"No, I—I just want to go home now."

"Sorry, Whitey, you're not going home for awhile. There's someone else who'd like to make your acquaintance. You're going to have to hang around here until he arrives."

Vic grabbed the phone from the night table and dialed out.

"Sheriff Bodie please. Tell him it's Vic Johns calling." Vic noticed the tortured look on Whitey's face as he contemplated meeting the local sheriff.

"Sheriff, Vic Johns here. I'm over at the Shamrock Motel, Room Seven, visiting one of the guests. I think you might want to get over here and talk to this young fella yourself. His name's Whitey, and he has some interesting things to tell you about chopping down trees and harassing people." Vic turned his back on Whitey and spoke in a hushed tone. "Sheriff, I know who the leader of this pack is. He's over in the outskirts of D.C. . . . Yes, I figured you didn't have jurisdiction over there. But listen, before you call in the local police , will you give me some time to try to find out what I can? . . . No, I won't take the law into my own hands. I just want answers, Sheriff. I'll fill you in on the details when I can. By the way, Sheriff, can you post a guard at the hospital for Sally, just in case? . . . Yes. Thanks, Bodie, I owe you one." He raised his voice again, "Come on over and meet Whitey, Sheriff. He's even got a pizza for you."

Vic pulled a Polaroid photo from his vest pocket and stuck it in the frame of the mirror in Room Seven. It was a photograph of a boot print.

❧

Vic could already hear the distant wail of the police sirens as he pulled away from the Shamrock Motel and headed home. The phone was ringing as he entered the house. Kim must be still at the hospital.

"Hello?" Vic answered.

A quiet woman's voice spoke hesitantly. "Mr. Johns? Victor Johns?"

"Yes, who is this?"

"I can't tell you, at least not yet. Mr. Johns, I saw the newspaper story about your wife's car accident. I'm sorry to hear about that."

Vic was impatient to know who this was. "What do you want?" he snapped.

"I have some information about the accident. I know who caused it."

"Why don't you go to the police?" Vic demanded.

There was a long pause.

"I'm afraid to. This is bigger than one isolated incident."

"I'm listening." Vic wanted to hear more.

"No, not over the phone. It's too dangerous. We have to meet."

"All right, name the time and place, I'll be there." Vic was anxious now.

"Do you have a cell phone?"

"Yes."

"Then get in your car and drive toward the Capital. Give me your cell number, and I'll call you with directions. Make sure you're not being followed."

This could be a setup, Vic thought, but fueled by a need to know, he gave her the number. "I'm leaving in five minutes," he said and hung up.

"Leaving to go where?" Kim asked as she walked into the kitchen.

"To meet someone who says she has information about Mom's accident."

"Shouldn't you be calling the police?" Kim reasoned as she tossed her keys and purse on the counter.

"Already have," Vic replied. "I caught one of their thugs tonight."

"You caught one of them?"

Vic related the capture of Whitey. "And as soon as I talk to this lady," he added, "I'm going after the rest of the gang."

"What? Are you crazy? Dad, this isn't a war, you know."

"It is to me. And I intend to win."

"Dad, you're not being reasonable. Let the police handle it. This isn't Vietnam."

"Sorry, it's already decided. The sheriff is giving me 48 hours to see what I can find out, then he calls in the local police in D.C."

"This is insane." Kim was pacing now. "I can't believe the sheriff actually agreed to back off and let you play commando!" She glared at Vic. "He's as crazy as you are." Vic shrugged his shoulders and smiled.

"I'm coming with you," Kim blurted out.

The refusal registered immediately on Vic's face. "No way, Kim. It's too dangerous. Besides, I need you to stay here and look after the place and Mom, too."

Kim began to protest, but Vic interrupted. "I promise, I'll be careful. No hero stuff. But I have to go alone. I have to do this, Kim."

He stepped forward, planted a kiss on her forehead and gave her a quick hug. "I'll be in touch," he said as he snatched up the cell phone and disappeared into the garage.

The call had come only minutes after he started out for D.C. This lady was obviously nervous and anxious. Vic had no trouble finding the meeting place, Denny's restaurant. He was actually relieved that the mystery woman had chosen such a public place to meet. Not a likely ambush site. Still, an air of extreme caution compelled Vic to scan the few late hour patrons of the establishment as he entered. An old man with gray whiskers, wrinkled skin and thinning, unkempt hair, occupied the second booth from the door. His eyes were riveted to the daily newspaper. An overweight truck driver perched on a stool at the bar, sipping coffee. A young couple in another booth held hands and stared lovingly into each other's eyes.

Down at the end booth, as in the directions given him by phone, was a young and very attractive blonde. This was his mystery woman? She smiled at Vic as he slipped into the booth.

"Mr. Johns, I presume?"

"Yes, call me Vic. And you are?" He extended a hand.

"Holly. Holly Fenton," she replied, slipping her thin hand into Vic's. He gave it a token squeeze and barged ahead.

"So, Holly, what do you have to tell me?"

"I'm not sure where to begin. I saw the story about your wife's accident and it bothered me so much—"

"Because you knew something about it, right?" Vic said with a trace of insinuation.

"Mr. Johns—Vic, believe me, I was in no way involved in the accident. I came upon the information quite by chance."

The arrival of the waitress cut off the conversation. "What can I get you folks?"

"Just coffee for me," offered Holly, looking at Vic.

"Yeah, two coffees, that's fine," Vic uttered impatiently, with a wave of his hand to dismiss the woman. "Go on, Holly," he said, when the waitress was out of hearing range.

"How is your wife, anyway, Vic?"

"About the same, I guess—I don't go to the hospital much. Can't stand to see her in a coma like that. They don't know if she's going to make it." A tear formed in the corner of Vic's eye. He shook off the emotion and pressed on with the business at hand. "So, what's the news?" he asked bluntly.

"I believe the person who orchestrated your wife's car accident is a man named Jake—Jake Crapper. He and his hired hands have been harassing you and your wife for some time now. They want to force you off your land."

"Why?" Vic demanded impatiently. This was the mystery question. Without an answer, none of it made any sense.

Holly hesitated. Her hands were trembling. Vic could tell she was reluctant to go there, but he also knew that she had contacted him. She needed to tell what she knew—for her own peace of mind. Besides, he had a right to know why he and his family were being terrorized. So, he pressed her for an answer.

"Why, Holly? Why do they want me off my land?"

"My boss, Dr. Ambrose Lapain, a professor at Georgetown University, has discovered that there may be buried treasure from the Civil War on your property. He has confirmed the location already but needs your land in order to properly document the findings and claim the wealth that goes with it. He's been using Jake Crapper and his thugs to provide the muscle to convince you to sell out."

"How do you know all this?"

"Mr. Johns, I assure you I have no part in this sick plot. I'm Dr. Lapain's research assistant at the University. I'm working on my Ph.D. Dr. Lapain and I made the discovery together through our research—" She stopped abruptly as the waitress dropped off the coffees and left. "But I had no idea until a few weeks ago that he had actually located the site. And I certainly didn't know that he was using those thugs to leverage you into selling. I swear to you, I have come upon all this information by accident."

Now it was starting to make sense to Vic. The escalating offers on the property, the tree, the mailbox, the harassment, and the car accident. All connected as he suspected. An elaborate plot to take over his land and this mystery treasure.

"So, where is the treasure?" Vic asked, as he lifted the cup to his lips.

"I don't know—except that it's on your property somewhere."

"I thought I knew every square inch of that land," Vic shook his head.

"It's supposedly marked by three rocks, Mr. Johns. During the Civil War, the Federal army ambushed a detachment of Colonel John Mosby's Rangers near the Rappahannock River. For some reason, Mosby's men took the booty from their raid the previous day and buried it near their camp. Apparently, the hidden treasure remained a secret until a few months ago when Professor Lapain located it on your land."

"And killed one of my dogs doing it," Vic replied bitterly. "So what's buried there that makes it so valuable?"

"I don't know. The professor hasn't excavated it yet because he wants it all properly documented as a historical find, so he'll get the credit for it." Holly paused, staring into her coffee cup. "Then there's the matter of the potential wealth. That's the other reason he wants the deed to your land."

"It must be pretty valuable if he's willing to destroy personal property, threaten lives and maybe even kill someone," Vic said, as the sight of Sally lying in that hospital bed, hooked up to life support, rushed back to mind.

"It surprises me, Vic, but I wouldn't be shocked to hear that Jake Crapper is behind all the serious violence. He's a vile, repulsive man. I wouldn't trust him one inch. There's no telling what he might do."

When the coffee cups were empty and the conversation had slowed, Vic reached in his pocket to pay the tab. "Are you all right, Holly?" he asked with genuine concern. "I mean are you going to be safe?"

"Oh sure," Holly replied quickly. "They don't know that I'm meeting you. In fact, they don't even know that I have as much inside information as I do."

"Well, be careful, and if you need any help, let me know, will you?" He reached out and shook her hand firmly. "And, Holly, thanks for the information."

"You're welcome." She smiled. "What are you going to do now?"

"I'm going to pay a little visit to Mr. Crapper's salvage company."

"Right now? In the middle of the night?"

Vic smiled grimly. "Yes. I want to leave a message for Mr. Crapper."

"Well, watch out for the guard dog. It's a vicious animal."

"I will. Thanks again, Holly. Keep in touch if you hear anything more."

She nodded. Vic slid out of the booth and walked briskly to the door.

Sheriff Bodie and Deputy Nate Peters arrived at the Shamrock Motel simultaneously. The twin cruisers, red and blue lights flashing, lurched to a stop in front of Room Seven, and their sirens faded into the still night air. Both men pulled their revolvers as they moved toward the door. Bodie knocked loudly, but the only audible response was a muffled sound. Standing to the side of the doorway, he turned the doorknob and gently swung the door open.

When Bodie nodded, Deputy Peters swung into the doorway, pistol at the ready. He quickly scanned the room and saw Whitey Thompson on the bed, trussed up like a roped calf in a rodeo.

"Untie the boy," Bodie ordered, as he inspected the room. He checked the dresser drawers, the desk, lifted the lid of the pizza box.

"Son," he said, turning to face Whitey, who was untied now and standing, "the way I see it, you're in a lot of trouble." Without warning, Bodie drove his fist into the lad's midsection, doubling him up in pain. He nodded to Nate, who stood behind Whitey, and Nate pounded his fist into the kid's kidneys, sending him sprawling in agony to the floor.

"You're gonna thank us for this later, boy," Bodie said as he booted Whitey in the ribs.

Nate dragged the groaning young man to his feet and slugged him across the face with a bare fist. Blood immediately trickled down Whitey's face from a wound next to his eye. Nate caught him from falling and cuffed him again, opening a gash in Whitey's lip. A knee in the groin and a couple more blows to the head, and Whitey was just about unconscious.

Bodie grabbed the shock of tousled white hair and lifted the limp head to make eye contact. "It's too bad that crazy man, Vic Johns, beat you up so badly, isn't it, kid?" He shook the limp body. "Isn't it?" He shook again until Whitey nodded. "Just beat you to a pulp and left you strung up like a piece of meat. That's the story, boy. You got that?" He shook the sagging body again. A faint nod indicated that Whitey heard. "Like I said, you're in a whole lotta trouble, boy, but you play this story out with us, we'll go easy on ya, hear?" Another barely visible nod.

"Deputy Peters, I think you'd better call an ambulance for our friend, Whitey, here. I'm afraid Victor Johns has been pretty rough on the boy."

Nate put the call in from the radio in his police cruiser. The motel manager and a few brave patrons had ventured out into the parking lot. Curiosity drew them toward Room Seven, but Nate quickly moved to disperse them, assuring them there had simply been a minor disturbance, nothing for them to worry about. He convinced the manager that no damage had been done to the room, that the guest had suffered minor injuries and would be taken to hospital for observation. Not really wanting to get involved anyway, the manager beat a hasty retreat to his office. Sheriff Bodie stepped out into the night air just as the last stragglers headed back to their rooms.

Nate spoke first. "I told the EMTs to skip the siren. No use attracting any more attention."

"Smart move, Nate. Listen, I want to put out an APB on Vic Johns. We'll issue a warrant for his arrest for the brutal assault on Whitey here." He smiled. "Johns comes anywhere near Culpeper, we'll have his butt in jail so fast he won't know what hit him."

"What about the kid, this harassment thing and the accident?"

"All in good time, Nate. When the hospital gets Whitey patched up, we'll have a little talk with him, find out what he and his friends are up to, and drill the party line into him again. Vic Johns has played right into our hands this time."

TWELVE

C lad in army fatigues, Vic crouched before the chain link fence surrounding Crazy Jake's Salvage Company. His calmness surprised him but probably shouldn't have. He had planned this carefully. Now all he had to do was carry out the plan. He noticed the sign posted on the gate, BEWARE GUARD DOG ON DUTY. That was the part that worried him the most. Animals are always unpredictable. The old highway was totally deserted at this hour, no one was around at any of the places of business, so any barking would not be a problem.

He reviewed the plan once more in his mind as he checked his equipment one last time. He came well-armed — bolt cutters, lead pipe, a noose, muzzle, leash and meat for the dog. He glanced at the building again. A couple of dim external security lights illuminated the main entrance and the bay areas around back. He doubted whether Crazy Jake would have some fancy alarm system in place. The guard dog was probably considered ample security for this run-down establishment.

As soon as the bolt cutters snapped the chain on the gate, the beast Holly had warned about emerged from behind the main building, teeth bared in an aggressive warning. Vic readied the meat. He gently swung the gate open only enough for the dog to pass through. That brought a snarl from the other side of the fence, but the dog, sensing Vic's fearlessness, advanced cautiously. Slowly, Vic placed the steak on the end of the steel pole and extended it toward the open gate. The dog had the scent now and moved toward the meat. Vic lured the animal out through the open gate and away from the fence. At the same time, he was rotating until his back was to the gate. He carefully set the steak on the ground in front of the dog and gently inched backwards through the gate into the compound and pulled the gate closed behind him. The dog was too busy tearing into the red meat to notice that he and the stranger had exchanged places.

Vic ran softly to the shadows at the rear of the main building and smashed in a window to gain access. As expected, no audible alarm sounded. He went to work quickly, swinging the lead pipe, reducing the showcase in the outer office to a shambles of broken glass. Paperwork and records he tossed wildly across the room, knocked the coffee machine off its table, overturned chairs and desks in both offices. Moving into the service bays, Vic flung tools and auto parts everywhere. He thought of Sally, suffering in her hospital bed, and vented the pent-up anger in a fury of revenge. He dumped workbenches and tool boxes, ripped posters and shelves from the walls. When the waves of anger subsided, Vic snatched a can of red spray paint and scrawled a message on the wall that, moments before, was adorned with flashy posters of racy cars and risqué women.

VENGEANCE IS MINE . . . WE'VE GOT WHITEY GIVE IT
UP OR ELSE. V.J.

Vic returned to the entrance gate satisfied. He'd made his
point. It felt good to trash Crazy Jake's place, to finally vent
the deepening frustration and anger. He wished he could be
around to see this Jake character in the morning when he
discovers the extensive remodeling job. Back at the gate,
there was no sign of the guard dog or the meat. He must
have decided to take advantage of his new found freedom.
Probably off dallying with some bitch in heat.

Vic drove back to his motel room, feeling the high of
pulling off the counterattack without a hitch. "I love it when
a plan comes together," he shouted, slapping the steering
wheel and grinning widely.

"Mornin', miss." Sheriff Bodie, hat in hand, smiled warmly
as the door opened to reveal an attractive young woman he
recognized as Kim Johns. "Sheriff Bodie," he said by way of
introduction. "I do hope it's not too early to come callin'."

"Not at all," Kim replied. "Is there some problem,
Sheriff?"

"Would your daddy happen to be home, miss?"

Kim was confused. "I'm afraid not, Sheriff, but you
already know that. Dad said you gave him 48 hours to
investigate the guy behind this harassment thing."

Now the sheriff looked confused. "No, miss, I did nothin'
of the sort. In fact, I'm here to take your daddy in. Seems
there was some trouble last evenin' — "

"Trouble! What kind of trouble?" Kim's heart skipped a
beat.

"Some young fella got beat up pretty bad. Says your daddy was the one that did it. I've got a warrant for his arrest."

"What?! On what charges?" Kim demanded defiantly.

"Assault and battery for starters—maybe even attempted murder. We'll see how the prosecutor decides to handle it."

"I don't believe it." Kim was scared and angry. "My Dad wouldn't do such a thing."

Bodie shrugged sheepishly. "Well, miss, you have to admit he's been under a lot of stress lately, what with the accident and all."

"But he still wouldn't assault anyone, not without provocation. I know him, Sheriff, he wouldn't do it. There's obviously been some mistake."

"Well, miss, I'm sorry to have to break this news to you, but broken ribs, facial contusions and concussions don't lie. I'm afraid the evidence stacks up pretty heavily against your daddy. And the victim's already named him as his attacker. I'm just doin' my duty. If your daddy shows up here, miss, I'd advise you to tell him to turn himself in. Maybe the judge will go easy on him."

The finality of it left Kim shaken, but she tried not to let the sheriff see her reaction. Dad had been acting rather strange lately, and there was no question stress levels had been high for months now. Maybe Mom's accident sent him over the edge. He didn't seem upset last night before he left for Washington. He wasn't belligerent at all. And he didn't say anything about any trouble with the guy he caught.

"You OK, miss?" The Sheriff's voice interrupted Kim's thoughts.

"Yeah. I—I'm fine, thanks sheriff." Kim nodded absentmindedly.

"Well, then, I'd best be goin', miss. By the way, how's your momma?"

A cloud immediately shadowed Kim's face. "About the same," she said. "Still in a coma. They don't know if she's going to pull out of it."

"Sorry about that, miss. I do hope she recovers." He donned his hat and turned to leave. "Remember, if your daddy shows up, you'd best talk him into turnin' himself in. Have a nice day, miss." There was just a tinge of sarcasm in his voice. Kim suddenly realized that he was enjoying laying this news on her. He wanted to see her squirm and make excuses, maybe even fall apart in front of him. Well, there was no way she'd ever give him that pleasure. Maybe Dad's impression of the sheriff was right after all.

The call came soon after the sheriff had departed. It caught Kim, drenched with sweat, near the end of her aerobic workout. Frantically, she grabbed a towel and ran for the phone. She pushed the speakerphone button and sponged the perspiration from her eyes.

"Hello?"

"Hi, Kim. It's me, Dad—"

"Dad, where are you?"

"In D.C. at a motel, why?"

"The sheriff's been here, and he has a warrant out for your arrest. Says you beat up some kid last night."

"What? I did nothing of the sort! I left him tied up and called the sheriff to pick him up at the motel."

"That's not what the sheriff says. Claims the boy identified you as his attacker. Apparently, he's got broken ribs, a concussion—sounds like he's pretty bad, Dad. Are you sure—?"

"Kim, listen to me. I never touched that boy. You have to believe me. The kid gave me all the information I needed. I didn't have to force it out of him, just scared him a bit."

"Then what's the sheriff talking about? He can't arrest you for nothing. If the kid's not hurt, he has no basis to charge you."

"Yeah, if the kid's not hurt. Those are the operative words. All I know is when I left that motel room, Whitey was fine—scared, yes, but physically he was unhurt. I just tied him and cuffed him to the headboard of the bed."

Kim mopped her brow again. "You don't think the sheriff—"

"Nothing would surprise me, Kim. The man is quite capable of doing just about anything."

"That means he set you up. Made you a fugitive in Culpeper County."

"That's right, Kim. Listen, I'm going to have to stay away from Culpeper for awhile until we can get this cleared up. You be extra careful now, OK? Looks like we have enemies in high places."

"Dad, be careful."

"I will. I'll try to call you later this evening."

"OK, but I'm heading to the hospital for evening visiting hours."

"All right, I'll catch up with you after that."

A click and the vacant hum of the dialtone told her he was gone. A sudden cold shudder shook Kim. She headed for the shower.

The morning sun beamed brightly as Jake Crapper and his crew arrived at the salvage company simultaneously, but foreboding black clouds to the west hinted of an approaching storm. However, long before nature unleashed her fury, Crazy Jake exploded into a rage of his own. He knew something was wrong when the compound gate was ajar, but one look at his demolished operation and he lived up to his name. His face beet red, he exploded in a flurry of expletives, screaming and flinging his arms wildly, kicking nearby objects and grabbing his head in grief and anger, as if a sudden migraine threatened to explode in his head.

Zeke, Willie and Charlie backed out of Jake's way. They had never seen their boss this angry before. He was out of control, and they dared not speak or move until the initial wave of wrath subsided. In shock and fear, the young men glanced about, wondering who had done this. Zeke was the first to spy the spray-painted message. He merely pointed to it and the others turned to take it in. Jake, though still livid, saw it, too, and grew strangely calmer. A sardonic smile crossed his face and another expletive rolled off his tongue.

"That S.O.B. has just declared war, boys. And we're gonna take him down." He broke into a crazy, uncontrolled belly laugh.

Willie, Zeke and Charlie just looked at each other and shrugged.

"Let's get this place back in shape, boys," Jake shouted. "Then the fun will begin. I've got a plan."

He flipped on the stereo, about the only item to weather Vic Johns' onslaught unscathed, and cranked up the volume until the windows rattled.

"You were lucky to catch me in D.C., Vic. I don't spend much time here anymore. By the way, what are you doing here?"

The judge had been surprised when Vic Johns intercepted him in the marble lobby of the FBI building.

"I called your house, and Esther said I could probably find you here. I need to talk."

The judge motioned to a private corner of the lobby, away from the reception desk and the elevators. Vic glanced about, feeling conspicuous in the knowledge that he was now a wanted man in Culpeper, Virginia.

"So, what's up, Vic? You look a little anxious." The judge smoothed his silvery hair as he sunk into an easy chair across from Vic.

"I'm in some trouble," Vic began. "Bodie has a warrant out for my arrest in Culpeper." He wrung his hands as he continued, "I captured one of the gang that has been harassing us—found his surveillance van and followed him to the old Shamrock Motel. I tied him up and threatened him so he'd tell me who his leader is. The kid was so scared, he spilled the beans right away. I didn't lay a hand on him, but Kim says the sheriff came by the house looking to take me in on charges of assault and battery. Fred, I didn't touch the kid, I swear."

"I believe you, Vic, don't worry." He patted his friend reassuringly on the shoulder. "So, what do you think happened?"

"Kim and I figure the sheriff beat the kid and put the blame on me."

"That wouldn't surprise me, after the stories I've heard," the judge nodded.

"Anyway, Fred, I tracked down one of the leaders of the group, a Jake Crapper, and trashed his business last night." He noticed his friend's furrowed brow and felt the disapproval immediately. "I know I shouldn't have, but I wanted to give him a wake-up call, a little warning to back off, hoping maybe that would be the end of it since we had one of his goons in jail."

Speaking from a deep wisdom garnered by years on the bench, the judge replied, "Experience tells me this kind doesn't give up that easily. You may have stirred up a hornet's nest, Vic, not to mention breaking the law."

Vic was defiant. "Well, maybe so, but they deserved it after what they've done to Sally and me. It felt good to fight back."

"Vic," he reached out and grabbed Vic's shoulders in his big, black hands, and stared his friend in the eyes. "I can understand the desire to get revenge, but remember Nam." He gently squeezed the muscular shoulders. "You've got to keep your head at all times. Don't let your emotions run away with you. You might get yourself killed."

"You're right," Vic sounded apologetic. "I'll be careful from now on." He paused, glancing around again, then carried on. "I want you to do me a favor, Fred."

"Anything. Just ask. You know that." The judge was sincere.

"Would you try to straighten this thing out with Bodie? I don't know who else to turn to, and I can't just turn myself in. I don't know how much control he has in the county." Vic pulled a slip of paper from his pocket and handed it to the judge. "You can reach me at this number over here in D.C. It's a motel on the west side."

The judge nodded and slipped the note in his shirt pocket. "I'll see what I can do." He shook a thick finger in Vic's face. "Now, you be careful, you hear?"

Vic smiled and nodded submissively, then patted his big friend on the back and walked out into the sunshine. He never did ask the judge what he was doing in Washington.

The few minutes spent with the judge lifted Vic's spirits immensely. The man had a way of revitalizing a person, instilling hope and energy where despair and emotional fatigue had prevailed. With a little more spring in his step and less weight on his shoulders, Vic hurried to his car in the underground parking and set his mind to the next order of business on the day's agenda. Remembering the judge's reprimand, he began to carefully plan the next step. He determined to execute the plan with mind over emotion at all times. Safety first, revenge second.

A wave of nostalgia rushed over Vic as he drove, window down, through the neighborhoods of downtown Washington, D.C. He missed the sights and sounds of the city—the corner hot dog vendors, the newspaper stands, the rush of people. It had always been a thrill to work in the shadow of the

Washington Monument, the Capital, and the White House, of course. What an inspiration to be so near the Jefferson and Lincoln Memorials, too. Vic had often relaxed, on his lunch break, beside the reflecting pool and pondered the greatness of a man like Abe Lincoln. As he inched his way along Pennsylvania Avenue, hitting every traffic light red it seemed, he realized one thing he did not miss—the city traffic.

It was three o'clock in the afternoon by the time Vic found the History Department and strolled the hallways searching for the right office. His heart was beating wildly as he finally knocked on the heavy wooden door.

"Come in," a cheery voice answered.

As he stepped into the room, Vic's jaw dropped as he recognized the face of Holly Fenton. Holly, however, was far more shocked to see Vic on her turf.

"What are you doing here, Vic?" she said in a panic.

"Came to pay Dr. Lapain a little visit."

"He can't see us together." Holly was almost out of control.

"Why not? He doesn't know we've met before. Don't worry, I won't give you away," Vic said reassuringly.

"He'll be here any minute." Holly held her head as if to get control of herself and think this through. "OK, just relax," she said. "We'll pretend we've never met before. I have no idea who you are—just some stranger dropping in for a visit. We'll stay cool, not give anything away."

"Holly, relax," Vic spoke soothingly. "It'll be okay. When he gets here just tell him some gentleman is here to see him and dismiss yourself."

"OK." She began to regain her composure.

In seconds, the door swung open and Ambrose Lapain entered with a stack of folders under one arm. Holly practically leaped toward him.

"Dr. Lapain, you have a visitor. This gentleman just arrived. In fact, I have not even made his acquaintance yet, but I'll go now and come back later. I sorted through those folders on the bookcases over there." She motioned to the far wall and Vic could see her hand was shaking noticeably. Fortunately, Lapain appeared to be preoccupied and missed the obvious uneasiness of Holly. She was gone before he paid any attention to her.

Vic stood and faced the professor. He reached out a hand.

"Vic Johns, Dr. Lapain. I've been wanting to meet you for some time now." Lapain froze in his tracks and swallowed hard. Vic thought the tall man was going to pass out. The blood drained from his face, leaving him a sickly pale color. He couldn't speak.

"Surprised to see me, Professor?" Vic was enjoying this.

Finally getting a grip, Lapain nonchalantly asked, "What brings you here, Mr. Johns?"

"Let's cut the crap and get right to the point, shall we, Lapain? I don't seem to have much patience lately." Vic's bitter tone cut into Lapain like a knife. The professor flinched. Fear was clearly etched on his face as he retreated behind the heavy desk.

"I know all about your game, Lapain. In fact, I've got one of Crazy Jake's goons sitting in the jail in Culpeper as we speak. Nice kid, but not too smart."

Composure, Vic thought. Stay calm, he urged himself. He wanted nothing more than to beat this nerdy professor to a pulp. But the judge's words kept coming back to him. If he couldn't avenge the physical and emotional torment, at least not right at this moment, then he at least wanted some answers.

"Why, Professor? Why Jake and his goons? Why all the misery and suffering? How come you didn't just come to me openly and talk about the buried treasure?"

Lapain's throat was dry. He stared at the floor. "I don't know. I guess it was greed. I wanted the discovery all to myself. Fame and fortune, I suppose." He paused, then raised his eyes to look at Vic. "It wasn't supposed to turn out like this."

"Oh, so you didn't really intend to destroy my house, harass my wife and try to kill her in a car wreck?" Vic spit the words out bitterly.

"It got out of hand—"

"Out of hand! Out of hand! I've got a wife lying in a hospital bed in a coma, full of tubes, fighting for her life!" Vic was getting angrier by the moment.

"Jake says he didn't do that. They had no part in it." Lapain shrugged. "Swears they weren't even in Virginia when the accident happened. It was just what it was—an accident. A freaky, tragic accident."

Vic wasn't prepared to hear that. It struck him like a train. He didn't want to believe it. They had to be at fault. The anger and hatred he had piled up inside balked. *He's lying to protect himself,* Vic thought. *It was too much of a coincidence to be some random road accident. Somebody has to pay for this. Sally is teetering at death's door.* Vic fought the tumultuous emotions tearing at his insides. He wanted to grab this spineless excuse for a human being and squeeze the life right out of him. But suddenly an image of the judge popped into his mind. The ghostly specter stared into Vic's soul and shook its finger disapprovingly. The rage subsided.

The professor's phone rang, giving Vic more time to gather himself as the angry fury spun away like a spent tornado rising back into the sky.

"Excuse me," Lapain said, as he reached to take the call. "Hello?" He froze, again turning white as a ghost. "Yeah, it's me," he said quietly. "What do you want, Jake?" Vic's eyes locked on Lapain's. He watched as a new wave of fear crept across the professor's face. No doubt Jake was filling him in on the remodeling job Vic had done. Lapain simply sat and listened. After a long moment, he spoke matter-of-factly. "Why don't you tell him yourself? He's sitting right here in front of me."

Lapain flipped on the speakerphone and Crazy Jake's husky voice boomed forth. "Johns, you there?"

"Yeah, I'm here, Jake. How's business?"

"Very funny, you snake," Jake hissed. "Johns, you're goin' down. You hear that? I'm takin' you down, man. You're gonna wish you were never born, you hear me?"

"I hear you, Jake, and I gotta tell you," his words dripped with sarcasm, "I'm literally shaking in my boots here."

A loud click told them an angry Jake had hung up. Lapain winced.

"I would take his threat seriously, Johns."

"What's he gonna do, Professor? Mess up my life?" Vic laughed.

"I lost control of Jake some time ago," Lapain admitted. "Believe me, the man is capable of anything. I wouldn't be antagonizing him, especially when he's already angry. They don't call him Crazy Jake for nothing."

"Funny," Vic responded with defiance, "I was just thinking that Jake ought to be smart and not mess with ME, while I'm this angry."

"So, what happens now?"

"That all depends on our friend Jake. If he backs off, maybe things will cool down a bit."

Lapain stared hard at Vic. "Believe me, Johns, Jake will never back down."

"Then I guess the war continues."

THIRTEEN

Sheriff Bodie sniffed contemptuously at the thought of that little weasel, the mayor, summoning him for a meeting. Nevertheless, he obediently made his way to the mayor's fancy home in the Brandenburg Estates on the edge of town. Bodie resented the pompous residents of these three-acre properties and fine homes. They think they're so much better than the rest of us, he thought, just because they have money.

He adjusted the toothpick in his mouth as he pulled into the driveway of the mayor's massive two-story Tudor-style estate. He found his host around back, as planned, reclining on a lounge next to the kidney-shaped pool.

"Afternoon, Sam. Nice day isn't it?"

Bodie nodded. "Can't complain. So, what's on your mind, Quint?"

"I've got a few concerns. Thought we should iron them out before it's too late." He gestured to the chair next to him. "Have a seat, Sam. Relax. How about a drink?"

"No, I'm on duty."

"Never stopped you before," Quint teased.

"Well, OK, maybe a light beer."

Smiling, Quint reached into a small cooler next to his chair and tossed a cold can to Bodie.

"So, what are your concerns?" Bodie asked with a trace of irritation.

"I've heard about the kid you've got in jail and the warrant out for Vic Johns. Sounds kind of messy to me. Bound to attract a lot of unwanted attention, I'd say."

Bodie felt the color rise on his neck. He wished the mayor would keep his nose out of this sort of thing. The irritation spilled over.

"Are you questioning my judgment?"

"Well, I—"

"I certainly hope not," Bodie pushed on heatedly, "because it really is none of your business."

"It is if it affects our program." The mayor refused to be steamrollered by Bodie this time.

"Our program? And who do you think is the mastermind of 'our program'?" Bodie lectured. "Me. I'm the brains and the brawn behind it. Look around you, Quint. Nice little spot you have here, isn't it? Never forget where a lot of the money came from."

Bodie could see that his words had struck a nerve, but Quint wasn't giving in that easy. "Johns had nothing to do with that kid getting beaten up, did he?"

"It doesn't concern you, Quint."

"That's what I thought," the mayor nodded knowingly. He stood and walked toward the pool.

"I saw an opportunity to bring Johns down, and I took it." Bodie explained defensively. "Don't worry about it."

The mayor stared out across the sparkling water and the lush gardens. "When you bring him in, how are you going to make the charges stick in the courtroom? It's a risky proposition."

"There's no risk. I've got the kid's testimony all sewn up. And the hospital treated him, so I've got their testimony, too. Johns doesn't have a leg to stand on. It's his word against the kid's, and the medical report gives the edge to the kid. I'd say it's an open-and-shut case."

Quint spun around to face Bodie. He was visibly uneasy now, but waded in a little deeper. "I don't like the brutality and deception, Sam. It's bound to come back to haunt us."

"Now, don't you go gettin' soft on me now, Quint." He stood up and moved closer to the mayor. "We're too far into this to turn back now. We've got to keep a united front, understand?"

Quint nodded unconvincingly and began to pace. "What about Judge Hamilton? I've heard rumors that he's been nosing around some of the business establishments in town. Is that right?"

"Yeah, that's right, but I'm keepin' an eye on the judge. Don't you worry about him, Quint. Just do your job. Leave the details to me."

Bodie didn't like the troubled look on the mayor's face. Quint was a weak man. It meant Bodie could push him around, but it also made him a risk to the whole enterprise. He could cave in under the pressure. The sheriff made a hasty mental note to try to go easy on Quint from now on. The man was obviously having second thoughts about their coercive methods. The stress was beginning to show. He might be on the verge of cracking. A little positive reinforcement was in order.

"Now, don't go worryin' about any of this stuff, Quint. I've got everything under control." Bodie smiled warmly. "Maybe you should think about taking some time off and getting away with the wife for some R&R in the mountains. I can handle things here for awhile."

Judging by the faint smile, the mayor embraced that idea. He nodded. "I might just do that, Sam. A week in the Shenandoahs sounds mighty good right about now."

"Go for it." Bodie slapped the smaller man on the shoulder and turned to leave.

Neither sheriff nor mayor noticed the gray Olds parked on the street in front of the neighbor's home. The sheriff drove off, oblivious to the shadowy figure lurking behind the rhododendrons.

Kim stuck to her daily routine of maintaining the vigil at her Mom's bedside until evening visiting hours ended. Normally, she felt at ease in the hospital setting. It was her workplace, a familiar environment of monitors, stethoscopes and life-saving, high-tech equipment, a setting in which she excelled as a competent, and confident, professional caregiver. But now she found herself on the other side of the hospital drama — on the outside looking in. Cast in the cursed role of the trauma victim's next of kin. Consigned to the vigil of hope, watching, waiting, hoping and praying, but otherwise helpless to effect any change in the victim's status. Her extensive medical expertise only heightened the pain of anxiety by denying any false hope. Sometimes ignorance is bliss, Kim thought, as she kissed her mother's hand and left the room.

In the hallway, the utter loneliness of the experience swept over her as she pushed the elevator button. I wish Dad was here to share the burden, she thought as the doors opened and she stepped into the empty elevator. A big hug would feel so good right now. She bit her lip to fight back the tears as she passed through the automatic doors and out into the cool night air.

The parking lot was well lit but, out of habit, Kim glanced up and down each row she passed on the way to her own car. As she backed out of the parking spot, an old van appeared out of nowhere and plowed into the rear of her car. Instantly, the driver sprang from the van, cursing and swearing. When Kim emerged from her vehicle, he directed the verbal assault at her.

"What's the matter with you, lady? Are you crazy, backin' up without lookin'? I've got the right of way here, you know."

"I—I guess I didn't see you." Kim was flustered and a little afraid of the big man carrying on such a tirade, and he wasn't finished yet.

"Who taught you to drive, girl? Didn't they ever tell you about yielding to oncoming traffic?" He walked around to the front of his vehicle. "Now, look at my van. I just got the front end repaired last week and now look at it. All because of some dim-wit broad who doesn't know how to drive."

Kim couldn't understand what he was so upset about. Her car had fared much worse in the collision. The rear corner was a crumpled mess. The van, on the other hand, had a slight crease in the fender and a broken headlight.

"First of all, I'm not a dim-wit broad, mister." She had to set the record straight on that first. "I'm really sorry. I didn't do it on purpose, believe me. I honestly didn't see you behind me." She was willing to concede her own blame.

"Witnesses." The big man scoured the lot for anyone who might have seen the accident. "Just my luck, not a single witness in this whole parking lot. Just my buddy, Zeke." He nodded in the direction of the van where a handsome young man was peering at them from the front passenger seat.

"Zeke, get out here, will ya'?" He summoned his friend from the van.

The younger man got out and began to inspect the damage. "Sure did a number on the car," he whistled. Then he moved in for a closer look at the van.

"My, oh, my," he whistled again. "Look at this." He pointed behind the bumper.

The big man leaned over to take a closer look, too. "Oh, no," he moaned. "Look at this, lady," he motioned for her to come and look, too.

Obediently, Kim stepped forward and leaned toward the bumper to inspect the damage. "I don't see—"

A meaty hand clamped a vise grip over her mouth, and a powerful arm grabbed her around the waist, lifting her right off the ground. The younger man quickly flung the van's sliding door open, and the big man hauled his catch inside. With a resounding clunk, the door was closed again. The young man jumped into the driver's seat and sped from the parking lot. With his bulk, Kim's captor had her pinned to the floor. She gasped to catch her breath and struggled to break loose, but it was hopeless. The hands were far too powerful. Her shoulder ached from the rough collision with the floor of the van. She was frightened but surprisingly calm.

"Anybody follow us?" the big man on top of Kim asked.

"No," was the reply from the driver's seat.

"OK, missy, here's the deal." Her captor loosened his grip slightly. "If you behave yourself and do as I say, nobody's gonna hurt you, understand?"

Kim nodded. He took his hand from her mouth.

"Who are you? What do you want with me?" Kim demanded.

"I'm Jake, and that boy drivin' up there is my employee, Zeke." Jake grinned and whispered, "He thinks he's God's gift to women, but don't go gettin' any ideas about him."

"Don't worry," Kim replied with disgust.

"Not your type, huh?" Jake laughed heartily.

"Let me up, you big ox," Kim commanded and Jake complied.

"What do you want with me, anyway?" There was fire in her words.

"Well, let's just say you're our bargaining chip."

"Bargaining chip?" Kim glared at the big man. "Listen, mister, I'm nobody's bargaining chip, you understand? Whatever this sick game of yours is, deal me out."

"I can't do that, miss. We're goin' fishin' and you're the bait. Kinda figure your daddy will pay handsomely to get his daughter back in one piece, especially since his wife is already, shall we say, vegetating?" His callous laugh echoed off the van walls.

"You pig," Kim sneered. She reared back to slug Jake, but he caught her fist in midair.

"Feisty one, eh? I like that."

"So, you're the piece of dirt that tried to kill my mother."

Suddenly, Jake's smile faded to a sinister sneer. "You'd better watch your tongue, girlie, or you might get hurt." The words were cold, malicious. End of conversation. He proceeded to tie her hands behind her back and blindfold and gag her with a couple of tattered old rags. Leaving her on the floor of the van, he moved to the front seat next to Zeke. They traveled in silence for a long time.

So, these were the losers responsible for all the damage and harassment over the past months. Scarcely seemed like hardened criminals. Were they capable of murder? Kim's heart grew cold as she remembered that they were responsible for running her mom off the road in an obvious attempt to kill her. They would pay for that. She was determined to survive to see to it.

She struggled with the ropes for awhile, but it was futile. They only chafed her wrists all the more. She decided to save her strength since it seemed she was safe for now at least. They wouldn't harm her as long as they had some use for her. Trade bait, huh? Me for Dad's land? He'd never go for it. But she would never tell them that. Kim settled back and relaxed. She whispered prayers for Mom and Dad and herself, and eventually the motion of the van brought sleep.

The jolting of the van on a rough road startled Kim awake. For a moment, disoriented, she didn't know where she was, but the ropes and blindfold were ample reminder of the living nightmare she had awakened to. In the chill of the van, she shuddered. Or was it fear that made her shake so uncontrollably? She stretched her limbs. Not the most comfortable sleep she'd ever had.

Before long, the van came to a halt and big Jake was hauling Kim out of the van. He removed the blindfold and gag. Silhouetted against the night sky, Kim could see the outline of tall trees.

"This here's your new home for awhile, missy," he said, pointing to a small wooden cabin. He practically dragged her toward the front door. Kim glanced about. In the darkness she could see very little, but they were in the mountains somewhere. The temperature was quite cold. She noted traces of snow on the ground. Not another dwelling was in sight—they had brought their bargaining chip to some remote location for safe keeping.

Jake headed inside with Kim in tow. The cabin was primitive but comfortable—wood floors, stone fireplace, an open kitchen area off to one side with table and chairs, and some other sparse furniture scattered around the living room. Two doors off the main room led to other rooms. A blazing fire in the hearth made it quite cozy.

Jake plunked Kim, hands still bound, on a chair at the table and banged on the adjoining doors. "Charlie. Willie. Rise and shine," he shouted. In seconds, two sleepy-eyed young men emerged from the rooms.

"Charlie, Willie, meet our guest, Kim Johns. Kim, this is Charlie and Willie, two more of my boys. They're gonna keep you company here for awhile. I know you're gonna be great friends in no time."

Charlie rubbed his eyes to be sure he wasn't still dreaming. "Hi, Miss Kim," he said, offering a nervous partial wave.

Willie nodded sullenly, saying nothing. He obviously had an attitude.

Zeke burst through the door, arms loaded with supplies from the van. "Gimme a hand, boys," he said. They sprang into action, relieving Zeke of most of the goods and helping him stow it in the kitchen. Jake retreated to the van.

"So, what do you think of our guest, boys?" Zeke half-whispered.

"She's real purty," Charlie offered.

"A fox," added Willie.

"She's mine," Zeke declared quietly, "I saw her first. Besides, she's a cultured lady. You two ain't got no experience with such fine women."

"Gotta start somewhere," Willie interjected. He pulled a nickel from his pocket. "I'll flip ya for her."

Zeke pushed him playfully. "Get lost, Willie, she's mine."

"Forget it, buddy." Kim had overhead the entire conversation. "None of you has a prayer with me—least of all you, Romeo." She laughed at Zeke.

The rebuff stung Zeke's pride. "Is that so?" He grabbed Kim's hair, forcing her head back, then traced her cheek with his other hand, slowly running the hand down her neck toward the V where her blouse was buttoned. Kim struggled and tried to kick Zeke, but to no avail. As his hand moved inside the blouse, Zeke suddenly jerked backward and was thrown across the room by Jake's massive arms.

"Keep your greasy paws off her, Zeke," Jake snarled. "Can't have you spoilin' the merchandise—not yet."

Zeke picked himself up from the floor and brushed off the dust, glaring at Kim the whole time. She shot back a smug smile. That should keep the lustful Don Juan at bay for awhile.

"Listen up, boys." Jake prepared to lay the ground rules. "We're gonna do this in eight-hour shifts. You stay inside and keep the girl tied at all times. You'll be relieved when your eight hours are up. You'll have a cell phone, and we'll use the van as the only transportation in and out. Got it?" They all nodded. Jake looked right at Zeke. "And no fraternizing."

To Kim, he said, "Don't bother tryin' to get away, missy. We're a long way from civilization, and there's a lot of bush out there. Not a nice place to be all alone. Like I said, do what I say and you won't be hurt."

He gathered up his things and lumbered to the door. "Willie, you take the first shift. Zeke and Charlie, get your stuff and come with me. I'm sure this won't take long. Vic Johns will be anxious to get his daughter back unharmed."

The judge strolled into the courthouse with all the confidence of a veteran of the law. Towering over the desk of dispatcher Chester Muldoon, his deep voice boomed. "I'm here to see a prisoner — Whitey Thompson."

A startled Chester flinched. "I'll have to check with the sheriff," he said and scurried away to one of the inner offices. He reappeared in seconds, it seemed, and ushered the judge to the sheriff's private office.

"Judge Hamilton, come right in." Sheriff Bodie was effusive. "Have a seat," he gushed as if the two were old friends. "It seems my deputy is a little confused. He said you wanted to see a prisoner of mine, a Whitey Thompson. Obviously, he misunderstood — "

"On the contrary, Sheriff, that's exactly who I came to see." The judge smiled.

"But, what business do you have with that kid, Judge?"

"I'm afraid that is none of your business, Sheriff Bodie."

"Well, I'm making it my business," Bodie declared bluntly. "If you want to see the kid you have to have my permission." The gauntlet was set.

No stranger to power struggles, the judge waded right in. He had gone toe-to-toe with far more formidable foes than this small-town cop.

"Does the lad have legal counsel, Sheriff?"

"No."

"What are you holding him for?" the judge probed.

"For questioning and suspicion of property damage, public nuisance and attempted murder."

"Have you questioned him?" the Judge kept pressing.

Bodie was getting impatient. "Of course, I've questioned him."

"Without providing the boy with legal counsel?"

The sheriff began to squirm in his seat. "He declined the right to have counsel present."

Judge Hamilton suspected that was a lie. The kid was probably never advised of his rights before being subjected to interrogation.

"What evidence do you have?"

"We've got a van decked out with some pretty sophisticated surveillance equipment and evidence linking him to the scene of significant property damage." Bodie took pleasure in delivering the next piece of information. "And we have his own testimony that Vic Johns brutally beat him at the Shamrock Motel just prior to our arrival to arrest him."

"So I've heard." The judge nodded with grave concern. "I understand you have a warrant out for Vic Johns' arrest?"

"That's right," Bodie replied. "If you have any contact with Johns, I suggest you advise him to turn himself in. Maybe the courts will go easy on him—first offense and all."

"I'll keep that in mind." He rose to his feet as if to leave. "Now, what about seeing that prisoner, Sheriff? I'm not leaving until I have a chance to talk to him. I'm gravely concerned that his rights may have been violated. You wouldn't want such allegations made public, now would you, Sheriff?" The judge grinned broadly.

"Don't try to threaten me," growled Bodie.

"Oh, believe me, Sheriff, it's not a threat. It's a promise. Either I get in to see the prisoner right now or I go public with the infringement of a young man's rights. Is that the kind of publicity you want, Sheriff?"

Bodie was furious. He hated to lose power struggles but had no choice but to back down on this one. Pressing the intercom button on his phone, he barked, "Chester, send Tom in here."

Within minutes, the judge was sitting in the interrogation room, looking across a table at a badly bruised Whitey Thompson. The poor kid was a mess—his face black and blue, left eye practically swollen shut. He winced at the abdominal pain incurred by merely sitting on a chair. This was not the work of Vic Johns—even an angry Vic Johns. The judge was indignant at the brutality inflicted on this young man. And the sheriff was trying to foist the blame on his friend, Vic. The judge seethed with anger.

"Whitey, I'm Judge Hamilton. I'm here to help, if I can."

The young man was silent, staring.

"Are you OK, son?" the judge asked with genuine concern.

Whitey shrugged.

"I know you've been through a terrible ordeal. I'm on your side, Whitey. What was done to you was wrong, and I want to right that wrong so no one else has to suffer like you're suffering. Do you understand?"

A faint nod and another shrug.

"Can I tape our conversation, Whitey?" The judge pulled a mini-recorder from his pocket but noticed the instant panic on Whitey's face. "I promise that nothing you say to me will get back to the sheriff, but I need the truth, Whitey. Can I record our talk?"

Whitey still wasn't sure. The judge looked straight into the battered face. "You can trust me, son," he said with deep assurance.

A tear welled in the corner of Whitey's good eye and rolled down his blackened cheek. He was a frightened, broken young man. He nodded.

The judge expelled a sigh of relief and started the recorder.

"Now, Whitey, I need the truth. Did Vic Johns do this to you?"

There was a long pause. The boy was still apprehensive about telling the truth.

"Whitey, did Vic Johns give you this brutal beating?" the judge repeated.

Another pause. "No," he finally answered.

"Then who did?"

Getting out that first word seemed to kindle Whitey's courage. He nervously glanced about as if afraid the sheriff was eavesdropping and would burst into the room any second to inflict another beating.

"The sheriff and another cop. They came to the motel after Vic Johns tied me up and left. He didn't do anything to me—just scared me some. He phoned the sheriff from the room and told him to come and get me. When they got there," Whitey cringed at the memory, "they started punching and kicking me and told me I had to say Vic Johns did it to me or else."

"Did the sheriff or any of his deputies read you your rights or advise you that you could have an attorney?"

"No."

"Did they question you?"

"Yes."

"Did they advise you that you had the right to have your attorney present at that interrogation?"

"No."

"Thanks, Whitey. That's all the questions for now." The judge stopped the recorder. "I realize you've done some things that were wrong, Whitey, but what you did today was right, very right, and it took a lot of courage to tell the truth. Now listen, son, you should have a lawyer to look out for you. Do you want me to find one for you?"

"Yes, sir." Whitey answered. "I'm scared in here, mister. I'm afraid of what that sheriff might do to me."

"Don't worry." The judge patted the young man on the shoulder. "I'll see to it that he doesn't touch you again, son."

The corridor on the way out passed the sheriff's office and, since the door was open, the judge stepped into the room. A conversation between the sheriff and a deputy halted abruptly. The awkward silence told the judge that they had been talking about him, but he didn't care. He pointed a finger at the sheriff and said, "Don't lay a finger on that kid again, or I will personally bring you down, Bodie." Message delivered, he marched out the door to find some fresh air.

Bodie looked at Nate Peters. "It's time we put the honorable Judge Hamilton in his place." The deputy nodded.

At a window seat in the coffee shop across the street from the courthouse, a stranger, mug in one hand and newspaper in the other, furtively observed the judge leaving the courthouse but did not move. He sipped coffee patiently until Sam Bodie emerged and drove off in the sheriff's squad car. Tossing a rumpled bill and a few coins on the table, the stranger hastily departed, newspaper under one arm. He sped off in a gray Olds.

FOURTEEN

Deputy **Chester Muldoon's chilling words** kept playing over and over in Vic's mind like a broken record. "Mr. Johns, we found your daughter's car abandoned in the hospital parking lot last night. The door was open, and her purse was on the front seat — that's how we got your cell number. Looks like she left in a hurry and probably not by her choice."

"Did you try calling my house?"

"Numerous times, but no answer. She was last seen leaving the hospital just after visiting hours ended at eight o'clock. It looks pretty suspicious, sir."

"Crapper," Vic muttered.

"What's that, sir?"

"Oh, nothing. Thanks for the call, Deputy."

"You're welcome. Just a word of advice, sir — I wouldn't come back to Culpeper right now if I were you. The sheriff's got a warrant for your arrest."

"Yeah, so I hear, Deputy. Thanks for the call — and the advice."

It had to be Crapper. Vic shuddered as he thought about Kim. Was she OK? What if someone else abducted her? No, he didn't even want to ponder that scenario. It had to be Crapper and his thugs, trying to even up the score for Whitey — probably want to trade Kim for Whitey.

This thing was far from over now. Crapper had really upped the ante this time. There's no way I'm folding, thought Vic, I'm in this to the bitter end. From here on, it would be all-out war, a high-stakes chess match. Vic's queen was in jeopardy — advantage Crazy Jake.

Vic stormed into the outer office of the salvage company.

"Where is he?" he shouted at Lil'.

"Where is who, sweetie?" Lil' replied, blowing smoke in Vic's general direction.

No time for games. Vic checked Jake's office in the corner first, then headed back to the work bays.

"Hey, you can't go in there," Lil' protested to no avail. Vic was already pushing his way through the 'Employees Only' doorway.

"Crapper, where are you?"

The big man appeared, as if on cue, in the doorway to the mechanics' kitchen. Vic felt like David facing Goliath.

"Johns. I thought you might show up here today." Vic wanted to wipe the sarcastic grin off Jake's face but resisted the urge.

"You kidnapped my daughter, didn't you, Crapper?"

"Kidnap? That's a pretty harsh word, Johns. I prefer to say we borrowed her for business purposes."

"Get to the point, you maniac. What do you want?"

"Oh, we're not too civil today, are we, Mr. Johns? What's the matter, fire gettin' a little too hot?"

"Listen, you—"

"No, you listen, Johns. I'm holding the cards in this little game, so I'll do the talking and you'll do the listening." Jake stepped over to a workbench and picked up a large wrench. He held it up, admiring it, as he talked. "Here's the deal, Johns, so listen up good. Your daughter is safe—for now. If you go to the cops, if you even look at a cop, she's history, got it?" Vic nodded outwardly but chafed inwardly at receiving orders from this thug.

"Now," Jake continued, "the deal is straightforward—one daughter in exchange for one deed. That's it. Plain and simple. The title to your land signed over to me, and you get your precious daughter back in one piece."

"What about your boy, Whitey?" Vic figured it was worth a shot. "How about a trade—Kim for Whitey?"

"Whitey? Who's Whitey?" Jake sneered. "No, you're not listening, Johns. The deal—the only deal—is one daughter for one deed. That's it, take it or leave it."

Vic needed time to think this through. "I'll need some time to get the papers drawn up," he stammered.

"You've got seventy-two hours. You call Lil' in the office here when they're ready and bring the papers here."

"When do I get Kim back?"

"After the papers are signed, I'll have her brought here and turned over to you."

"How do I know I can trust you? Maybe she's dead already. I need proof that she's alive or there's no deal." Vic knew he had no real bargaining power—Jake did hold all the cards for now — but he had to press this point, he had to know that Kim was OK.

"Well, since you're being so cooperative, I think we can handle that one little request." He pulled a cell phone from his pocket and dialed a number. "Zeke, it's Jake. How's the girl . . . Good, glad to hear it. Listen, put her on, will ya? I've got her daddy here, and he's worried about her." Jake handed the phone over to Vic.

"Kim? Is that you? Are you OK . . . Listen, Kim, I'll take care of this. You're going to be all right. Hang in there, OK? I love you."

Jake snatched the phone away. "That's all, missy, daddy's gotta go now. He's got some paperwork to take care of." Jake hung up, grinning.

"Where is she, Jake?"

"Oh, I'll never tell," Jake answered playfully. "Let's just say she's in a nice, safe place."

Vic wanted a piece of Goliath. He wanted to pounce on this madman and beat the hell out of him, but the man was wielding a six-pound wrench and weighed in at probably a hundred pounds more than Vic. Besides, Kim was the important one now. Her life was on the line. He had to keep his wits about him and think this through.

"See ya later, Johns." The meeting was over. Class dismissed.

Vic departed with Crazy Jake's mad laughter ringing in his ears. He worried for Kim. If they harm her in any way, Vic vowed, I'll kill them.

❧

Under any other circumstances, the cabin would be the consummate, rustic getaway—a fine place to unwind, do some hiking and fishing, and enjoy the great outdoors. But, as Kim quickly discovered, it was not a good place to be cooped up—hands constantly tied, guarded by a crew of mindless adolescents.

Not that they were treating her badly. The food was palatable, the cabin warm. It was the uncertainty of her welfare and the boredom of sitting around doing nothing that frayed Kim's nerves. She also wondered about her mom, even felt guilty about not being at the hospital. What if she dies while I'm held hostage?

Kim shook her head, knowing she had to get her mind off the things she couldn't change and focus on the challenge before her—captivity. She turned her attention to the pony-tailed teenage guard sprawled on the couch across the room. A mini CD player pumped raucous heavy metal tunes through the headphones lodged on Willie's head. Boredom was not a problem for him at the moment.

"So, Willie, what's your story?" Kim had to yell to be heard.

Unhappy with the interruption, he jerked the headphones off. "Whaddya say?"

"How did you get mixed up with Jake?"

"I needed a job. Jake was lookin' for another worker."

"So, how did you two get linked up?"

"I was livin' on the street, panhandlin' and stealin' mostly, just to get by. Sleepin' in cardboard boxes in alleys with a bunch of drunks. I hated it, but I had no choice. There was nowhere else to go."

"It must have been awful for you."

"You have no idea, lady. It's a jungle out there — survival of the fittest."

"What got you out on the street? Did you run away from home?"

"Yeah. When I was thirteen. Had enough of the beatings from my step-father. He was a mean son-of-a-bitch. Came home drunk two or three nights a week and beat up one of us — usually me, but I didn't mind so long as he didn't hurt my momma."

"So you finally left?"

"Yeah, one night he come home drunk as a skunk and took to beatin' on me with a baseball bat. He woulda killed me if I hadn't gotten away. I never looked back, just kept runnin' ever since."

"Have you been on the street all that time since then?"

"Mostly. I shacked up for awhile with a few guys in a run-down, old hotel room but didn't get along too good with them. Figured I was better off on my own. Then one day I was eatin' in the Big Mac Lounge — after a good day of panhandlin' — and got lookin' at a newspaper somebody left layin' on the next table. I saw this ad for a mechanic's helper — will train, no experience necessary, it said. I figured this was a chance for me to get off the street."

"And now you're linked with Jake as part of a criminal gang — harassment, kidnapping, attempted murder. They put people in jail for that kind of stuff, Willie."

The words stung. Willie was visibly agitated. "You don't know nothin'. Jake's been good to all of us — gave us jobs when we needed them. He treats us all right. And now we got us a chance to make it big."

"But at what cost?" Kim fired back. She knew she had gotten under his skin. Beneath the sullen exterior was a lot of pain and anger but also a good side, a sensitive young man with a moral sense of right and wrong. Kim had touched that nerve.

"Lady, you don't know what it's like. A guy like me gets maybe one chance like this in a lifetime."

"Willie, there are other ways to get ahead, without the risk of spending years in jail. What would your mother think if she saw you involved in criminal behavior like this?"

That jab hurt. Willie's anger exploded. "Why don't you just shut up?" he shouted as he stomped outside and slammed the door behind him.

It was collection day. Nate Peters was doing the honors today. As he made his rounds, the first three places of business — Wong's Chinese Restaurant, Ralston's Hardware and Coltrane's Furniture Repair — were closed. Strange at this time of day, Nate thought, but he continued on to Long's Fabric Shop.

The protocol was in place. Wait until all the customers leave, turn the lock on the door and pick up the envelope from the owner. Everyone knew the procedure. It was quick and easy and rarely attracted any unusual attention. Patricia Long always played along without a whimper of complaint. She was waiting behind the counter when Nate entered.

"Morning, Patricia." Nate smiled.

"Deputy," she replied with a nod.

"You have an envelope for me?" Nate inquired.

Patricia shook her head. "Actually, no I don't. Not today, Nate."

"What do you mean?" said Nate with genuine surprise. "This is not good, Patricia. Missing payments has proven to be a health risk, you know that."

"I'll take my chances, Deputy, and so will a few of my friends." She waved her hand in the general direction of the back of the store where a dozen other merchants were suddenly streaming from the back room. Nate knew them all — the Wongs, Findlay Ralston, Hank Coltrane . . . It was a mutiny.

"You people don't know what you're doing. You're gonna be in a lot of trouble over this," Nate threatened. "I suggest you all just turn around and head on back to your own stores and mind your own business."

"This is our business," replied Findlay Ralston. "At least, we intend to make it our business from now on. So, we suggest that you walk right out that door and don't bother coming back again."

Outnumbered and pride stung, Nate Peters made an abrupt turn and headed for the door. "There'll be hell to pay for this," he mumbled as he left.

The merchants looked at one another, smiling with pride. "We did it," they cheered, amid much back-slapping and hand-shaking. Findlay Ralston winked at Patricia.

"Culpeper Regional Hospital. How may I direct your call?" chimed the cheerful receptionist.

"I'm calling for an update on the condition of my wife — Sally Johns," Vic replied.

"What floor is she on, sir?"

"Third. Intensive Care."

"One moment, sir, I'll connect you with the floor nurse."

Moments later a familiar voice came to Vic. "ICU. Nurse Calloway speaking."

"Nurse Calloway, this is Vic Johns. I don't know whether you remember me or not, but my wife is Sally Johns — the auto accident victim . . ."

"Yes, I remember, Mr. Johns."

"So, how is Sally, Nurse?"

"Still comatose but stable. Her injuries are beginning to heal nicely. We're just not sure yet about the possibility of long-term brain damage."

"Is she going to make it?" Vic inquired.

"I would say she has a good chance, but again, it's too early to predict what quality of life she may experience."

Vic sighed deeply. "Thanks for the update, Miss Calloway. And thanks for the care you're giving Sally. I'll call again."

"Anytime, Mr. Johns. Of course, why not come in and see her yourself? Personal contact — a familiar voice — can be very important to the recovery of coma victims."

"I understand. I've got some other things to do right now, but I'll certainly try to drop in. Goodbye, miss."

Ralston's Hardware had been a fixture in Culpeper since long before the town's oldest residents could remember. The plain storefront with its tall glass windows and double doors had changed little over the years that it occupied its prominent space on Main Street. The oiled wooden floors showed the wear of decades of daily traffic, but the cluttered shelves and narrow aisles had changed little. Sales were still rung up on the old cash register with the push keys and black-on-white numbers that popped up at the top of the machine to indicate the sales totals.

It was nearly closing time when Deputy Nate Peters entered the shop. At the sound of the bell, Findlay Ralston, who was packaging some birdseed for Mrs. Lewis, peered over his spectacles from behind the counter. He shuddered slightly at the sight of the Deputy.

"Afternoon, Deputy," he said, trying not to appear nervous.

Peters nodded and proceeded to browse the merchandise.

"There you go, Mrs. Lewis," the storeowner said, as he handed over the neatly folded sack of birdseed. The little old lady smiled and headed for the door. Nate Peters politely nodded and tipped his hat as she passed by on her way out to the street. The deputy locked the door behind Mrs. Lewis, flipped the open sign to the closed side and pulled the shade down over the door. "Time to close up, Ralston," he said scowling.

"Now wait a minute, Nate," protested Findlay.

"I'll do the talking, Ralston." The sternness of the voice silenced any further protests. "We have a little matter to settle — this week's payment."

Findlay swallowed hard. He wanted to sound tough but was sure his voice came out at least an octave higher than usual. "Not really, Deputy. You see, I don't intend to pay — ever."

That brought a smug grin to Nate Peters' face. "You don't know what you're saying. You will pay—one way or the other."

"No, I won't. I'm not giving you another red cent. So you can just leave now."

Peters glared at the smaller man. "I'm not going anywhere and neither are you, Ralston. Not 'til this little misunderstanding is cleared up. Now, I've had enough of your tough-guy act. We both know the smartest thing to do is just hand over the money. Do it the easy way and save yourself a lot of pain, pops."

Determined not to cave in to the pressure, Ralston shook his head. But he winced as Nate Peters flew into a rage and swept the entire contents of one shelf onto the floor. Nate kicked a toaster lying in his path. He grabbed a broom and and with one swing sent a neatly stacked display of tools showering to the floor. Light bulbs and plumbing supplies were next. Findlay Ralston stood helpless as his store was turned upside down.

"Nate, please . . ." The words fell on deaf ears. The deputy was bent on destruction. Finally, in desperation, Findlay stepped forward to restrain Nate by grabbing his arm, but the bigger man simply flung him to the floor like a rag doll. The storekeeper crumpled in a lifeless heap as a trail of blood trickled from behind his head. Seeing the blood, Nate Peters hastily cleaned out the cash register and beat it out the back door into the alley.

The changing of the guard took place in the afternoon. Charlie would be Kim's new challenge for the next eight hours. Having succeeded only in alienating Willie, she was determined not to blow it with her new sentry. He looked amiable enough. Reminded her of a kid who never grew up. The spiky red hair, chubby cheeks and freckles, made him look like a typical ten-year-old at summer camp.

"So, Charlie, what do you like to do?"

A shy smile broke on his face immediately. "Lots of things," he said.

"Like what?" Kim persisted.

"Like drinking beer with Willie and Zeke when Jake's not around." He laughed profusely.

"What else?"

"I like takin' things apart and fixin' 'em."

"What kinds of things?" Kim kept the conversation going.

"Well, cars and TVs and machines and stuff. Mostly we fix cars at work, though."

"What do you do for fun, Charlie?" Kim asked.

"For fun?" He laughed at nothing in particular. "Special assignments are fun. I like making fires and chopping down trees." He grinned foolishly.

"You made a fire, Charlie? Where?" Kim probed gently.

"At a place."

"What place, Charlie? Do you remember?"

"It was out in the country someplace. A mailbox, yeah, a big mailbox that looked like a house. Jake let me burn it."

"What about the tree? Did Jake let you chop down the tree, too?"

"Yeah," Charlie said. "It was a big tree, and it made a really loud noise when it fell down. I was scared, but I laughed. Jake said we did really good."

"How do you think the owner of the mailbox and the tree felt when he found them ruined?" Kim asked.

Charlie stared blankly at her. He had obviously never thought about the victims. "I dunno," he stammered. "Am I in trouble now?" he asked sheepishly as he stared at the floor.

"Yes, I think you're in some trouble, Charlie. You and Jake, Zeke and Willie are doing some bad things, but I think Jake is probably in the most trouble because he told you guys what to do. You know, Charlie, you could make things better by letting me go."

Fear swept across the simple man's face. "Oh, no," he protested, "I could never do that. Jake said if I let you get away we'd all end up in jail. He said the tough guys in jail would gouge my eyes out and cut my fingers off. I don't wanna go to jail. Don't make me go to jail." Charlie was sobbing.

The emotional outburst caught Kim by surprise. "Okay. Okay, Charlie, I won't make you go to jail. Maybe there's another way to get you out of trouble."

The tears dried up immediately. "Really?"

"Yeah," Kim replied, "let me think about it for awhile."

A tiny field mouse suddenly tore across the middle of the floor in front of them, heading for the kitchen area. Charlie reached for the fireplace utensils and came up with the shovel. He swung it in one fluid motion, bringing the brunt of it down on the fleeing mouse's head. It lay there either stunned or half-dead.

"Take it outside, Charlie, I hate mice," shouted Kim.

So Charlie scooped it up in the shovel and carried the twitching creature outside. Kim watched from the window as Charlie laid the mouse on the porch and deliberately decapitated it. Then, laughing loudly, he savagely pounded the mouse's remains into a pancake. Kim shuddered. Simple Charlie was a loose cannon. Unstable, unpredictable, with a lust for destruction. A powder keg waiting to blow. Best not to be lighting matches around this volatile young man.

FIFTEEN

Vic felt a little silly in the get-up, but a glance in the mirror told him the people at the costume and make-up shop had done a superior job of disguising him. He just couldn't be too careful setting foot back in Culpeper. The rental car was a further precaution — he even scraped off the rental company's bumper sticker just to avoid suspicion.

The adrenaline was pumping as Vic carefully backed into a space in the parking lot then headed for the front entrance of the Culpeper Regional Hospital. He felt conspicuous, imagining that everyone in the busy lobby was staring at him. No security guards were in sight. That was promising. The elevators were straight ahead, and Vic wanted to make a mad dash for them and hide behind their brightly polished steel doors but resisted the urge. Instead, he strolled, with shaking knees, toward the up and down buttons.

A crowd was gathering in front of the two elevators as Vic waited. He silently cursed the slow service and avoided direct eye contact. The close proximity to so many people was nerve-wracking. If anyone recognized him, he'd have to make a run for it. The ding of the arriving elevator spooked Vic. He panicked. As the steel doors began to open, he pushed his way through the crowd and fled down an adjoining hall lined with administrative offices. He ducked into a washroom and heaved a sigh of relief. He had to get control of himself. He took a couple of deep breaths. The mirror over the sink gave him a waist-up view, and he hardly recognized himself. The fake beard and eyebrows looked so real. No one could possibly recognize him. A sudden rush of mingled fear and exhilaration came over him. He had not felt the buzz this intently since Vietnam. It would sweep over the platoon on the eve of a combat mission. The men would grow strangely quiet, as the gravity of combat enveloped them. At the same time, a strange eagerness to get on with it would have them pawing the ground like skittish thoroughbreds before a big race.

Vic saw himself in the mirror applying the grease paint to camouflage white skin. The familiar khaki and green fatigues melded his physique into a mound of underbrush and foliage. There was security in hiding behind the paint and camouflage, a kind of invincibility. Vic felt it, as he straightened up and turned for the door.

Avoiding the elevators this time, he took the stairs to the third floor. According to the signs, the ICU was down the hall to the left. Vic turned the corner and faced large double doors with frosted windows. A sign instructed visitors to use the intercom for clearance to enter the ward. Now what? There had to be another way in. One of the big doors suddenly swung open, and two smiling nurses emerged from the unit. Vic instinctively turned away to avoid eye contact, but the nurses hardly noticed him. Their conversation about some medication regimen continued unbroken as they boarded a nearby elevator. Vic strolled the hallway in the opposite direction from the ICU in search of some creative way to slip past the security clearance. Halfway down the hall, he passed an older man wearing a blue lab coat and pushing a cleaning cart equipped with brooms, mops and sundry cleaning supplies. As Vic watched, the custodian guided his cart through a door labeled Housekeeping. After several minutes, the man reappeared minus the cart and blue coat and entered the elevator.

As soon as the elevator doors closed, Vic was on his way into the housekeeping room. The walls were lined with shelves stacked with cleaning supplies. At the far end of the narrow room were several lockers and a single bench. Vic grabbed a blue coat hanging on a hook beside the lockers and pulled it on. A cleaning cart was parked next to the door, and he rolled it ahead of him as he left the room. He shuffled along with his head down as if deep in thought. This would be risky, but he had to see Sally. She was just beyond those big doors, all alone in her struggle to hang on, now that Kim had been taken. Vic braced himself as he pushed through the big doors.

The nurses' station loomed on the left, and the first thing Vic noticed was a tall security guard dressed in the unmistakable dark blue uniform. He was leaning over the counter making conversation with one of the duty nurses. Vic sized up the situation. His brain said, Turn around and get out of here. But his heart said, Keep going, you can slip past the preoccupied staff. He followed his heart. Every step seemed like a city block. As inconspicuously as possible, Vic searched the windowed rooms as he passed, looking for his Sally.

Vic's heart froze when, without warning, a nurse rushed from a room and nearly collided with the cart. She swore under her breath and marched off toward the nurses' station. With a sigh of relief, Vic shuffled on down the hall.

"Hey, you there," shouted the security guard.

Vic turned and saw the guard approaching. His cover was blown. He wheeled the cart around.

"Where's your photo I.D.?" demanded the guard.

Vic drove the cart hard into the unsuspecting guard, throwing him off balance. Mops and bottles of cleaners went flying and so did Vic. He raced from the unit, plunged down the stairway to the lobby and walked briskly to the door. Once outside, he ran for the car and was racing from the parking lot before security could get a read on the license plate.

Ambrose Lapain bore the tell-tale signs of a troubled conscience. An endless string of sleepless nights was taking its toll. Black circles ringed his sleep-starved eyes, and his normally thin frame looked especially gaunt. What should have been a high point in his professional career—an incredible discovery—had turned into his worst nightmare. His own conniving greed had unleashed a runaway train of destruction and violence. The pangs of conscience had become a rasping, squeaky wheel that grated on his nerves incessantly. He felt personally responsible for Jake's actions—even the heinous and brutal—and the consequent heartache heaped on the Johns family. It had tainted the noble pursuit of history, the sheer thrill of the discovery. Somehow, he had to do something about it. For the sake of justice and his own integrity, he had to stop the train he had set in motion.

Kidnapping Kim Johns and threatening her life was the last straw. He now knew beyond a shadow of doubt that Jake was out of control. The man mirrored Lapain's own greed but with a more dangerous at-all-costs bent. The sickening part was the knowledge that Jake cared nothing for the historical significance of the find. Only the lure of lucrative returns kept him in the hunt. Yes, greed was the primary appetite of Jake Crapper, and Lapain knew that motivation, too. Visions of cold cash had also danced in his head since the discovery, but always co-mingled with an intense craving for the fame that discovery could bestow.

But now, something spoke to him from within— something deeper and more momentous than money and fame. A growing dislike for Jake and his tactics was clearly present, but Lapain knew what propelled him now was purer than that. It conjured up a childhood image of his grandmother's glowing pride in him when, as a skinny eight-year-old, he turned in that lost wallet stuffed with hundred dollar bills. He could easily have taken the cash, and no one would ever have known. But he did the right thing, and Grandma's praise had indelibly registered on his young mind the greater good of honesty and integrity. Such lessons are never lost. They simply get submersed in the flurry of daily living. Lapain could see Grandma smiling now as he, the valiant gladiator, strode into the arena.

Another meeting on Jake's turf. Not smart, but what choice was there? It could get ugly, and a local coffee shop was certainly no place to air the dirty laundry. He breezed right past the chain-smoking Lil' in the reception area and found Jake in his run-down office.

"You've gone too far this time," he exclaimed.

"Well, Professor, where have you been? Chasing that pretty young thing that works for you over there at the university?"

"Shut up, Jake. Let's talk."

"Talk? About what? I've got nothin' to say to you."

"I want you to let that Johns girl go."

"What? Give up my collateral? Toss in my bargaining chip?" Jake flipped his pen onto the desktop. "Not in a million years. I'm in the driver's seat, Doc, and I've got no intention of givin' up that leverage. Pay attention, and you might just learn something. You might find out how to get real results."

"She's not a party to this, Jake. Let her go. She's an innocent bystander."

"Boy, you've really gone soft, haven't you?" Jake sneered. "I can see the headlines now: 'College Professor Gets Conscience.'"

"I'm not going to backpedal on this one," Lapain said, coolly.

"You're outta this game, partner." Jake paused to light a cigar. "You don't have a say anymore."

"Don't try to freeze me out," Lapain replied. He was surprised by the steadiness of his own voice.

"Try? This is my gig now, Professor. Though I must admit, I'll be eternally grateful for the invite to join this crap game." An uncontrollable belly laugh shook the big man.

But Lapain wasn't ready to fold his cards quite yet. He still had an ace up his sleeve and the time had come to play it.

"Hold on, Jake. I'm not finished yet." He took a deep breath and plowed ahead. "Either you set that girl free — unharmed — or I blow the lid off this whole plan. It'll be plastered all over the front page of every major newspaper in the country. You won't be able to get near the Johns place."

"Are you threatening me, Professor?" Jake growled.

Lapain stared right back. "It's not a threat; it's a promise. Free the girl or everything goes up in smoke."

The trump card worked. Jake's brow furrowed. The silly grin and mocking sarcasm vanished. He was deadly serious now.

"Don't go too far with this, Lapain. You might find you're in over your head." The words were icy. Lapain could feel Jake's eyes boring into him, but seeing Jake rattled was exhilarating. It gave him a strange sense of inner strength.

"I'll give you forty-eight hours to release the girl, then I start talking to the Washington Post," he declared flatly.

Without another word, Lapain strode out of Jake's office, leaving his shaken rival to brood. He felt a lot taller as he stepped out into the sunshine.

Sheriff Bodie ducked beneath the yellow police tape strung across the doorway of Ralston's Hardware store. A zealous young reporter waved a microphone in his face. Bodie made no attempt to hide his irritation.

"Sheriff, are you treating this as a homicide?"

"Of course we're treatin' it as a homicide. A man doesn't just fall down in his own store, bust his head hard enough to kill himself and leave the cash register open and empty. It's kind of a no-brainer, don't you think?"

"So, you suspect robbery was the motive?" asked the reporter.

"I didn't say that, but it might be." Bodie rubbed his forehead.

The reporter stuck the microphone in the sheriff's face again. "Do you have any suspects yet?" she persisted.

"No," Bodie snapped. He shoved the microphone aside and waded through the crowd to the solitude of his cruiser.

A few minutes later, in the privacy of his office, he vented his frustration on Nate Peters.

"What the hell happened over there, Nate?"

"Sam, it was an accident. The old man got in the way. I didn't mean to do him in. He just fell and hit his head. I panicked when I saw the blood and grabbed the money to make it look like a robbery. What else could I do?"

"You could have been more careful. You could have thought before you acted." He was incensed at Nate's stupidity. Normally, his deputy was more reliable, but now he had them in a real predicament. The merchants in town would surely link Ralston's death to their strong-armed coercion.

"Sam, I said it was an accident. The old guy fell. I didn't mean to hurt him."

"Alright. It's done. He's dead. We can't change that, so let's figure out how we're gonna handle this." His mind was already working on ideas.

"I could go before the inquiry and tell them it was an accident," Nate offered.

"Forget that, Nate," Bodie snapped. "There's no way you can take the fall for this. It'll focus too much attention on our activities here in town. The merchants will be talkin', there'll be questions raised . . . We just can't have it. Besides, how do you explain takin' the money outta the till?"

"Oh yeah. I guess that was kind of stupid, in hindsight," Nate confessed.

"We've still got the robbery motive. Maybe we can do somethin' with that." But nothing was jumping out at him.

"Are you sure no one saw you come outta the store?" Bodie asked.

Nate nodded vigorously. "I'm sure. I went out the back into the alley. There was no one around." He thought for a moment, then something came to him. "There was a lady in the store when I entered. An old lady. What was her name?" He searched his memory banks. "Mrs. Lewis, I think."

"Old Mrs. Lewis? The bird lady? Why, she won't be any problem. She's so senile, she probably doesn't know what day it is," Bodie laughed.

The intercom buzzed, and the voice of dispatcher Chester Muldoon interrupted the discussion.

"Sheriff, I just had a call from hospital security. Seems they had an incident a few minutes ago in the ICU. A man masquerading as a member of the custodial staff. Wasn't wearing hospital I.D. and took off when a security officer accosted him in the hallway. He got away clean—nobody recognized him, no license plate number, but they're wondering if it was that Vic Johns fellow."

A light went on in Bodie's head. Just when things were spinning out of control, behold, a bolt of inspiration.

"Thanks, Muldoon. I'll check it out later," Bodie said. He signed off and turned to face Deputy Peters. "Nate, I think I know who we're gonna pin this murder charge on."

"You mean Vic Johns?" Nate didn't see the point yet.

"It's perfect," Bodie continued, "he's on the run, wanted for assault, probably running out of resources. So he comes back to Culpeper, where we least expect to see him, knocks off Ralston's Hardware Store for some quick cash, then hits the hospital to try to see his wife."

"Sounds plausible to me, Sam."

"Plausible? It's ingenious." Bodie basked in his own brilliance. "Now, let's see what we need to do to make the charges stick."

He pressed the intercom switch. "Muldoon, I want you to put out an APB on Victor Johns. He's wanted for questioning and suspicion of murder in the death of Findlay Ralston. And prepare a press release stating that Sheriff Sam Bodie is launching a murder investigation to find the perpetrator of the brutal slaying of long-time Culpeper resident and businessman Findlay Ralston. Get it to me in writing ASAP."

"Will do, Sheriff."

Bodie and Nate Peters savored the moment.

"To every problem, there is a viable solution," Bodie announced with an air of triumph. He slapped Nate on the shoulder and sent him back to work.

❧

Judge Hamilton waited in the visitors lounge of the hospital. The chairs were plush, but the coffee was old. So were the magazines. The hallmark of institutional waiting rooms — outdated news magazines. Finding nothing current to read, his mind wandered to his friend, Vic Johns. The call had come early this morning while he was sipping his first coffee. Two requests, Vic said. They were simple enough things, but now that he was here to fulfill the first, the judge wasn't so sure. How would Sally look? What should he say or do? Butterflies waged war in his stomach. This was a little out of his league. But Vic wanted to know how she was. He wanted her to have contact with someone she knew. His own ill advised and botched attempt at visiting her had left him no choice, he said. The judge was more than happy to do what he could, or so he thought at the time. Funny how places like hospitals suck the courage out of grown men. He'd sat on the bench for years, meting out justice to hardened criminals, yet here he was, palms sweating and heart thumping, in anticipation of a simple hospital visit.

This wait, while the nurses completed some procedure on Sally, didn't help either. He'd rather get on with it. Just get it over with. Of course, maybe Esther would arrive before he had to go in. He'd left a message for her at her mother's place in Baltimore, asking her to come straight to the hospital on her way back into town this afternoon, if she could get here sometime around three o'clock.

"Mr. Hamilton, she's ready now. Follow me, if you like." The nurse's pleasant voice oozed warmth and compassion. The judge felt safer in her presence. He would have followed that voice into the flames of war. He wished she would stay in the room to choreograph the visit and utter the occasional soothing word to calm his butterflies. But she merely pointed the way and set off on matters more pressing.

The judge entered the brightly colored room with its pale green walls. The machines and tubes grabbed his attention first. Like silent sentries, machines he knew nothing about flanked the bed, tethered by tubes to a reclining human form, a body he barely recognized as Sally. Her eyes were closed, her face discolored by bruising and her head heavily bandaged. He had seen some horrific sights in his time, but this scene shocked him. He managed to speak and touched her fragile hand, but there was no response. He spoke his name and mentioned Esther. He told her that Vic had sent him, that he had wanted to come himself but was unable because of problems with the sheriff. He told her not to worry though, that everything would be sorted out soon—he was working on that. He mentioned Kim, too, and said she would be back in to see her soon.

"Don't stop fighting, Sally," he said. "We all love you. You're going to pull out of this, you'll see. You'll be okay. We'll have a big barbecue in your honor when you get out of here, and I'll cook you the biggest and best steak you've ever seen. And Vic and I will whip you two girls in bridge, too. Now there's a challenge you can't ignore."

Still no response. He whispered a silent prayer and fought back the tears as he left the room. The kind nurse was passing by.

"Any questions I can answer for you, Mr. Hamilton?" Her gentleness reassured him that Sally was in the best of hands.

"What's the prognosis?" the judge inquired.

"It's hard to say," she replied in that wonderful, soothing voice. "Some victims of this kind of trauma come out of their coma and live relatively normal lives. It all depends on the extent of any brain damage suffered. Her other injuries are healing nicely, so when and if she awakens from the coma, we'll be better able to assess any long-term consequences. Don't give up hope, yet."

"Oh, I won't. Believe me, none of us will. Thanks for your help, Nurse. You've been very kind. And thank you for the care you're giving Sally."

She nodded bashfully, and the judge headed for the elevator.

SIXTEEN

The monotony of life as a hostage and the intense yearning to return to the hospital to be with her mom had Kim locked in the throes of big-time cabin fever. She couldn't stand wasting another day with these I.Q.-deprived adolescents while her mother lay in hospital, hovering at death's door, needing her. Kim had studied each of her guards carefully. Idle chatter during the long hours of confinement had netted valuable insights. She had constructed profiles of each of them, complete with predictable reactions to various circumstances. In the long hours of the night, when sleep eluded her, Kim would pore over the files stored in her memory banks, assessing the pros and cons of making a break with her various keepers.

Now, sensing her patience waning and feeling ever more strongly the need to get back to her mother, Kim decided it was time to finalize her analysis and plan her escape. She had ruled out doing it on Charlie's shift solely because of his unpredictable volatility. Though simple of mind and therefore probably easily duped, one could never be sure how Charlie would react at any time. He could be as docile as a kitten one minute and in the next, explode like a hand grenade with little or no provocation. No, Charlie was definitely at the bottom of the list.

Kim concluded that Willie's pent-up anger made him a bad risk, too. She had tried to penetrate that icy exterior, but the young man carried too much painful baggage to let anyone in. All advances were met with heavy resistance, even angry outbursts. Though she felt sorry for Willie, she knew his chip-on-the-shoulder attitude and unresolved anger were a dangerous mix in any potential escape attempt.

She had also eliminated any thought of making a run on Jake's shift. Though he would be the easiest to outrun, he was the smartest of the three, and Kim didn't like the thought of him knowing about her escape immediately. Besides, she would not want to get in any sort of wrestling match with the man. The tonnage would be an unfair and insurmountable advantage. Not only that, Jake was cold-blooded. He cared nothing for the feelings of others. He'd just as soon gut his best friend if it meant a paltry financial gain for himself. No, when she made her break, Kim wanted Jake Crapper as far away from the cabin as possible.

That left Zeke. Physically, he was the strongest of the three young guys, but Kim liked his straightforward approach to life. He was predictable. Sex and women dominated the functioning portions of his brain. There was no mean streak in the man. No latent pool of resentment or anger. No scores to settle. He was delusional — thinking he was God's gift to women — but it was a harmless delusion and one that might just play into Kim's hand.

&

The guards changed again about mid-morning. Jake hauled his formidable carcass out to the van and left a smiling Zeke in charge. Kim opted for a daytime break to allow a chance to put some distance between herself and her captors before dark. The opportunity came right after lunch. An unsuspecting Zeke, in the act of retrieving a battered copy of *Car and Driver* from the floor, leaned a little too closely to a napping Kim. With lightning speed, Kim's right foot swung ferociously, cracking Zeke's head with a sickening thud that sent him sprawling to the floor unconscious. Kim leaped over the motionless body and dashed for the door. Every second counted. She flew off the porch and disappeared into the bush behind the cabin, bounding downhill like a scared rabbit in full flight, branches slapping face and legs, twigs snapping underfoot. The adrenaline rush kicked Kim's competitive drive into high gear, and the exhilaration of sudden freedom fueled the charge downhill. The finish line was out there somewhere. For a time, she heard only the commotion of her own clamoring through the bush but, on stopping for a quick breather, she picked up the distant screaming of Zeke, desperately warning her to come back to the cabin before it was too late. Kim kicked herself for not grabbing the cell phone on the way out. She knew Zeke would be ringing Jake any minute. Oh well, by the time he arrived, she'd be miles away.

She continued her descent, calculating that eventually the forest would spit her out into some more highly populated area down below. For now, she was immersed in a sea of tall hardwoods and thankful for any cover it afforded. She dodged fallen limbs and debris, scrambled over downed logs and fought to keep her balance on the slippery bed of dried leaves carpeting the forest floor. She ran until her lungs were bursting. Panting and gasping for air, she fell to her knees, fighting to suck in precious oxygen. As her breathing leveled off, an eerie silence hung about like the smoke from a nearby campfire. During sporadic gusts, the wind whispered secret lullabies in the treetops. Then only deathly silence until wind and trees conspired to raise their chorus once more.

Kim suddenly felt like the lone survivor on a deserted island but fought back the self-pity, willing herself to focus. Survival depended on it. A clear mind and careful decision-making would be required. This was no deserted island, she told herself. These were hunting grounds, and she was the prey. At any moment, the hounds might surface in hot pursuit. The thought kept her moving.

Jake was livid. Such a simple assignment. How could anybody with half a brain screw it up? Leave it to Zeke. Probably came on to the chick and let her get the upper hand. None of that mattered now. He had to come up with a new plan. Pursue the girl in the woods and hope to get her before she gets to help or increase the pressure on Vic Johns and get this thing settled once and for all? The leveraged position appealed to him the most. Having Johns' daughter in custody ensured a much stronger bargaining position. Besides, it would be tough to hide Kim's disappearance. Johns had already asked to speak to her once to verify that she was still alive. He would ask again.

Thus, Jake and his boys ended up combing the deep woods around the cabin in the late evening hours. As the forest shadows deepened to a sinister ebony, Jake began to rethink the strategy.

"Boys, come on in," he shouted. "Over here. Take a load off. Let's think about this. She can't go far in the dark. She'll be holed up somewhere 'til morning."

Charlie shivered. "No way I'd want to be out in these woods all alone at night," he said. "I'm kinda scared even being here with you guys."

"You wimp," Willie said as he lightly shoved Charlie.

"Yes, you are," Zeke declared. "You probably want your momma to come and rescue you."

"No, I don't," Charlie said. "I'm braver than you, Zeke."

Zeke couldn't let that go. "Prove it," he challenged, shoving Charlie hard.

Charlie shoved Zeke back, and the two came chin to chin, ready to fight.

"Knock it off, you two," Jake barked as he took control. "Here's what we're gonna do. The girl will be runnin' down the mountain, headin' for the nearest town. I figure it'll take her another day to get outta this thick bush, if she doesn't get lost. Eventually, she'll have to cross the highway somewhere around Snake Creek. We're gonna go down there and stake out that section of the highway and let her come right to us."

"That's a good idea, boss," Zeke said, feeling the need to suck up to Jake after his gaffe this afternoon.

"This time, no mistakes, you hear me?" Jake said, as he glared at them one by one. "We snatch her and get her back to the cabin right away, understand?"

They all nodded.

"Let's go." The bear led the way back to the cabin.

Climbing fallen logs and high-stepping thick undergrowth was beginning to take its toll. Kim's pace slowed considerably. Pangs of hunger gnawed in her belly as waves of mild light-headedness swept over her. Fortunately, fresh water was in abundance. She had already traversed several mountain streams and paused long enough to drink deeply of nature's essential liquid. The need now was for sustenance—solid food.

As the sun began its slide toward the horizon, Kim turned her thoughts to shelter for the night. The forest was far too treacherous to roam after dark. She began searching for some protection. She felt so vulnerable and alone as the darkness closed in on all sides. In the waning light, Kim could distinguish the outline of a rocky overhang just ahead. The protruding rock formed a natural canopy. The space beneath the overhang had been a catch-all for blowing leaves, judging by the mounds of brittle leaves tucked into the fold of rock. A bed of leaves sounded just fine to Kim after a long day of arduous trekking, so she nestled in to wait out the night and hopefully sleep some. The night sounds reminded her of camping out under the stars on their property before the cabin was built. A symphony of crickets and a hooting owl lulled her into a deep slumber.

Judge Hamilton worried about his friend Vic. It wasn't in Vic's nature to sit tight and wait for events to unfold. He was a doer, a man of action. The best defense to him was an aggressive offense. Turn the tide in one's favor by diving in headfirst. Take the bull by the horns. Make things happen rather than sit on the ropes and take life's punches. It was unrealistic to expect Vic to sit patiently for long, while he, the judge, tried to sort matters out. This fact-finding mission had better yield some tangible results — for Vic's sake. No telling what he might do otherwise.

The clamminess of the judge's shirt had him second-guessing the decision to walk to the courthouse from the hardware store at the other end of town. As he approached the courthouse steps, the sheriff's car pulled into a reserved parking spot. How convenient. No need to meet on Bodie's turf. Although, at the moment, the thought of an air-conditioned office outweighed all other considerations.

The judge waited politely at the curb for the sheriff to haul himself out of the squad car. Bodie didn't look very enthusiastic about his sidewalk greeter. Of course, he never seemed overjoyed to see the judge. The sheriff performed the obligatory hitching of his pants and stepped to the curb.

"I hope you're not standin' there waitin' for me," he said bluntly.

"Why, Sheriff, is that any way to greet one of your good law-abiding citizens?"

"What is it you want, Hamilton?" an obviously irritated Bodie demanded.

"Just some information. Any clues or developments in the disappearance of Vic Johns' daughter?"

"What's it to you?" Bodie fired off.

"Let's just say I have a personal interest in Kim's well-being, Sheriff."

"Johns sent you trottin' down here to find out what's goin' on, is that it?" Bodie grinned.

"It doesn't matter. So, what's the latest, Bodie?" The judge's disdain for Bodie oozed from every word. He certainly wasn't going to try to hide it. Bodie would get his comeuppance one of these days. Until then, he, Judge Hamilton, would merely tolerate the arrogant small town sheriff.

"Nothin's the latest. That's what we've got—zilch, zero, zip. She disappeared out of the clear blue, left her car and purse behind in the hospital parking lot. No clues. No suspects. Nothing."

"Surely somebody must have seen something, Sheriff. People don't just disappear—especially leaving a purse and a car behind."

"If you're suggestin' we're not doin' our job, Hamilton, you can turn around and get the hell outta here." Bodie turned to walk away.

The judge reached out and caught Bodie by the arm. "Wait, Sheriff . . ."

Bodie spun around, shaking his arm free. His eyes were daggers.

"Don't you ever touch me again," he growled.

"Come on, Bodie, an innocent young lady's life is at stake here. You must have something. Look, we both know who took Kim—the same thugs who've been making threats against Vic Johns."

"Maybe so, but without some clues or evidence, there's little I can do about it."

"What about your prisoner in the jail? He know anything?"

"I haven't gotten around to questionin' him yet."

"Might be a good place to start, don't you think? Where is the car?" the judge asked.

"Over at the compound on Sherman Street."

"Mind if I have a look at it?"

"Be my guest, Judge. I'll send one of my boys over there with you."

The judge knew Bodie couldn't get rid of him fast enough.

"I'll set it up right now," Bodie said as he turned to head inside.

"By the way, I think I'll come back and have a little chat with Whitey after this, OK, Sheriff?"

Bodie shrugged and disappeared inside.

Vic cut into the sirloin getting cold on his plate. He was growing restless. He'd been over and over the situation in his mind. Turning over the deed was no guarantee of Kim's safety. This Crapper fellow was a real psycho—definitely not to be trusted. Yet, what options did he have? Defy the deadline, and Crapper would be crazy enough to carry through on the threat. Trying to find Kim's whereabouts would be a long shot. There just wasn't enough time for a thorough search. Besides, they could have her stashed anywhere. And any attempt to free her might bring the same tragic result. There had to be another way.

Vic mindlessly carved his steak and washed down each bite with a swig of beer. Finally, a plan was beginning to take shape in his mind. He was so absorbed in it that he hardly noticed his cell phone ringing in the pocket of his jacket.

"Yeah," he said, answering on the fourth ring. "Oh, hi, Fred. Yeah, I'm OK. Just having some grub. Of course I'm alone. In case you haven't noticed, I'm not too popular these days . . . Very funny, Fred. Seriously, though, what did you find out today? . . . OK, give me the bad news first . . . What? You're not serious. How can they charge me with a murder I didn't even commit? What a joke . . . What about Kim? Any leads? . . . Somehow that doesn't surprise me. I'm sure we're well down Bodie's list of priorities."

Vic waved the waitress away with his payment and a hefty tip.

"So, Fred, what do you think I should do? I can't just sit around and wait. I've only got a matter of hours . . . Well, listen, Fred, I need the phone number for that lawyer buddy of yours up here in the city. Do you think he can be trusted? . . . I thought so. I need him to do me a favor . . . OK, I got it. Thanks, Fred, I knew I could count on you. You're just about the only friend I have right now . . . Yeah, I'll be careful. Talk to you later."

SEVENTEEN

A **concert of birds heralded the dawn** of the new day. A much gentler wake-up call than the abrasive buzz of her alarm clock at home. Kim rose from the bed of leaves to continue the descent to civilization. The heavy morning dew soon had her shoes soaked, but hunger was her most pressing need. After a half-hour of determined downhill hiking, she spied an isolated cabin tucked among guardian pines. Not at all your traditional-looking cabin. This one looked like an alien spaceship that landed in the clearing, setting down on the welcoming bed of pine needles. It was round, like a mushroom, with a pointed roof made of oblong shingles, like a dreamy cottage from a childhood fable. Kim half-expected to see tiny dwarfs come marching from this whimsical hut. But seeing neither dwarfs nor smoke coming from the chimney nor vehicles parked outside, Kim inched her way to the front door. Food was her primary objective. She knocked loudly on the door, then peered in through a window. The place was closed up--front door locked and windows secured. She had to get in. With no other recourse, she grabbed a log from the woodpile stacked about twenty feet from the front door and threw it at the pane to the left of the door. The glass shattered in a million pieces, and Kim carefully stepped through the window, avoiding the jagged shards still lodged in the frame. Glass crunched underfoot as she tiptoed to the kitchen at the back of the cabin. The air was heavy with wood smoke and tobacco, and the walls were decked out in animal skins—beaver pelts, deerskins, even a wolf with head intact. Kim was sure the eyes were following her every movement. She pulled open a cabinet door. What a glorious sight! Rows of canned beans and vegetables stared her in the face. A quick search turned up a can opener and a spoon, and in seconds, she was gorging herself on cold pork and beans. They never tasted so good.

As she ate, Kim planned her next move. Feeling guilty about the broken window, she thought about trying to repair it but soon nixed that idea for want of materials and because of the urgency of continuing her flight. She also considered leaving a note for the owner with an explanation, an apology, and a promise to make good on it—if she survived this perilous escape. But lacking pen and paper, she quickly nixed that idea, too. She would also take some supplies with her—mostly food—to last at least a couple of days. She rummaged around the cabin, thinking how much it reminded her of their first cabin on the property. The lingering odor of the wood smoke carried her back to childhood days when Dad would be the first one up in the mornings, collecting firewood and getting a roaring fire going in the fireplace. The morning chill could not compete. But when Dad started cooking bacon on the open fire, that's when Kim got interested in crawling out from under the warm blankets.

The memories dissolved as she found a deerskin pack large enough to tote a couple of day's worth of supplies. She stuffed tins of beans and some crackers into the pack. The tins would be a little heavy but she had no alternative. On some hooks next to the door, Kim grabbed a down-filled hunter's vest—light but warm, with some protection in case of rain. She crammed the pockets with the can opener, some spoons, matches and first-aid items she found stuffed in another drawer. She rolled up a heavy wool blanket, tied it with string and lashed it to the leather bag. Not bad for a city girl, she thought.

A quick glance about, then out onto the mountain she went again, feeling much more confident with the leather bag strapped to her back. She decided to follow the rough road leading from the cabin, hoping it would take her to a main road where help could be flagged down.

Jake was losing patience. He took a long, hard drag on his cigar and blew smoke rings across the cab of the pick-up truck. Too bad all of life couldn't be as simple and pleasurable as a good cigar. No rush, no stress, just slow and quiet gratification. When a man has a cigar in hand, the troubles of the world seem to take a back seat.

Unfortunately, even a cigar wasn't bringing Jake the usual satisfaction today. Too much had gone wrong. They had to find the Johns girl quickly, so they could deal with Lapain's threat. The professor had to be taken seriously. Going to the papers to blow the story wide open was something Lapain would do. And the press would have a heyday. That was not going to happen. Not while Jake Crapper was still breathing. Time for a little meeting with Professor Lapain—a persuasive meeting.

Jake fingered the .38 tucked into his belt, ensured that it was well concealed beneath his jacket, then ambled into the lecture hall. He slipped into the back row undetected while Professor Lapain, back to the class, wrote on the blackboard. The tiered classroom was nearly packed with students of every size, shape and age. Jake guessed there must be close to two hundred people fervently scratching notes on lined notepads. Lapain must be pretty popular. Too bad, Jake thought, in mock concern. He'll be sorely missed.

Somewhere near the end of the class, Lapain caught a glimpse of his unwanted newcomer. Jake noticed how visibly shaken Lapain was at the sight of him hunkered down in the back row. He wanted to stand up and shout some rude greeting to the professor but fought the urge. Best not to draw unneeded attention.

Lapain quickly capped off the lecture and dismissed the class. After everyone had left, he grabbed a sheaf of notes and made his way up the aisle to confront his new student. Jake waited. Everything was playing out perfectly so far.

"What are you doing here, Jake?" The words were caustic.

"Figured it was time we had another meeting, Professor." Jake smiled.

"I told you never to come here!"

"Oh, don't worry. The meeting isn't takin' place here, Lapain."

Jake stood up, quickly pulling the pistol from his belt and pointing it at Lapain's stomach. "We're goin' for a little drive. You're gonna walk out this door with me as if we're old buddies headin' for a beer together. My truck's in the lot in front of the building. Any heroics and I blow a hole in your gut. Got it?"

He waved the pistol at the professor's head until he nodded. Then, shoving him toward the door, Jake barked, "Now move!"

Fifteen fear-stricken faces stared at the judge from around the conference table. The eyes begging for assurances. Not one Culpeper merchant in attendance believed that Findlay Ralston's death was robbery related. They wondered aloud who would be carried out in a body bag next. Findlay had been the driving force behind the uprising against Sheriff Bodie's extortion ring. The deflated morale hung in the room like stale smoke. The others had looked to Ralston as their leader, the judge now knew. How could he re-ignite their passion for justice when fear had such a stranglehold? His booming, self-assured voice intruded on the panicky conversations around the table, immediately silencing all other voices.

"First of all, there is no hard evidence that Bodie and his thugs had anything to do with Findlay Ralston's death."

"We don't need evidence," Patricia Long declared. "Every one of us knows in our heart that Bodie is behind this."

"That why we so afraid," added Kai Chui Wong. The others nodded in agreement.

"If Bodie is capable of doing this to Findlay, then none of us is safe," Patricia Long continued.

"But you're basing your fear on the unknown," the judge said. "What if Bodie had nothing to do with Ralston's death? What if it truly was a robbery related death? If that's the case, you have locked yourselves in imaginary cells of fear."

"Call us pessimistic or gutless or whatever you want, Judge, but that's the reality we have to live with right now," said Jim Owens of the Framing Shop.

"Yes. And we have to think of our families, too," Patricia chipped in. "We can't just think of ourselves here." Nods of agreement all around.

Patricia Long summarized it for everyone. "We know Bodie is dirty. We know what he's capable of. End of story. None of us wants to end up like Ralston."

"So, why did you call me here then, if you've already decided to pack it in and concede victory to Bodie?" the judge asked.

"You're the only one we can turn to," confessed a short, stubby fellow the judge didn't recognize.

"But you've already made up your minds from the sound of it," the judge insisted.

"That's because we're so scared, Judge," a voice from the far end of the table declared.

"Yeah, we don't know what to do," added another. "We fear for our families, for our businesses, for our town."

"What if Bodie did do it, Judge?" asked Jim Owens.

"Well, if he did, then he needs to pay," the judge replied. "Otherwise, Ralston's death is meaningless. If Bodie is guilty, and you retreat like scared pups with your tails between your legs, then his extortion and brutality will only continue, and a courageous, good man like Findlay Ralston will have died needlessly in a losing cause. I think you owe it to Findlay to stand up for the cause he spearheaded and believed in so strongly. Findlay Ralston was afraid, too. But he wanted to free Culpeper of the likes of Bodie and restore it to the kind, caring, safe town it used to be."

The words were hitting the mark, chipping away the icy resistance. Their slain leader could be the rallying point so sorely needed, so the judge carried on.

"Folks, you are in a war here. A war against injustice. A battle for freedom. I believe justice will prevail. But no war is without casualties. And no victory is won without a cost. Findlay Ralston may be a casualty of this war—we can't be sure—but either way, his blood cries out for justice, for freedom, for a Culpeper he believed in and spent his life building. Are you willing to turn your backs on him now?"

The flame had been rekindled. The judge could see it in their eyes even before they began to verbalize their recommitment to the cause. It spread like wildfire around the table. No one was immune. All resistance melted. They were one again in their resolve.

"Tell us what to do," Patricia Long pleaded.

"Keep up your united front," the judge replied. "Don't give Bodie an inch. Remember, your strength is in your unity. I'll follow up on Ralston's death—see what I can dig up. In the meantime, take extra precautions—don't be caught alone in your shops. Always have extra staff on hand, even if it's not your usual practice. Maybe you can set up a rotating monitoring system to check up on each other during the day. Or how about hiring your own security people to keep tabs on your members? Let Bodie know he's in for a fight. Sooner or later, he's going to make a mistake that will cost him dearly."

By the time the judge left the meeting, the merchants were fired up and totally unified in their resolve to resist Sheriff Bodie's extortion. The judge figured his performance on this night ranked up there with the stirring speeches of Patton, Churchill and Martin Luther King, Jr.

Kim continued her descent from the mountain, following the rough road leading away from the plundered cabin. Though strewn with potholes, the road afforded much easier transit than the forest bed. And it must link up with a main road soon. The vision of her mom's battered body lying in that hospital bed drove her to press on, despite muscle pain and fatigue.

"I'm coming, Mom. Hang in there. You can make it." The imaginary conversations fueled her resolve. "You'll see, Mom. Before you know it, we'll be sipping lattes at Starbucks after a big day of shopping."

The distant drone of an engine interrupted the monologue. It sounded like a truck approaching and grew louder and louder until, in a whoosh, it seemed to pass nearby and began to fade away again Kim ran toward the sound. The highway was just ahead. She burst onto the asphalt in a state of euphoria. With arms raised in triumphant salute, she paced the yellow centerline—a victory lap. This ribbon of asphalt leads home, she thought, as her eye followed the yellow stripe until it disappeared around the next bend. Now, just a ride.

❦

Willie saw the whole thing. From his position uphill, at the bend in the road, he saw a figure dart onto the highway. At first, he thought it was just some hunter crossing over, but the blond hair and the victory dance told him otherwise.

"I found her," Willie barked into the walkie-talkie. "Hurry up, Zeke. Get your ass down here. She's walkin' right down the middle of the road, just waitin' for us to nab her."

Within minutes, the van slowed to pick up Willie and then accelerated in pursuit of the solitary figure jogging along the yellow line. As the van neared, the runner moved to the shoulder of the road and turned to extend a thumb in hopes of hitching a ride. The shock of recognition registered on Kim's face as the van slid off the road in a shower of gravel. The doors flew open, and Jake's boys hit the ground running. But Kim was already sprinting like a scared rabbit.

The Hamilton estate sprawled across several acres of fine Virginia forest with a pillared brick house befitting someone of the judge's stature in the community. The mansion was Esther's baby. She had chosen the plan, supervised its construction, designed the stunning landscape treatments, front and rear, and furnished the home using an eighteenth-century aristocratic motif. It was her castle, her pride and joy. But the judge had his own sanctuary. To get there, you followed the driveway to the attached double garage where it branched off, circled around the garage and headed deeper into the property. Passing between twin rows of overhanging trees, you soon came upon a second clearing, where a modest clapboard structure huddled against a cluster of towering oaks. An oversized, automatic door opened the way to the judge's shrine.

Rows of shiny wrenches and ratchets hung above an organized workbench. An engine hoist hung menacingly from the rafters like a giant spider. Vintage license plates and advertising signs on the walls clashed with modern diagnostic equipment and power tools. The judge's auto workshop, his private Shangri-La, was the stuff of dreams. Every tool of the trade for dissecting and restoring cars could be found here. For twenty-five years, the Judge had retreated to this sanctuary to tweak a carburetor or paint a fender.

His interest in cars began at the age of seven when young Freddie took a shine to collecting stray hubcaps. Scouring the ditches along old Route 42 near his home, he would drag home a half-dozen wheel covers every other day. It didn't take long for Freddie to discover that his recycled hubcaps were a gold mine. The young entrepreneur set up shop, selling his "refurbished" merchandise and salting away the profits to save up for his first car.

As he hit the teen years, Freddie began to hang out at ol' Moses' garage over on Liberty Avenue. Moses was a pudgy, little man who loved to laugh. He was always smiling, and he treated Freddie like one of his own kin. Taught him how to tear apart a carburetor and put it back together again. Even helped Freddie buy his first tools. When the school day ended, without fail, Freddie Hamilton could be seen racing down Main Street past the malt shop and around the corner onto Liberty Avenue. Everything Fred Hamilton learned about auto mechanics, he traced back to ol' Moses.

Years later, when Moses was confined to a wheelchair, Fred would bring him out to his private sanctuary, and they'd talk cars 'til sunset. Moses would coach Fred on his techniques and dish up diagnostic tips. The two men were kindred spirits. Fred still felt the presence of ol' Moses in the workshop, even though the old guy had been gone now for nearly eight years.

Moses would have liked this latest restoration masterpiece—a '57 Chevy in robin's egg blue with white flares on the fender wings. He'd brought it back from a rusty shell. Hunted far and wide for the upholstery and seats. And he put the wide whitewalls on her, too, because Moses always liked that. Now just a few adjustments on the transmission, and she'd be ready for a road test.

Fred jacked up the front end and slid underneath his latest piece of art. With the stereo blaring the smoky blues of Muddy Waters, he didn't hear the footsteps approaching from the open door. Didn't see the hand grasp the handle of the hydraulic jack. A twist and, instantly, the jack collapsed, dropping two tons of steel onto his unsuspecting body. The moody blues strains drowned out the final wheeze of the crushed body. The footsteps retreated hastily, racing across the back of the property.

Kim vaulted the guardrail and slid twenty feet down the embankment. She hurdled a fallen tree and shot into the forest once again. Underbrush grabbed at her ankles, but like a spooked white-tailed deer, she tore through it and plunged on deeper and deeper into the solitude of the woods. She glanced back only once and saw that Jake's boys just didn't have the heart to chase her into the forest. She slowed her pace only slightly and only when her lungs began screaming for oxygen.

After a half-hour, Kim allowed herself to slow to a walk. The rapture of reaching the highway was abandoned somewhere back around the guardrail. Now what? She'd have to avoid the highway. Progress would be considerably slower. She'd been so close to getting back. The disappointment was a bitter pill, but Kim was glad she'd eluded Zeke and the boys. The good news was, she still had the backpack and supplies.

EIGHTEEN

Holly froze at the sight of Jake Crapper and Ambrose Lapain leaving the history building together. She watched as Jake shoved Lapain into a pick-up truck. When the truck pulled away seconds later, Holly raced for her own car. Tossing files on the passenger seat, she fired up the yellow Miata and raced from the parking lot in pursuit of Jake's vehicle. On the edge of campus, she caught up with it but decided to trail Jake for awhile. The old pick-up was an easy mark anyway. Wouldn't be a problem tracking it from a distance.

Inside the abduction vehicle, Ambrose Lapain probed Jake Crapper's motives.

"Where are we going?" he demanded.

"Someplace nice and quiet so we can have a man to man."

"About what?"

"About your threats to open your big mouth and blow this whole operation out of the sky, that's what!" Jake snorted. "I can't let that happen."

"What are you planning to do with me?" the professor asked.

"Whatever it takes to keep you quiet."

Lapain felt the chill of those words. He knew Jake meant exactly what he said. The pistol pointed in Lapain's direction was proof enough.

"What do you expect me to do, Jake? You try to take over the whole deal and go way overboard on the use of force. Do you really expect me to just sit tight and let you ruin it all because you don't have the patience to let the plans play out?"

"Patience," Jake sneered. "It's not a matter of patience, it's about you not havin' a plan. It's about goin' and getting' what's out there. Maybe it doesn't mean so much to you, what with your six-figure salary and all, but for me 'n' the boys, this is the chance of a lifetime to move up in the world. I can't let that slip through my hands because of your friggin' botched up plans. It's time for action. No more sittin' around waitin'."

"You just don't get it, do you, Jake? The more you push this Johns fellow, the more he gets his back up. He's a tough nut. He's not going to roll over and let you walk in and plunder his land. We need diplomacy and tact, not threats and brute force."

"I'll decide what we need. Consider yourself semi-retired, Professor. From now on, you're one of the foot soldiers taking orders from me, the drill sergeant. Understand?" Jake waved the pistol for emphasis.

"I still say . . ."

"No, you don't have anything to say," Jake interrupted. "Just obey the orders you're given. That's it. Plain and simple."

"But . . ."

"I can see I'm gonna have to put you out of commission, Professor. You just refuse to listen, don't you?"

Jake's emotionless words seized Ambrose Lapain's throat. The professor had felt fear before, but this sensation was different. Something was constricting his airway. He felt himself fighting for air, gasping like a drowning man. He had to get out. Had to get away from this madman, from the pistol barrel leveled at his chest. The panic had his chest pounding and eyes wildly searching for an escape plan. It was then that the canary yellow in the side mirror caught his eye. Top down, humming along in dogged pursuit. Waves of angelic golden hair blowing in the wind told him Holly was at the wheel. An angel of deliverance. His angel.

There was no premeditation to the act. It was instinct — survival instinct — nothing more. As Jake slowed before a red light at the approaching intersection, Lapain popped the door latch and, in one motion, rolled out of the van, hitting the pavement hard. He bounced up and leaped into the yellow convertible, screaming, "Drive, Holly! Gun it! Get out of here!"

Holly tromped the accelerator and flew around Jake's van. She ripped through second and third gears in a flash and tore off down a side street, narrowly missing getting blindsided by oncoming traffic. In a hail of horns and screeching brakes, angry and astonished drivers skidded across the intersection.

৵

The legal profession had become so specialized, they probably had specific lawyers to handle the defendants in cafeteria brawls at the elementary schools. Vic was too stressed to handle much more of this referral game. The judge's lawyer buddy in Washington, Jonas Filberg, while sympathetic, admitted he could not handle any real estate matters, nor could any of the partners in his firm. However, he knew someone across the state line in Richmond, Virginia — a Benjamin Goldberg, a personal friend and highly skilled real estate attorney. So, Vic continued on the referral conveyor belt hoping this next stop would be the last. Goldberg's offices were located in a stately antebellum mansion with tastefully redone interior. Plush carpeting and extensive use of the original plank floors and carved oak moldings preserved the flavor of 1800s Americana. A marble staircase led to Mr. Goldberg's personal suite on the second floor.

Vic immediately felt at ease as Ben Goldberg acknowledged that he, too, knew Fred Hamilton well. In fact, he and Fred were debating team partners years before in pre-law studies at Georgetown U. They had chummed together during law school and even clerked together in the same firm for a year. Ben was a balding man of about sixty with a pointed nose upon which tiny, black-rimmed glasses perched. He had an air of quiet confidence and a casual demeanor, as evidenced by rolled up sleeves and a loosened tie. Ben's heavy nasal inflection reminded Vic of childhood days, talking with his nostrils pinched.

"Jonas said you have a sensitive real estate matter that you need handled in a hurry with few questions asked," Goldberg said, shifting the conversation to business.

"Yes, I do," Vic replied. "I know you're a busy man, Ben, and I appreciate you seeing me on such short notice. I need this property deed prepared so that it can be signed over to new ownership, and I desperately need it done right away. I know it's asking a lot . . ." Vic pulled some papers from a large manila envelope.

"Don't give it another thought, Vic. Any friend of Fred's—you know?" He took the documents from Vic and retreated behind his massive desk to peruse them. "So you want a simple transfer of ownership from your name to . . ."

"Jake Crapper."

"Well, that's a strange one."

"Actually, if you knew the man, you'd say it was a very appropriate name."

"I see. Well, it's a highly unusual request, but I don't see any reason why we can't get the paperwork ready for you in a couple of hours. I'll put my administrative assistant on it right away. Why don't you drop back in this afternoon, say about 2 o'clock?"

"That will be terrific, Ben. Like I said, I really appreciate it."

Finally, a chance to do something, Vic thought as he descended the marble staircase. Now to figure out the actual exchange of deed for daughter. There was no way he would trust Jake Crapper with a signed deed transfer without Kim being present for the exchange. That snake was a double cross waiting to happen.

Over pizza and root beer at a café down the street from the law offices, the enormity of what he was arranging began to sink in. He was about to turn over his entire estate to some lowlife scumbag. All the years of hard labor developing the land and building their dream retirement home would be down the drain in minutes. Handed on a silver platter to an undeserving criminal. The injustice of it rankled Vic. He would do anything to avoid this, but Kim's life was in jeopardy. Her safety had to come first. They would sort it all out later, once she was free of Crapper's grasp.

Halfway through the second slice of pepperoni pizza, the brainstorm hit. This wasn't the only way. Why play by Crapper's rules? There were other cards to be played. Vic swallowed hard, grabbed his phone and dialed feverishly.

"Yes, it's Vic Johns. I was just in the office for a meeting with Mr. Goldberg—he's preparing some paperwork for me. Would you please ask him to leave the names blank on all copies of the deed transfer . . . Yes, we'll fill in the names by hand when we sign them . . . That's right. Thank you."

The rest of the pizza and root beer went down a little more smoothly.

The haunting image of her mom lying helpless and alone in that hospital bed dissolved Kim's disappointment. The image once again fueled her descent, sending her plunging on through the gnarly underbrush. She stopped once to devour another tin of pork and beans and a handful of crackers. Then it was off and running again.

By late afternoon, another remote cabin came into view. A curling waft of smoke from the chimney told her this cabin was occupied. It was a primitive log structure with small windows. A few cords of firewood leaned against one wall, and animal skins stretched on frames stood off to one side of the cabin door. Kim noticed two weathered crosses, primitive grave markers, over near the edge of the clearing. The graves were not fresh.

She boldly approached the door, intending to knock, but hesitated. For a long moment, she stood pondering the wisdom of this plan. Maybe she should just pass by and keep going. There was no sign of a vehicle or a road, so little hope of speeding her descent from this mountain.

Then she heard a click—the unmistakable cocking of a trigger. Her breath caught in her throat. She slowly turned her head to stare down the muzzle of a shotgun. From the other end of the barrel, the creepy face of an old man stared back. He had a scruffy, gray beard, caterpillar eyebrows and glazed eyes—crazy glazed eyes—shrouded beneath a tattered hat. The fingernails of the hand clutching the barrel were caked with dirt.

"Thou shalt not trespass." The words thundered from a mouth full of bad teeth.

Kim instinctively raised her arms as the shotgun poked at her. Oh great, she thought, a religious fanatic. That's all she needed right now.

"Listen, mister. I'm not really trespassing. I'm just passing by and stumbled across your cabin here."

The bushy eyebrows furrowed, and the shotgun waved in Kim's face. "Thou shalt not bear false witness."

"Look, I don't want any trouble," Kim responded, gently pushing the gun barrel away from her face.

But the old man persisted. He shoved the gun right back in her face.

"A false witness shall not be unpunished, and he that speaketh lies shall not escape," he roared.

The glare of his wild eyes sent shivers up Kim's spine. She'd had enough of this old Bible-thumper already and had no intention of wasting her time with him. Judging by his wiry frame, she figured she could overtake him physically, but the shotgun gave him a decided edge at this moment.

"Mister, I'm trying to get off this mountain. I was kidnapped, understand? But I got away, and I'm trying to get to the nearest town."

"Ye have sinned against the Lord; and be sure thy sin will find thee out."

"Cut the hyper-religious crap. All I want to do is leave, OK?"

Kim pushed the gun away again and stepped back in a conciliatory manner.

"I'm not a threat," she continued. "I don't want anything from you unless you can help me get to town. I won't hurt you, and I'm not intentionally trespassing on your property. The men who kidnapped me are following me—that's why I'm on the run. I haven't done anything wrong."

"Let the wicked forsake his way," came the thunderous reply.

The man had a one-track mind. If he didn't look so stark raving mad, it would actually be comical, Kim thought. He was motioning for her to enter the cabin. Not wanting to argue with the shotgun, she complied. The stench of the place made her gag. It was dark and dirty. As her eyes adjusted to the light, she realized she stood on a dirt floor.

The furnishings were simple and rough, all hand-carved. A fire crackled in the hearth of a stone fireplace. The old man shoved her into a chair beside the table.

He sat across the room, shotgun cradled on his lap, as if pondering what to do with her. He took up a corncob pipe and proceeded to pack and light it. The circles of smoke wreathed his head like exhaust from a brain laboring overtime to sort out the situation.

Finally, he grunted and nodded toward Kim. "Pack. What's in it?"

She removed the backpack and plopped it on the table — unzipped the main compartment and pulled out the contents, spreading them across the tabletop. The old man nodded and gestured at her again. "Coat," he said.

She took off the vest and tossed it to him. He checked the pockets and tossed it to the floor.

"Shirt and pants," he grunted.

She began to object, but the shotgun waved again. Obediently Kim unbuttoned her shirt, tossed it over and slipped out of her pants. She felt his eyes on her as she stood self-consciously in her underwear in front of him. He probably hadn't seen a woman for sometime — especially a half-naked one. After staring at her briefly, he rummaged through the rest of her pockets, then tossed the pile of clothes back to her. With relief, Kim dressed quickly.

The old man packed and lit his pipe again. Kim could tell none of this was coming easy to him. Obviously, he was not accustomed to dealing with intruders. Evidently, with no previous experiences, he was making this up as he went along. Kim carefully returned the items on the table to her backpack. She noticed a framed black and white photograph on a small table beside the bed. It was a woman—a simple but attractive woman with a little girl perched on her lap. Flowing natural curls ringed the child's radiant face.

"That's a nice picture," Kim said. "Is that your wife and daughter?"

The old man glanced at the frame, nodded and kept puffing.

"They are very beautiful," Kim added. "Are those their graves outside?"

The pain etched on his lonely face was Kim's answer.

"I'm sorry," she said. "How did they die?"

"'Twas a long time ago now," he replied, as if reluctant to revisit those dark days.

"You don't have to tell me about it," Kim said.

"Me and brother Jed was off huntin'. A couple o' drunk hunters come upon the cabin." He paused, choking on the words. "Them devil workers done raped my wife and little girl, and butchered 'em both with a huntin' knife."

A single tear ran down the old man's cheek.

"They done it a long time ago. 'Spect my little girl'd be 'bout your age now."

He wiped away the tear.

"'Vengeance is mine,' saith the Lord." His voice turned harsh again. "Ain't gonna bring the wife and girl back ag'in, but they's some comfort in knowin' them murderin' renegades is gonna burn in hell for what they's done."

"I'm truly sorry for your loss, mister. I'm trying to get back to my mother. She's in the hospital in Culpeper—in a coma. It was a car wreck. We think some crazy person ran her off the road. She's in bad shape. I love her, and she needs me there when she wakes up. That's why I have to walk out that door now, even at the risk of you shooting me. My mother needs me."

Kim grabbed the backpack and stood. The old man didn't move. She moved to the door, opened it and stepped out into the brisk evening air.

NINETEEN

The shock waves nearly buckled Vic's knees. He shook his head in disbelief as the tears welled in his eyes.

"Sorry to give you the bad news, Vic," Esther Hamilton was saying. "He was a good man."

Vic fought the lump in his throat. "When did it happen?" he asked.

"Yesterday. He was out in the shop working on that old car he was restoring. Apparently the hydraulic lift failed . . ." She sobbed.

"I'm so sorry, Esther. Fred was always so careful. He knew what he was doing."

Esther pulled herself together enough to talk. "The police came and investigated. Said they had little to go on. They're calling it a terrible, unfortunate accident."

A long pause. "Vic, I'm gonna miss him. I don't know if I can take this. I sure wish Sally was around. I could use her shoulder right about now."

"You're a strong woman, Esther Hamilton. You can't let this beat you. You know what the judge would say."

"Yes, I know. He'd say, 'Hold your head high and rise above the problem.'"

"Yeah, something like that," Vic agreed. "When is the funeral?"

"Tomorrow afternoon at three. It's going to be a simple graveside service—the judge didn't want a lot of hoopla. Can you be here for it, Vic? It sure would be nice if you could say a few words, seeing as you were his best friend and all."

She was fighting back the tears again.

"I'll plan on it, Esther. See you then."

I must be out of my mind, Vic thought after hanging up. The sheriff has posted a warrant for my arrest, and I'm committing myself to walking right into Culpeper to attend a funeral at the cemetery. Maybe if it was in a church, there would be some sort of understood truce—respect for holy ground or the deceased—that would prompt the law to back off just this once. But can't count on that—not as long as Sam Bodie is sheriff. This calls for a plan.

The troops convened in Sheriff Sam Bodie's office for a strategy session. Bodie fancied himself Robert E. Lee laying out battle plans for a major engagement with the Federal army from up north. It didn't matter that the enemy was one solitary man holed up in Washington, who might not even show up for fear of arrest. They would be ready just in case.

"The cemetery will be the focal point of our operation, men. We'll lay the trap, and if Johns is crazy enough to walk into it, we'll nab him. Nate and I will be attendin' the graveside service as representatives for the Department. The rest of you will be stationed at the entrances to the cemetery. No one touches Johns during the service, understood? I don't wanna create a scene at the grave. We'll give them their chance to grieve unhindered, but as soon as Johns exits the cemetery, we nab him. Got it?"

"Do we use force if necessary, Sheriff?" Chester Muldoon asked.

"Yes, if necessary," Bodie replied. "Remember, this guy is wanted for assault and murder. He's a dangerous criminal, and he's well-trained in hand-to-hand combat, so don't try to be heroes out there. I don't want him slippin' past our net."

Bodie unfurled a map of the Culpeper cemetery on the table in front of him.

"Now, here are the assignments. There are two entrances to the cemetery. This one," he said, stabbing the map with a stubby finger, "at the north end. That's the main gate. I want Chester and Floyd there. Dodie, you and Tom will take the east entrance, over here. You'll take up your positions as soon as the service begins. Nate will radio you from the squad car just before it all starts. I want both exits sealed off. Leave only enough room for a single car to barely pass through the gates. If Johns is ridin' in one of the limousines, the procedure will be to stop the limo at the gate and take Johns with as little fanfare as possible. If he's in his own car, it gets even easier because we won't have to disturb any other guests. Of course, that means he'll be drivin', so be prepared for some heroics. Nate and I'll be part of the crowd leavin' the cemetery, so we'll serve as backup. We'll ID Johns and relay a heads-up to your positions so you'll know what vehicle he's in. Any questions?"

"What if he does slip by the roadblocks at the gates, Sheriff?" Tom Porter asked.

"It better not happen, but if it does, Bobby will be parked in a squad car outside the main gate and he'll lead the pursuit with the rest of us following."

"Do you really expect Vic Johns to show up, Sir?" Dodie Anderson asked.

"My gut tells me he wouldn't miss this for the world. He and the judge were pretty close—former combat buddies and all. Those kinds of guys stick together. He'll be here. I'd bet on it."

Bodie eyed his troops. "Any more questions?" All heads were shaking, every face etched with intensity. They were ready.

Ambrose Lapain winced as Holly dabbed yet another abrasion with antiseptic.

"Sorry, Professor," she said, wetting another cotton swab with the fiery ointment. "Isn't it amazing how bruised and battered a body can get jumping from a moving vehicle?"

The professor flinched again in response.

"That was pretty exciting, wasn't it? Smart thinking, Professor, leaping from the truck like that. I've never seen you move so quickly."

"Fear and panic make us do all kinds of strange things. I just want to thank you, Holly, for being there for me. Without you, I probably wouldn't have gotten away at all." He didn't really want to contemplate being Jake Crapper's prisoner.

Holly continued to nurse the wounds. She was leaning in so close, Lapain couldn't help but smell the sweetness of her hair and notice the soft contours of her cleavage. It aroused him. He felt her arm brush lightly against his. Her fingers were so gentle, so warm and tender. He wanted to reach out and touch her, to take her in his arms, hold her and kiss her lips.

"That Jake Crapper is something, isn't he?" Holly asked, breaking the spell. "I don't know if I've ever seen such a vile person in my entire life."

"Yeah, me neither." Lapain thought a moment. "I don't know what I'm going to do now, Holly. What do you think? About the whole situation, I mean."

"Good question, Professor. I'd definitely steer clear of Jake, if I were you. He's crazy."

"I'm beginning to regret the discovery of the letter and especially getting Jake involved." Lapain pressed a bandage in place, unrolled his sleeve and buttoned the cuff.

"I can understand that," Holly replied, "but you can't lose perspective here. That letter is an important find and so is whatever is buried over there in Virginia. From a historical point of view, it's important to our field of study, to history, but it's also important for the American people. This is part of our heritage—another glimpse into our past. Professor, we can't just turn our backs on this now. It's not about us or about any sort of personal fame or wealth. It's about opening the doors of the past, about doing our jobs. We can't let one crazy person like Jake defile this monumental opportunity."

"So, what do we do?"

"Is there some way we can work around Jake? Leave him out of it?" Holly suggested.

"I'd love to leave him out of it. I don't want that snake to get a penny out of this," Lapain said. "What if I go to Vic Johns and level with him? Apologize and let him know that Jake is the one who went way overboard into the violence, that I never intended for it to get out of hand."

"That could work," Holly nodded. "Of course, then the ball would be in Vic John's court. He would have to agree to excavating the sight."

"Yeah, I realize that, but what choice do we have? It's his land. It'll have to be his decision. Maybe you can convince him of the importance of this for the American people, Holly. You know, the same speech you just gave me. He's a patriot, a veteran. It might just work."

"Well, I'm willing to give it a shot. Just tell me when and where. Vic Johns is a reasonable man from what I've seen. I think he'll do the right thing."

"That still leaves Jake, though. How do we get him out of the picture?" Lapain asked.

Holly scratched her head. "Yes, and he's so full of greed right now. Nothing's going to slow him down."

Lapain, deep in thought, suddenly brightened. "Unless we use that greed against him." He broke into a smile. "Nurse Holly, how about a drink?"

"Sure," Holly smiled. Lapain again felt the urge to kiss her, but he headed to the refrigerator instead.

A tidal wave of emotional strain swept over Vic Johns, the pounding breakers stinging and chafing raw nerves. He felt himself going under, totally immersed, gasping, choking, fighting for air, reaching for the surface, desperate to stay afloat. Shadowy images passed before his eyes: Sally, ashen, comatose, alone, on the brink of death in the Culpeper hospital; Kim, shackled and lost, calling for his help; Sheriff Sam Bodie, angrily waving a wanted poster bearing his image; Fred Hamilton, staring corpse-like and sinking beyond reach, disappearing into the darkness below. How much can a man take?

Vic pounded the motel mattress and sobbed. Anger, grief, disbelief. A strange cocktail he'd never tasted before. Even combat was more comprehensible. Comrades fell, slaughtered by enemy fire, but at least you knew the cause. You could see and hear the enemy in the foxhole over the ridge. It was war, and casualties were expected. You killed some of them, and they killed some on your side. It was insanity and sheer terror, but at least you could process it. War meant death and suffering—end of story. But this domestic brand of suffering was something else. Who could understand any of it? It tore at your insides, little by little, piece by piece, like buzzards ripping into a dead carcass. The enemy was a faceless coward hiding behind the curtain of heaven, pulling levers, pushing buttons and sending helpless victims into the swirling abyss.

Vic dangled over the chasm, clutching and grabbing. Defiantly, he vowed to claw his way out of this misery. He'd never succumb. He may not understand the why of it, but he would, by sheer determination and willpower, shape his own destiny and secure a future for himself and his family. No devil of hell would deter him from that path. He pounded the pillow once more, this time to seal the vow of a personal pledge to prevail or die trying.

Vic sloshed cold water on his face—a wake-up call to rejoin the battle. From behind the hand towel, ringed eyes glared back in the mirror, a testament to stressful days and sleepless nights. Not since combat days had he seen such a haggard image. His cell phone sprang into action, ringing and vibrating from a table by the bed. He snatched it up.

"Hello . . . Yes, this is Johns . . . Professor, what do you want? . . . Yes, I can be there, but I don't see why . . . Okay, I understand . . . Yeah, sure, I'll be glad to talk about any plan to end this thing . . . All right, I'll be there, but this better be on the level."

The King's Quaff, a rare English-style pub complete with Tudor exterior and medieval furnishings, would be the meeting place. Vic felt more at ease in the semi-darkness of the pub. Once his eyes adjusted to the light, he walked slowly to the last booth, looking for Lapain. Even in the sooty blackness, his eye caught Holly's brilliant blond hair. She smiled and nudged Lapain, nodding in Vic's direction. Lapain leaped to his feet, extending a hand. Vic shook it apprehensively and sat across the table from the university duo.

"Mr. Johns—Vic, may I call you Vic?" Lapain asked awkwardly. Vic shrugged. "I think you already know Holly, my teaching assistant?"

Holly smiled again. Vic nodded.

"Vic, I want you to know that I feel badly about the way this has turned out. I never intended it to get out of hand like this. Jake has gone crazy. He's obsessed with getting the treasure that we believe is buried on your land. He's convinced it will make him a rich man. I've tried to reason with him, but he won't listen. He tried to kidnap me but, thanks to Holly here, I managed to escape after jumping from a moving truck."

"That would explain the bruises," Vic replied. He had noticed the bandages and abrasions.

A waiter approached with paper coasters and a bowl of unshelled peanuts. "Drinks, folks?" he said as he laid the items on the table.

"I'll have a gin and tonic," Holly said.

"Me, too," Lapain said as he looked at Vic.

"That's fine with me," Vic nodded.

"Comin' right up." The waiter was gone as quickly as he'd arrived.

Holly grabbed a peanut. "Mr. Johns—I mean Vic—we've been talking it over, and we think we can use Jake's obsessive greed against him."

Lapain interrupted. "I feel so bad about this that I want to try to make it up to you, Vic. First, let me apologize. Like I said, I never intended to cause you or your family any harm. Jake is the perpetrator of the violence, and I can't control him any longer. I've created a monster, and I feel responsible. So I want to try to set things right."

"What do you have in mind?" Vic asked.

"We're thinking that Ambrose—I mean, Dr. Lapain—could go crawling back to Jake, apologizing for threatening to blow the lid off this thing, and offer to rejoin the quest for the treasure as the historian to keep the whole thing authenticated."

"That could be dangerous if he's already tried to kidnap you," Vic said.

"I realize that," Lapain replied, "but it seems the best choice we have. Of course, you would have to carry through with pretending to sign over the land so Jake would think he's getting ownership of whatever we dig up."

"Yes, without that, the plan doesn't work," Holly added.

Vic rubbed his chin. "I've got the papers ready. They're not signed yet, but I've got them."

"So, we could go ahead with the plan right away." Holly smiled and looked at Lapain.

"That's right," Lapain agreed. "And the sooner the better, since Jake has your daughter, Vic."

Vic was warming up to the idea. He would have to have some guarantee of Kim's safety, of course. He wondered whether he should trust Lapain, but with Holly involved, it seemed okay. She seemed so sincere, and even Lapain's remorse seemed genuine. It was the best chance of bringing this thing to some sort of final resolution and hopefully freeing Kim.

The waiter returned with the drinks. Vic used the pause to shell a couple of peanuts.

"So, how do you see this unfolding?" he asked after the waiter left.

Lapain took a sip of his drink and returned the glass to the paper coaster. "I will meet with Jake, apologize and attempt to convince him that this is the only way to go."

Holly jumped in, "Then we'll arrange the swap of the deed for your daughter."

"As soon as that transaction is done," Lapain added, "we'll arrange to dig up the treasure and have the police ready to move in and arrest Jake at the site."

"Do you really think Jake will go for this?" Vic wondered aloud.

"I think he's so obsessed about this, he'll jump at it. It streamlines the whole thing for him—he wouldn't have to deal with Kim or you any longer. He'll figure he gets what he wants and can walk away a wealthy man." Lapain grinned.

"Almost sounds too easy, too good to be true," Vic said, "but, hey, let's go for it."

The three conspirators drank a toast to bringing down Jake Crapper.

TWENTY

The day dawned bright and clear. A whisper of a wind, but not a cloud in the sky. The memorial service was slated for 10 a.m. Everything was in place early, and Vic joined Esther in the family limousine for the ride to the cemetery. The Culpeper cemetery consisted of lovely treed grounds surrounded by an eight-foot wrought iron fence. Two stately entrances blended stone walls with ornate steel gates and bronzed signs. It was an old cemetery that sheltered graves from the Civil War Era. Some formidable monuments occupied the old section near the front entrance, including a Confederate cavalry commander with sword drawn, mounted on a charging steed. There were crosses of every size and stones engraved with Confederate flags. In the newer section, grave markers were limited to flat stones, which made it easier for the unionized maintenance crews to mow the lawn.

Vic sized up the considerable crowd already gathered at the judge's grave. Dignitaries from all walks of Culpeper life were in attendance, including Sheriff Bodie and Deputy Nate

Peters, the mayor, and others. A veritable "Who's Who" of Washington society stood waiting at the grave as well. Vic recognized a few of them. The judge touched a lot of lives. He would be sorely missed.

Standing next to Esther, Vic stared at the empty space beneath the casket. It mirrored his own cold detachment from the proceedings. It was all like a dream, an out-of-body experience. He felt strangely displaced but managed, when his turn came, to speak heartfelt words of respect and admiration for the man who had been his best friend for decades.

He made eye contact with Sheriff Bodie several times during the speeches. Was there a plan in place to grab him? If so, Bodie wasn't giving anything away. Neither was Nate Peters, although both of them kept glancing at Vic throughout the service. When the preacher had pronounced the final benediction and Esther had tearfully placed a rose on the casket, Vic led her back to the limo. Before climbing in, he glanced at Bodie and noticed he was already on the radio, sending a message from his squad car. Showtime!

The limousine began the winding crawl toward the main entrance gate. Just as it reached the old section, a door flung open and a man fled among the marble monuments. Immediately, Sheriff Bodie and Nate Peters jumped from their squad car and pursued on foot. They chased the man toward the northeast corner of the cemetery.

The limousine continued on its winding path. Inside, Esther smiled and said, "Fred would have enjoyed this."

"Yes, he would have," Vic said, squeezing Esther's hand. "I'll be in touch," he said, then leaped from the door on the driver's side and disappeared among the monuments. He ran toward the west side of the cemetery and his waiting rental car on the other side of the fence. The decoy was working.

By the time Sheriff Bodie and Nate Peters caught up with their quarry, Vic Johns had disappeared over the fence and into the busy streets of Culpeper. Bodie slammed his hat to the ground and kicked the dirt. Outsmarted by Johns. He shoved the decoy and told him to get the hell out of there or he'd be shot. The well-dressed derelict left, anxious to spend his fifty dollars on a good meal and a bottle of Southern Comfort.

Lapain was nervous. He wiped his sweating palms on his khakis and glanced at Holly. Outwardly, she seemed calm, but he detected a slight waver in her voice. They walked into the outer office of Crazy Jake's Salvage Company, determined to pull this off. The owner entered from the back. The man always seemed so much bigger indoors. He filled the average doorway and dominated the room.

"What's she doin' here?" he said, practically spitting the words.

"She's in on this as my witness and partner," Lapain replied.

"Oh, I get it," Jake sneered, "she's your bodyguard. Is that it?" His belly jiggled as he laughed. "Pretty brave of you two to come walkin' in here like this. I didn't think you had the balls for somethin' like this, Professor."

"There's a lot at stake here," Lapain said. "Some risks are in order."

Jake nodded. "Fair enough. I can't argue with that."

"I got to thinking about everything, Jake. Actually, Holly helped me see things more clearly. So, I've come to make amends. I'm sorry about the threat to blow the whistle on this whole thing. I now realize that doesn't do either of us any good. This is a once-in-a-lifetime opportunity. Why should I throw that away?"

"Exactly," agreed the big man.

"So, I want you to sort of reinstate me, so we can get on with our original plan. Holly and I will be the official historians on the project to ensure the findings are properly recorded, catalogued and authenticated. I get my fame and, hopefully, some fortune and you get your share, too. No questions asked. Finders keepers. We all walk away winners. What do you say?"

Jake stared at them for a long time. Lapain could feel the beads of sweat forming on his forehead. He wanted to grab Holly's hand and run away from there. Jake pulled a cigar from his shirt pocket and lit up. Still staring, he took a few long pulls and blew smoke rings in their faces. Holly fought the urge to cough but couldn't. She wheezed and succumbed to a violent coughing spell. Jake loved it and started laughing. It broke the tension. Lapain laughed, too.

"You caught me in a good mood," Jake said smiling. "I just got off the phone with the one and only Vic Johns. Seems he has some paperwork that needs signin'."

Lapain acted surprised. "You're kidding! That's perfect! I never thought I'd see the day."

"Okay, Professor, you're back in. But the girl stays with me as collateral just so you won't suddenly change your mind again."

Lapain started to protest, but Holly piped up, "That's fair enough. As long as I get treated right." She looked at Jake for some assurance. He shrugged and nodded.

"All I want is to dig up that treasure," he said. He took another long pull on the stogie and exhaled a contented blue cloud.

Lapain looked questioningly at Holly. "Let's do it," she said patting his arm.

"All right," he nodded, "Let's go for it."

Kim awoke cold, stiff and hungry. The only shelter she'd been able to find by nightfall was the narrow gap between two massive fallen trees. The logs had only recently come crashing down, so there was little decay. They provided a windbreak but little else. She stood and did some basic stretches to get the kinks out. Breakfast would be beans and crackers once again, but she was thankful anyway.

By midmorning, she approached another intersection with the road. Caution would guide her this time. She slowly made her way toward the road, hoping a vehicle would suddenly appear and afford her a ride off this crazy mountain. She picked her way through the weeds lining the asphalt strip, constantly watching left and right for any sign of her pursuers.

"There she is!" The shout came from across the road. It was Charlie, dancing up and down, shouting and pointing right at her. Kim froze like a deer caught in oncoming headlights. From the corner of her eye, she spotted Willie emerging from the woods about three hundred yards up the road. Instinctively, she began to run in the opposite direction with Charlie loudly joining the chase. She had seen Charlie run and was confident that she could easily outdistance him. She looked back to confirm the substantial lead over both Charlie and Willie when suddenly something landed on her from overhead, tangling her feet and sending her sprawling in a cloud of dust on the gravel shoulder.

A smiling Zeke gamboled into the middle of the road.

"What a perfect throw!" he congratulated himself.

Kim struggled to free herself, but the net had her hopelessly fettered.

"Zeke, let me go!" she yelled.

"Can't do that, miss," he replied, grinning from ear to ear.

Charlie and Willie arrived to give Zeke a few high-fives. They all stared and laughed as Kim struggled like a caged animal.

"Let me go, you fools!" she practically screamed. That only brought a louder chorus of jeers and laughter.

Willie and Zeke dragged her to her feet just as Jake's ugly van appeared from around a curve up the road. Kim's spirits sank when she saw Jake haul his butt out of the van and pull out a handgun.

"Good work, boys," the big man gloated. A toothpick hung from his lips like an exclamation point on his smug grin. He trained the gun on Kim. "Get the net off her, boys, and we'll load her in the van."

Zeke and Willie worked to unravel her from the net. As they finally lifted it from her head, Kim heard a familiar sound—click. The others heard it, too. Their heads turned to see a scruffy old-timer standing at the edge of the woods with a shotgun aimed at Jake.

"Let her go," the old man growled in a voice familiar to Kim.

Kim edged away from Jake and the boys. The old man looked at her with a wry smile and nodded toward the van. He wanted her to take it as her getaway vehicle. She didn't hesitate—mouthed a quick "Thank you" to the old man and jumped behind the wheel of the van. Kim heard the pistol fire as she started the engine. Her liberator slumped to his knees, grabbing his chest where a crimson stain was spreading. Kim didn't know what to do. She couldn't leave him here like this, bleeding to death. But then the old man looked at her, face ashen and contorted, and waved her away.

She slammed the gearshift into drive. Jake had his pistol aimed right at her. She ducked as she stomped on the accelerator. A bullet exploded through the windshield as the van hurtled forward, sending Jake and his boys diving for the ditch. In the mirror, Kim saw Jake fire at the old man's head. Shaking and sobbing, she sped away without looking back again.

The van careened around one bend after another. Panic pressed Kim's accelerator foot to the floor. She fought to hold the road, but after about a mile, the tires surrendered their grip, sending the van ricocheting off a guardrail. The right front tire blew but, miraculously, Kim reeled in the vehicle and brought it safely to a halt. Jake and his boys wouldn't be far behind, even on foot. No time to change the tire. Back into the woods she charged, up a steep ridge to a crevice that afforded shelter and a sightline to the van. She settled down to wait.

Maybe twenty minutes passed before she heard the voices approaching. She picked out Charlie's shrill exclamation first, "There's the van! Jake, the van, I see the van!" The group came into view, Jake wielding the handgun as they cautiously approached the vehicle. The others stood back as Jake flung open the driver's door and thrust the pistol forward. He climbed into the seat and checked the cargo area. Finding no sign of Kim, he shouted to the boys to look around for her. Willie pointed out the flat tire and Jake ordered him and Zeke to put the spare on.

Jake and Charlie fanned out to search the area. Jake was heading directly toward Kim's ridge.

"And hurry up with it, boys," he yelled back toward the van. "I've got to get to an important meeting this afternoon." He stopped to survey the steep rise. Kim ducked lower in her hiding place. "Damn, I needed that Johns girl," she heard Jake mutter. Then he turned away. The hill was apparently too daunting a climb for his corpulent frame.

He called Charlie back. The search was over. Within minutes, Zeke and Willie had the van rolling again. Kim heaved a big sigh of relief as they drove off.

TWENTY-ONE

Vic had insisted on the public meeting place. Less chance of Jake pulling a fast one with plenty of witnesses around. With papers in hand, he arrived at the greasy spoon early. He'd reserved a table down at the end with a view of the street. A friendly waitress ushered him to the booth and fetched him a coffee while he waited for the others. Just a few more minutes and at least one part of this nightmare would be over. He couldn't wait to see Kim safe and sound. The report from the hospital just hours before had been no change. He felt a sudden longing to see Sally, to hug her, to tell her how much he loved her and needed her. He made up his mind to go with Kim to the hospital as soon as the transaction was completed. The hell with Bodie and the guards. If they wanted him, they'd have to drag him out of that hospital — but not before he got to see Sally.

An ugly van pulled up to the curb in front of the diner, and Vic recognized the hulking figure that spilled out of the driver's door. A blue Volvo swept in behind the van, and

Professor Lapain hopped out from behind the wheel to greet Jake. Together they walked to the entrance. Jake was all smiles. Lapain looked a little tense—but gave a knowing glance. They slid into the booth opposite Vic. Once coffees were ordered, the talk shifted to business.

"So, where's Kim?" Vic asked bluntly.

Jake motioned with his head toward the window. "Right outside in the van. What about the papers?" he asked.

Vic patted the manila envelope at his elbow. "I'll need to see Kim before I sign anything," he said.

"Figured you might make that demand," Jake replied. "The boys have her in the van. When I give them the word, they'll give you a glimpse of her. Then we sign the papers, you leave and they'll deliver your daughter from the van as you hit the street. I stay here until you're safely on your way."

"Sounds reasonable to me," Vic nodded. He just wanted to get this over with and get away with Kim safely at his side. He slid his mug to the side, pulled the papers from the envelope and spread them on the table.

The waitress dropped off coffees for Jake and Lapain and asked if they wanted to order any food. Jake impatiently dismissed her. Lapain nervously tapped the table with his fingers.

"Okay, let's see Kim," Vic demanded.

Jake grabbed his cell phone and quickly dialed. "Zeke, give us a quick peek at your girly friend there, will ya?"

A blond figure with a blindfold appeared briefly in the passenger's seat. Vic's heart skipped a beat. He wanted to run outside and take Kim in his arms, get her far away from these madmen.

"How do I know she's really okay?" Vic asked.

"I guess you have to take my word for it, Johns. It wasn't easy keepin' my boys away from her, you know. She's a pretty fine piece of flesh, if I say so myself — soft and round in all the right places and spunky, too. The boys kinda' like that combo in a woman."

"Oh shut up, Crapper. Let's get this done." He rummaged for a pen. His cell phone began to ring. "Hello?" he answered. "Kim! Where are you? But I thought . . . When did you escape?" Vic glared across the table at Jake, whose face had suddenly gone white. "Are you okay, Kim? . . . Good. Yes, get him to drop you off at the hospital. That's good. I'll call you there."

Vic rose slowly as he talked. Jake started to move, but Vic held up a hand. He slipped out of the booth and hit the street, leaving the unsigned papers strewn across the table before Jake and Lapain. Glancing at the booth as he passed by the window, he saw Jake pound the table with a meaty fist. Lapain looked bewildered.

"Now what?" Lapain asked aloud as he gathered up the unsigned papers.

"Now we say the hell with property deeds and paperwork. Come on."

Jake led the way back to the van for an impromptu meeting. "Okay, boys, change of plans. Johns flew the coop without signing the papers."

"You're kiddin'!" Willie moaned. "Now what are we gonna do?"

"We're gonna say the hell with Johns and go get that treasure. Today."

"But—" Lapain began.

"No buts, Professor. It's all over. No more talkin' and plannin'. It's time for action."

Charlie rubbed his hands with glee. "Action. Zeke, Willie, we're gonna have some action. I like action." He smiled.

"What's the plan, boss?" asked Zeke.

"Simple. We go in and dig up the treasure and live happily ever after. End of story."

"There must be some other way, Jake," Lapain said.

"No. I don't have any more leverage with Johns. It's too late. My mind's made up. We're going in there today. You can come with us if you want, Professor, but don't get in the way. I'm in charge and there's one goal now—to get that treasure and run."

Lapain looked at Holly. She shrugged. "You'll need me to show you where to dig," he said, looking at Jake.

"No, we don't. I'm not stupid, Professor. I already checked out the site. I thought it might come down to this. Those three rocks are sittin' there just beggin' for us to start diggin'."

"Take the girl and get lost, Lapain," he continued. "We don't need you any more."

The side door slid open, and Lapain and Holly were roughly shoved out onto the sidewalk. "Let's go, boys, we got work to do," they heard Jake say before they drove off.

Holly stood and brushed herself off. "Now what?" she asked.

"I don't know," Lapain replied. "This messes up everything. We've got to call Vic and let him know what Jake's planning to do."

They hopped in the Volvo and headed for Culpeper.

Vic scooped up his phone. "Hello?"

"Vic, it's Lapain. Where are you?"

"On my way back to the motel to check out, and then I'm heading for Culpeper. Why?"

"I just want to apologize. I'm sorry. I didn't realize Jake didn't have your daughter. I guess this wrecks our plan."

"I'm just glad Kim is safe," Vic replied.

"Yeah, that's good. By the way, Jake threw Holly and me out. Says he doesn't need us any more. He's planning to dig up the site today."

"Without you there?"

"Yeah. Says he's going to take the treasure all for himself."

"We can't let him do that."

"I know, but how do we stop him?"

"We don't have to," Vic said. "We can still use our plan, Professor. I'll call Sheriff Bodie and tell him to get over there to make the big arrest. I'll convince him by telling him I'll be there, too. I'm tired of running anyway."

"Okay, we'll meet you there. But be careful—Jake is desperate."

"I'm on my way."

Vic pulled the car off the road. Two quick calls to make. He dialed the first.

"Hello? Culpeper Regional Hospital, how may I direct your call?"

"Hello. Could you connect me to third floor, ICU nurses' station, please?"

"One moment please."

"ICU. Nurse Calloway speaking. May I help you?"

"Nurse Calloway, it's Vic Johns speaking. My daughter Kim will be arriving there any moment, and I need to leave her an urgent message. Please tell her that I've gone to the house instead of the hospital. Tell her it's all going down today. She'll understand."

"Okay, I'll tell her. But, Mr. Johns, I've got good . . ."

"Sorry, Nurse, but I really have to run. I'll be in later. Thanks."

He hung up and dialed again.

"Sheriff Bodie please. Tell him it's Vic Johns calling." Bodie was on the line in seconds. "Sheriff, I wanted to let you know what's going down today. Thought you might be interested in making a few arrests. Rally the troops—my place in a few hours. The bad guys will be there digging up treasure. In case that doesn't excite you enough, I'll be there, too. You can wrap up two cases at once--two birds with one stone, so to speak. Might be good publicity. See you there."

He hung up without waiting for a response.

TWENTY-TWO

The sun was setting quickly. Shadows lengthened and deepened, transforming the woods into a gloomy haunt. Jake and his boys arrived at the rear of the property and backed the van in along the creek side almost to the site. They tossed shovels and picks to the ground and carried twin gas cans up the hill to the clearing where the house stood. Charlie and Willie manned the cans while Zeke held one of the portable spotlights. They broke windows on two sides of the house and entered, pouring gas liberally as they walked. They each did a circle around the main floor, then Willie climbed the stairway to the second floor and down again. As soon as they stepped outside, Jake yelled, "Light it!"

With delight, Charlie struck a match and tossed it in through the broken window. The flames shot along the trail of gasoline like a hissing roller coaster. Willie's match sent a similar trail rushing to meet the first in an eruption of flaming energy. Within minutes, the entire interior was ablaze.

"Let's go, boys," Jake yelled, and led the way back down the hill into the woods and out of sight.

Vic swung around the familiar curves, hardly even braking. Lapain's Volvo had appeared out of nowhere and stuck close behind. In a shower of dust, both drivers skidded sharply into the lane and accelerated toward the house. By now, flames were licking at the roof and every window spewed fiery orange waves.

Vic slammed on the brakes and jumped from his car. He had a notion to run inside but quickly realized it was too late. Holly was already dialing 911.

Lapain joined Vic in staring at the house now engulfed in flames. The fire was mesmerizing in its destructive fury. It roared above the popping of wood and sizzling of melting plastics and vinyl.

After relaying the appropriate information to the 911 operator, Holly broke the spell, shouting, "Do you think Jake did this?"

Both men nodded. "It's got to be Jake's doing," Lapain said.

"I don't understand. Why burn the house?" Holly asked.

"As a diversion," Vic answered.

"He probably figures the fire will keep everybody occupied up here while he digs up the treasure down there and escapes the back way," Lapain added.

"I'm glad I didn't tell Kim to come here," Vic uttered, as if in a trance. He couldn't take his eyes off the inferno consuming his life's dream.

Holly glanced at Lapain and mouthed the word, "Shock." The professor nodded. Neither seemed to know what to do or say next.

Suddenly, Vic snapped out of it. "Where's the site?" he asked. "We've got to get to them before they get away with anything."

"It's down the hill behind the house." Lapain pointed in the general direction. "Into the trees about 500 yards."

"It must be near the creek, then," Vic replied. He knew just about every inch of this property.

"Yeah, pretty close," Lapain said. "What are we going to do? I mean, this could be dangerous. Shouldn't we have some sort of plan?"

Vic was into combat mode now. "First, Holly, we need you to stay here until the sheriff arrives. You'll have to lead him down to the site, OK?" She nodded.

"What about your dogs?" Lapain asked, remembering his own painful introduction to the massive Rottweilers.

"They're not here. I had a vet friend come and get them after Kim was abducted." He wished they were here now so he could send them in as an advance attack force. They might have even saved the house.

He continued, "We don't have any weapons, so we'll just have to use surprise and try to keep them talking until the sheriff gets here."

"And hope Jake doesn't shoot us," added Lapain.

"Right. Okay, let's go," Vic said and headed out like a platoon sergeant leading his troops into battle.

They crossed the clearing to the edge of the woods. Glancing back just before plunging into the woods, Vic saw Holly gleaming like an angel in the golden glow of the blaze.

The wail of approaching sirens broke through the bedlam of the fire. He and Lapain picked their way carefully in the failing light. About a hundred yards in, they spotted the lights. The hulking silhouette of Jake Crapper could not be mistaken. Two of the boys held the lights, and one was digging with a spade. Vic motioned to Lapain to proceed quietly. Hopefully, they could sneak up behind Jake before he heard them. The sirens got louder, and Jake turned to look in the direction of the house just as Vic and Lapain got to within twenty paces of the group. Jake wheeled and pulled a gun from his belt. Instinctively, Vic and Lapain raised their hands.

"We're unarmed, Jake," Vic said.

Jake waved the pistol. "Keep those hands in the air, boys," he said. He gestured for them to come over to the light.

"So, you decided to crash our little party, huh?" Jake loved being in control. "Well, you might as well watch, fellas."

All eyes turned to Willie, the excavator. He dug feverishly, tossing dirt onto nearby leaves. Vic glanced about, sizing up the situation. Jake had the only visible weapon, but he was too far away for any overthrow attempt. They'd need some sort of diversion.

Just then, Willie's shovel clanked on metal. He looked at Jake and broke into a big grin. "Maybe this is it, boss!"

"Get in there and help him, Charlie," shouted Jake.

The two got down on their knees and began scooping the dirt with their hands. Lapain got too excited and made a move toward the hole. Without hesitation, Jake shot him in the thigh, sending him reeling to the ground, shrieking in pain.

"Hold your fire, Crapper," Vic yelled. He knelt to console Lapain. The professor moaned, clutching the wound with both hands. Blood trickled over his fingers. Vic pulled off his belt and fashioned a tourniquet around the bleeding thigh.

"Don't move, either of you," Jake said. He was pointing the gun at them but eagerly looking at the treasure Willie and Charlie were lifting from the hole. It was a dark metal box with a lock on the front. Jake grabbed the lock and tried to wrestle it open.

"Stand back." He motioned to Willie and Charlie to step back. Aiming carefully, he fired a single round. The lock exploded. They all rushed forward to lift the lid, but the rustling of leaves back up the hill in the direction of the house froze them.

"Everybody drop your weapons and raise your hands." Vic recognized Sheriff Bodie's voice.

Nate Peters, Chester Muldoon and Bodie emerged from the shadows with Holly close behind. The officers had their revolvers drawn. Vic saw Jake raise his gun as he turned toward Bodie and the others. He leaped into action, chopping the gun from Jake's hand and throwing his weight into the bigger man. They fell together in a heap. Jake came up swinging, but Nate Peters quickly grabbed him from behind. He scuffled with Jake but, with Chester's help, finally got some cuffs on the big man. Jake cursed them the whole time.

Holly heard Lapain's moaning and, seeing the blood, ran to his aid. Bodie motioned to Zeke, Charlie and Willie. "Stand still, boys," he said. The three nodded.

"So, what do we have here?" Bodie asked, as he nudged the metal box with his boot.

"It's Civil War booty," Lapain moaned.

"It's mine," Jake snapped.

"The hell it is, Jake," Lapain shouted. "I'm the one who told you about it. It's my discovery."

"Doesn't look like either of you boys are in much shape for claimin' anything," Bodie said.

Knowing Bodie, Vic had a pretty good idea where this was going, so he jumped right in.

"This is my property," he said, "so I figure the box and anything in it belongs to me."

"Shut up, Johns," Bodie said. "You're under arrest, too, so you're not claimin' anything, either."

As Bodie leaned over to flip the lid and expose the contents of the mystery box, a phalanx of black uniforms emerged from the murkiness near the creek. A S.W.A.T. team in full assault gear — helmets and flak jackets — with automatic weapons trained on the group around the excavation.

"FBI. Nobody move," an imperious voice shouted from behind the black wave. An agent in plain clothes and FBI jacket stepped forward.

"Don't touch that box, Sheriff," he ordered.

Wisely, Bodie complied. He holstered his gun, raised his hands and stepped back. "Who are you?" he asked.

"You'll find out soon enough, Sheriff Bodie." He gestured to his troops. "Cuff them all except that man and the lady." He was pointing at Vic and Holly. "And get an ambulance down here right away," he added.

Within moments, Sheriff Bodie, his deputies, and Jake and his boys were all handcuffed and lying flat on the ground at gunpoint.

Only Bodie was protesting. "You can't do this. This is my jurisdiction. I'm the law around here."

"Shut up, Sheriff. You're under arrest for extortion and suspicion of murder," the agent in charge said. "Read 'em their rights, guys, and haul 'em out of here."

Then he walked over to Vic, extending a hand. "Mr. Johns, Frank Reilly, FBI. I'm an old friend of Judge Hamilton. A while back, the Judge stopped by the Bureau and elicited my help to do some investigating into a suspected extortion ring here in Culpeper. He filled me in on the strange things happening to you, too. Seems there's a lot that's not quite right in Culpeper these days."

"Ain't that the truth," Vic said. He shook the agent's hand. "I'm sure glad to see you and the S.W.A.T. team, Frank. But how did you know about this?"

"We've been tapping a few sources for some time now. I had the team assembled and ready, and when we intercepted your call to Sheriff Bodie, we figured it was time to take action on this case. Looks like we've killed two birds with one stone," he said with a knowing smile.

"Well, thanks for the timely intervention. I was fresh out of options," Vic said.

Reilly turned to a couple of his agents. "Guys, secure that box. That property belongs to Mr. Johns here."

"Actually, Agent Reilly, it should belong to Miss Holly Fenton over there." He pointed at the surprised Ph.D. student. "Holly has been aiding me in dealing with Jake Crapper and his cronies. This is a pretty important discovery that needs to be properly documented and I can't think of a better person to handle it." He smiled and winked at a beaming Holly.

"I'm sure you can handle the box from here, Holly." He hugged her and whispered in her ear, "Thanks for everything you did. You're a brave young lady."

Holly smiled again and shrugged. "It was a real education," she said.

A couple of FBI agents helped Professor Lapain off the ground and partially carried him as the group made their way back up the hill toward the burning house.

"Sure was sorry to hear about Fred's death," Reilly said. "He was a good man."

"The best," Vic added. "We went back a long way. Served in Nam together."

They walked in silence for a few moments, reliving their memories of the judge.

Vic broke the silence. "You know, there was something strange about Fred's death. He was always so careful. I just have this gnawing suspicion that it wasn't accidental."

"It wasn't, Vic. We've got good evidence pointing to Sheriff Bodie. Seems Fred was making things a little too hot for his liking. So, Bodie decided to do away with him."

Silence again until they neared the clearing.

"What a raging inferno," Reilly said, as they watched the firemen battle the blaze.

"Yeah. Won't be much left," Vic replied.

Just as they emerged from the woods, Kim came running across the clearing.

"Dad, are you all right?" She ran into his arms.

"Yes, I'm fine. Are you okay? Agent Reilly, meet my daughter Kim."

Kim offered a perfunctory "Nice to meet you, Agent Reilly," and continued excitedly, "Dad, I've got great news! I just came from the hospital. Mom's awake, and she's asking for you!"

Vic couldn't believe it. Tears welled in his eyes. He hugged Kim again. He didn't know whether to laugh or cry or shout or pray. He put his arm around Kim's shoulder to lead her to the car.

"Let's get to the hospital then," he said. To Holly and Agent Reilly, he said, "You'll have to excuse us. We have an important visit to make at the hospital." They nodded in unison.

Arm in arm, he and Kim headed to the car. As they passed the burning home, Kim said, "What about the house, Dad?"

"It's only a house," Vic replied. "Let's go see Mom."

CPSIA information can be obtained at www.ICGtesting.com
Printed in the USA
BVOW021903220312

285857BV00001B/2/P

9 780985 151713